A Houseful of Girls

by

Mrs. George de Horne Vaizey

A Houseful of Girls
by Mrs. George de Horne Vaizey

ISBN: 978-93-62761-74-3

Published by

DOUBLE 9 BOOKS

2/13-B, Ansari Road
Daryaganj, New Delhi – 110002
info@double9books.com
www.double9books.com
Tel. 011-40042856

ABOUT THE AUTHOR

Mrs. George de Horne Vaizey, a prolific British writer best known for her domestic fiction, was born Jessie Bell. Her literary career started in the late 1800s, and she wrote several short tales and more than 100 books. Warmth, humour, and a sharp understanding of human nature defined Mrs. Vaizey's writing style, which won her readers' hearts both in the United States and Great Britain. She was baptised as Mrs. George de Horne Vaizey in 1879 after being wed to him. Mrs. Vaizey produced a large number of works, many of which dealt with themes of family relationships, romance, and societal issues, while leading a hectic life with her two daughters. Her most well-known pieces are "More About Peggy," "The Rebel of the Family," and "The Fortunes of the Farrells." The works of Mrs. Vaizey encapsulated the spirit of Victorian and Edwardian society, providing a window into the daily challenges and victories faced by common people.

CONTENTS

Chapter One
Half a Dozen Daughters

There were six of them altogether—six great big girls,—and they lived in a great big house, in the middle of a long high road, one end of which loses itself in London town, while the other goes stretching away over the county of Hertford. Years ago, John Gilpin had ridden his famous race down that very road, and Christabel loved to look out of her bedroom window and imagine that she saw him flying along, with his poor bald head bared to the *breeze*, and the bottles swinging on either side. She had cut a picture of him out of a book and tacked it on her wall, for, as she explained to Agatha, her special sister, she felt it a duty to support "local talent," and, so far as she could discover, Gilpin was the only celebrity who had ever patronised the neighbourhood.

Christabel was the youngest of the family—a position which, as every one knows, is only second in importance to that of the eldest, and, in this instance, Maud was so sweet and unassuming that the haughty young person of fourteen ruled her with a rod of iron.

Fair-haired Lilias was a full-fledged young lady, and Nan had had all her dresses let down, and was supposed to have her hair up; but as a matter of fact it was more often down than not, for it was heavy and plentiful, and Nan's ten thumbs could by no chance fasten it securely. Hair-pins littered the schoolroom floor, hair-pins stood out aggressively against the white paint on the stairs, hair-pins nestled in the little creases of velvet chairs: there were hair-pins, hair-pins everywhere, except just where they should have been—on Nan's dressing-table; and here there was such a dearth of these useful articles, that on one memorable occasion she had been compelled to effect a coiffure with the aid of a piece of string and a broken comb. The effect was striking for a good ten minutes, and then came the inevitable collapse; but, "Dear me," as Nan observed, "accidents will happen, and what is the use of making a fuss about a thing like that, when the world is full of suffering!"

Elsie thanked her stars that she was only sixteen, and need not be "grown-up" for two long years to come; but when her younger sisters grew obtrusive, she suddenly remembered that she would be seventeen in three months' time, and would have them know that she was to be treated with respect; and, in spite of daily discussions, feuds, and battles, the girls all loved each other dearly, and believed that such a charming and highly endowed family had never before existed in the annals of Christendom.

THE WAILS OF HER VIOLIN CAME FLOATING DOWNSTAIRS.

As a matter of fact, the Rendell girls had claim to one great distinction — promiscuous accomplishments had been discarded in their case, and each had been brought up to do some one thing well. Maud was musical, and practised scales two hours a day as a preliminary before settling down for another two or three hours of sonatas and fugues. Elsie locked herself in her bedroom for a like period, and the wails of her violin came floating downstairs like the lament of a lost soul. Nan appropriated a chilly attic, carved wood and her fingers at the same time, and clanged away at copper work, knocking her nails black and blue with ill-directed strokes of the hammer, as she manufactured the panels which were fitted into her oak carving with such artistic effect. Lilias declared sweetly that she was too stupid to do anything, but privately reflected that at least she had mastered the art of looking charming; and what did it matter if she *were* useless, since with her beauty she would certainly marry a duke on the first opportunity, and be spirited away to a life of luxury! As for Agatha and Christabel, they were supposed to devote themselves to the study of languages and the domestic arts, but in private conclave they had already decided on their future career. They were to keep a select academy for young ladies, in which they would correct all those glaring errors of governess and mother under which they themselves had groaned.

"I can bear it better when I feel it is for a good end. Our girls shall never suffer as I am suffering!" said Chrissie, with an air of martyrdom, when she was ordered to bed at nine o'clock, and remorselessly roused from slumber at seven a.m. "If grown-ups were sensible, they would allow a child to follow its own instinct. Nature must surely know better than mothers; and my nature tells me to sit up at nights and have breakfast in bed. To be sent off as if one were a child in arms is really too horribly trying!"

"And when Mr Barr was there too! So degrading! Last night he was talking to me about books, and I'm sure he thought I was quite grown up. The table was between us, you know, so he couldn't see my legs. I was enjoying myself so much, and saying that I thought Thackeray much over-rated, when mother came up and said, 'Time for bed, Chickie! Run away!' I assure you, I *blushed* with mortification."

"Piteous!" said Christabel, bringing out her pet word with emphasis. "They never think of our feelings. I shall make it a rule to study the characters of our young ladies, and avoid wounding their susceptibilities. I know how it feels!"

In spite of their many sufferings, however, the Rendells would one and all have been ready to declare that there never had been, might, could, would, or should be, such another father and mother as they possessed. To have a son at college, and yourself carry off a prize at a tennis tournament, was surely a feat to be proud of on the part of a father; and what joy to have a tiny little scrap of a mother, who could be petted like a child and lifted up in the arms of the youngest daughter—a mother who had solved the problem of eternal youth, and looked so pretty and so meek, that it was a constant marvel where on earth she managed to stow that colossal will-power before which every member of the household bowed and trembled.

The Rendells' house was at once the brightest, the airiest, and the noisiest in the neighbourhood. As there were only six daughters, it can truthfully be asserted that there were never more than half a dozen girls talking at the same moment. Strangers passing beneath the schoolroom window at a moment when the sisters were assembled together, had indeed been known to estimate the numbers present as from a dozen to twenty; but such a statement was obviously false, and tended to that painful habit of exaggeration which it is the duty of all good folk to deplore. They were girls of strong individuality, and each felt it a duty to state her own views on any given subject, which she proceeded to do, undaunted by the fact that her companions were too much engrossed in talking themselves to be able to listen to a word she said. Maud talked, pouring out tea and dropping sugar into the cups with tragic emphasis; Lilias prattled sweetly, waving her white hands to enforce a point which no one heard; Nan banged the table and upset her cup in violence of denunciation; Elsie squeaked away in melancholy treble; and Agatha's "Too bad!" and Christabel's "Horrid shame!" were heard uninterruptedly in every pause.

When the door of the Grange opened to admit a stranger, the wail of a violin, the jingle of the piano, and the clang of Nan's hammer greeted him on the threshold, and from morn till night the echo of laughter and of happy voices never died away. There was only one occasion when the Rendell girls subsided into silence, and that was when Jim—the brother, the typical man of the race—came home on a visit and shed the lustre of his presence on his native village. Then the Miss Rendells sat in rows at his feet, paying obeisance, and, meekly opening their mouths, swallowed all he said, not even Nan herself daring to raise a question.

Chapter Two
A Happy Thought

Thurston House, the abode of the Rendell family, was one of those curiously-constructed houses which are only to be met with in old-fashioned neighbourhoods. It stood directly on the high road, a big grey building which could boast of no architectural beauty, and which indeed presented a somewhat cheerless aspect, with its wire blinds and tall, straight windows. A gaunt, town-like house—such was the impression made upon the casual passer—by; but appearances are apt to be deceptive, and that same stranger would have speedily altered his impression, if he had been taken round the garden to view the other side of the house. It was almost impossible to believe in such a different aspect! From one side a busy high road, strings of cyclists, *char à bancs* driving past, bearing parties of brawling trippers, clouds of dust, the echo of the drivers' horns, and the continued whirl of wheels; and on the other—deep bay windows looking on to a lawn of softest green, winding paths shaded with grand old trees, and, beyond all, a meadow stretching down to the riverside, where punt and canoe stood waiting in happy proximity, and clumps of bamboos flourished in eastern luxuriance.

"Our country house," the girls called the rooms facing south, "Our town house," those at the front; but though they adored the garden, and spent every available moment out of doors, the busy high road still held an attraction of its own. Mrs Rendell had her own entertaining rooms at the back of the house, but the girls were faithful to the little porch chamber which had been their property since childhood—a quaint little den built over the doorway, with a window at each of the three sides, through which an extended view was afforded of the comings and goings of the neighbourhood.

"I love this dear little bower," sighed Lilias sentimentally. "There's something so quaint and old-world about it. I feel like Elaine in her turret-chamber, looking out upon the great wide world."

"And it's such sport watching the people pass, especially on rainy days when the wind is high, and they are trying to hold up their dresses, and carry an umbrella and half a dozen parcels at the same time!" cried Nan with a relish. "Last Saturday was the very worst day of the year, and all the good housewives went past to shop. Chrissie and Agatha and I offered a prize to go to the one who guessed rightly who would have the muddiest boots. It was lovely watching them! Old Mrs Rowe, clutching her dress in front, and showing all her ankles, while at the back it was trailing on the ground; Mrs Smith, stalking like a grenadier, with a skimpy skirt and snow-shoes a yard long; dear, sweet little Mrs Bruce, as neat as ever, with not a single splash; and Mrs Booth, splattered right up to her waist, with boots as white as that rag. I had her name on my paper, so I got the prize, and spent it in caramels. I'm getting rather tired of caramels—I've had such a run on them lately. I must turn to something else for a change."

"You are getting too old to eat sweets, Nan," said Lilias severely. "You ought to set the children a better example. If all the money you spend at the confectioner's was put together, you would be surprised to find how much it was. And it's bad for your teeth to eat so much sugar. Why don't you save up, and put it to some really good use?"

"Such as frilling, and ribbons, and combs for the hair!" suggested Nan slily, rolling her eyes at the younger girls, who chuckled in the consciousness that Lilias had got her answer this time at least, since every one knew well how her pocket-money went! "What is your idea of something useful, my dear? We'd be pleased to take into consideration any scheme which you may have to propose, but in its present form the suggestion is somewhat vague."

"My dear child, you know as well as I do that there are a hundred different ways. The only difficulty is to choose." Lilias stared out of the window, trying hard to cudgel up one idea out of the specified hundred, in case she should be pressed still further. That was the worst of Nan, she always persisted on pushing a subject to the end. "You—er—you might help the poor of the parish!"

"Just what we do! I heard the vicar say myself that Mrs Evans was a striving little woman who ought to be supported. If we took away our custom—"

"I mean the really poor. Mrs Evans would not shut up shop for the want of your threepenny-pieces, but the Mission at Sale is always short of funds. If you had a collecting-box, you could send in a subscription at Christmas."

"'The Misses Margaret, Elsa, Agatha, and Christabel Rendell—four and sixpence halfpenny,'" quoted Chrissie derisively. She marched across the room and stationed herself with her back to the fire, her thin face looking forth from a cloud of hair, an expression of dignified disdain curling her lips. "How important it sounds, to be sure! It's all very well talking about saving up, Lilias, but it's not so easy to do with sixpence a week, and birthdays every month, and Christmas presents, and pencils and indiarubbers, and always seeing fresh things in the shop-windows that you want to buy. It's not that I wouldn't like to help: if I had a sovereign, I'd give it at once, but I won't be put down in the list for eighteenpence, and that's all I could save, if I tried, from now to Christmas. I gave a threepenny-bit to old 'Chairs to mend' only last Saturday, and one the week before to a woman who was begging. I am most charitably disposed!"

"So am I," agreed Agatha—"especially when it's cold. Rags wouldn't be so bad in summer, but they must be awfully draughty in winter. And I spend less in sweets than any of the others, because my teeth ache. I've often wished we could do something for the Mission; but I'm so poor, and I sha'n't get any goose-money till autumn. I wish we could think of some plan by which we could make some more. Chrissie and I are always talking about it. There seems so few ways in which girls of fourteen can make money. We thought of writing and asking the editor of the employment column; but mother laughed at us, and said it was nonsense. It's not nonsense to us!"

"If we could only have a sale of work," said Lilias slowly. She was still staring dreamily out of the window, and hardly realised what she was saying, but the other four girls turned sharply towards each other, and a flash of delight passed from one pair of eyes to the other.

"Ah-ah!" sighed Elsie.

"Splendiferous!" cried Nan.

"How simp-lay love-lay!" drawled Christabel, with the languid elegance of manner for which she was distinguished; and Agatha beamed broadly all over her good-humoured face, oblivious of the sufferings of the poor in the prospect of her own amusement.

"What fun we should have! I'd bake the cakes and manage the refreshment stall! Tea and coffee, threepence a cup; lemonade, fourpence; fruit salad, sixpence a plate!"

"I'd sell toffee in tins, and have a pin-cushion table, and make every single soul I know give me a contribution."

"I'd give my new oak bracket. No, it's too big. I couldn't spare that; but I'd carve something else; and make little brass trays and panels. 'High art stall: Miss Margaret Rendell. Objects of bigotry and virtue to be handed over to her,' and don't you forget it!"

"I'll take visitors out in the punt at threepence a head. I'm so stupid that I can't do any work, but the idea is mine, and that ought to count for something," said Lilias; and a vision rose before her eyes of a slim white figure gracefully handling the pole as the punt glided down the stream. Punting was a most becoming occupation; on the whole she could not have hit on a pleasanter manner of helping the cause. "I daresay I shall make quite a lot of money!" she added cheerfully; and her sisters laughed with the half-indulgent, half-derisive laughter with which they were accustomed to greet Lilias's sayings. She was so sweetly unconscious of her own selfishness, and looked so pretty as she turned her big bewildered eyes from one to the other, that they had not the heart to disturb her equanimity.

"The punt is a good idea," admitted Nan, "for people are always pleased to go on the river, and we must turn our advantages to account. A garden sale, that's what we must have! Little tables dotted about the lawn beneath Japanese umbrellas; tea in a tent, and seats under the trees. We can use all the properties that mother keeps for her garden parties, and make it just as pretty and attractive as can be. I shouldn't wonder if we made a lot of money, for we shall be so original and ingenious. People are so stupid in this world. I always feel I could do things so much better myself. Who wants to go to a stuffy old bazaar in the Mission Room? No one does! They go from a sense of duty. Mother groans and says, 'Oh dear, if I could only give a subscription and be done with it! More cosies and chairbacks! I've a drawerful already!' And bazaar things are hideous! Father gave me ten shillings to spend at the Christmas sale, and I wandered round and round like a lost sheep, and couldn't see a single thing that I wanted. In the end I bought a cover for *Bradshaw*. It wasn't a bit useful, for I never have a *Bradshaw*; but it was the nicest thing I saw. Now, let us solemnly resolve not to have anything on our stalls that will not reflect credit on our judgment. Nothing ugly, nothing useless, nothing vulgar—"

"Impossible, my dear! Can't be managed. It's the law of Nature that the kindest-hearted people have the least taste. I don't know why it should be so, but it is, and I'll prove it to you. If we announced that we were going to have a sale of work and asked for contributions, who would be the first people to respond?" Christabel thrust out her left hand and began checking off the fingers with dramatic emphasis. "Miss Ross,—Mrs Hudson,—Mary Field,—old Jane Evans. 'So pleased to hear that the dear children are interesting themselves in the welfare of their poor brothers and sisters, and I've brought round a few wool mats as a little expression of sympathy!'—that's Mrs Ross! Then Mary Ann would hobble up with a parcel wrapped up in a handkerchief, and kiss us all twice over, and say, 'I've brought round a piece of my own fancy work, lovies, as a contribution for your sale. My sight is not what it used to be, and it's difficult to get the material one would like in this little place; but shaded silks always look well, and I made the fringe myself out of odd pieces of wool.' And *that's* not the worst!

Mrs Hudson would paint bulrushes on cream-pots, and forget-me-nots on tambourines, and come round bristling with importance. 'I always find fancy work is overdone at sales, so I thought a little of my hand-painting would be acceptable! No one needs more than a dozen cosies, but every one is glad of an extra tambourine!' ... It's easy to talk, my dear, but what could you do when it came to the point? There's nothing for it but to smile, and look pleased."

"I should say politely, but firmly, that I could not find it in my heart to deprive them of such treasures—that with so many deserving objects craving support, it would be pure selfishness on our part to monopolise all the good things! Such munificence was far, far more than we deserved, and would they kindly send a little cake instead? They would be delighted, for they are everlastingly giving to some mission or other, and are always in a rush to get work finished. But I don't propose to let things reach such a climax. I wouldn't hurt their dear old feelings for the world. So we will say at once that we want cake and fruit, and we shall get the very best of its kind. We must fix our date for the strawberry season; for the human heart is desperately wicked, and people will gladly pay sixpence to sit under trees and eat strawberries and cream, when wild horses wouldn't drag twopence out of them for a pen-wiper. I expect we shall succeed best with punting and refreshments."

"If it's fine! But it won't be fine—it will pour!" said Elsie gloomily, and wagged her head in the hopeless manner of one who has tasted deeply of the world, and knew its hollowness by heart. If there was by chance a cheerful *and* a melancholy view to be taken on any subject, Elsie invariably chose the melancholy one, and gloated over it with ghoulish enjoyment. She was never so happy as when she was miserable,—as an Irishman would have had it,—and hugged the conviction that she was "unappreciated" by her family, and a victim of fate. She shed tears over *Misunderstood* in the solitude of her chamber, and cultivated an expression of patient martyrdom, as most fitted for her condition. Occasionally she forgot herself so far as to be cheery and playful; but her feelings were so ultrasensitive that they were bound to be wounded by some thoughtlessness on the part of her sisters before many hours were over, when she would remember her own unhappiness, and roam away by herself to the other end of the garden to apostrophise the heavens and pity her hard lot. "It will be sure to pour! It always does pour when we want to do anything!" she declared; upon which Nan threw her book into the air and caught it again with a dexterous movement.

"Fiddle-de-dee! It's going to be a bright, glorious summer day, with just enough sun to be warm and not enough to be hot, and just enough wind to be cool and not enough to be cold. And the grass is going to be dry and the strawberries ripe; and all the pretty ladies and gentlemen are going to drive over from miles and miles around, and spend so much money that they will have none left to take them home. What is the use of croaking? If things go wrong, it's bad enough to have to bear them at the time; but until then imagination is our own, and we will make the most of it. It will not pour, my dear Raven; so don't let me hear you say so again! Make up your mind that this sale is going to be a success, and try to bear it as well as you can."

Elsie looked up at the corner of the ceiling, and arched her eyebrows in resigned and submissive fashion. When the rain did come,—as of course it would,—when all the fancy work was drenched and the pretty dresses spoiled, the girls would remember her prophecy, and be compelled to acknowledge its correctness; but till then she would suffer in silence, and refuse to be drawn into vulgar argument. So she determined, at least; but a fiery temptation assailed her in the form of another objection, so unanswerable that it was not in human nature to resist hurling it at the heads of her companions.

"I hope you are right, I am sure; but, all the same, it is rather early in the day to make arrangements. You are counting without your host. How can you tell that mother will consent to let you have the sale at all?"

And at that the listeners hung their heads and were silent, for it was indeed useless to build castles unless they were first assured of this foundation.

Chapter Three
A New Neighbour

After dinner that evening the six girls assembled in the drawing-room, and little Mrs Rendell sat in their midst on a low chair drawn up in the centre of the fireplace. A grey silk dress fitted closely to the lines of her tiny figure, two minute little slippers were placed upon the fender, and the diamonds flashed on her fingers as she held up a fan to protect her face from the blaze. She looked ridiculously young and pretty, to be the mother of those six big girls; and a stranger looking in at the scene would have put her down as a helpless little creature, too meek and gentle to cope with such heavy responsibilities. But the stranger would have been mistaken.

"Mother darling," said Christabel insinuatingly, "granting always that you are the kindest and most amiable of mothers, do you happen to feel in an extra specially angelic temper this evening?"

"An 'oh-certainly-my-darlings-do-whatever-you-please' temper!" chimed in Nan sweetly; "because if you do—"

"I hope I shall never be so forgetful of my duties as to say anything so indiscreet," replied Mrs Rendell firmly. "Margaret, your hair is tumbling down again! Kneel down, and let me fasten it for you at once!"

Nan knelt down meekly, her roguish face on a level with her mother's, and the brown coils were twisted and hair-pinned together with swift, decided fingers.

"You must do it like this—do you see!—tighter, closer, more firmly!"

"Yes, mother."

"It's disgraceful that a big girl like you—a girl nearly eighteen—should not be able to do her own hair!"

"Yes, mother."

"You wouldn't like to be known as the girl with the untidy hair, I suppose, or to have a collapse of this sort in church or in the street?"

"No, mother."

"Then pray, my dear, be more careful. Don't let me have to speak again."

"I'll try, mother. A rough head, but a loving heart! You might kiss me now and say you're sorry, for you stuck two hair-pins right into my scalp, and I never winced!"

Mrs Rendell smiled, and laid a gentle hand on the girl's cheek. For one moment her dignified airs seemed to vanish, and nothing but motherly tenderness shone in her eyes, but the next she drew herself up again, stiff as a little poker, and said lightly —

"Nonsense, nonsense! Get up, child, and don't be ridiculous! Sit on that high chair, and don't stoop! I can't endure to see a young girl lounging on a couch. What is this new scheme that you wish to ask me about to-night?"

"Mother dear, you know you like us to be charitable! You are always preaching—er, I mean impressing upon us—that we ought to remember the poah," said Christabel, standing up as stiff as a grenadier, and smiling at her mother in her most ingratiating manner. Mrs Rendell would have died rather than acknowledge a special weakness towards any member of her flock; but as a matter of fact her youngest-born possessed a power of wheedling favours which none of her sisters could boast, and was herself agreeably conscious of the fact, and fond of putting it to the test. "I am sure you will approve of our scheme, and feel pleased with us for thinking of it. It's for the Mission. We thought of getting up a little sale among ourselves, and giving the proceeds towards the funds."

"It is so little that we can give; but if we devote our time and strength" — murmured Lilias prettily.

"It all adds up when you put it together," said practical Agatha; "and you can stick on such awful prices. Chrissie and I thought we might have the refreshments and a pin-cushion stall, and set out little tables on the lawn."

"Such jolly fun!" gushed Nan. "Every one would come; and we would have games, and sports, and sails in the boats, and something to pay wherever they went. The young ones would stay, after the others had gone, to eat up the strawberries, and we would have pounds and pounds to give to the secretary."

"Of strawberries?" queried Mrs Rendell coldly. "Your English, Nan, is painful to hear. I think I shall write down some of your sentences and give them to you to parse. Then perhaps you may realise how they sound! A sale for the Mission! That is an ambitious idea. How do you propose to get together enough work to fill a single stall, much less three or four?"

"There are five months before July, and we would work like niggers all the time. Nan would carve, we would sew, all our friends would help, and we would make money by tea and refreshments. Really and truly, we could do very well, if you would only say 'Yes'."

"And we should so enjoy it! It's horrid having nothing to look forward to; and if there was this in prospect, we should be busy and occupied, and the wet days wouldn't seem half so long!"

"Now, let us understand each other," said Mrs Rendell briskly. "Is this scheme proposed for your own amusement, or for the good of the Mission? One says one thing, one another, and I can't make up my mind whether I am asked to consent to a charity or to a novel form of garden-party. I should like to have that point settled before we go any further. Are you thinking of yourselves or your neighbours?"

Silence. The sisters looked at one another askance. Elsie sighed and shook her head, Agatha flushed to the roots of her hair, only Nan retained her composure, and said daringly —

"Both, mother. We began by saying that we should like to give a contribution, but we had so little money that it seemed hardly worth while sending it; and then the sale was suggested. The first idea was to help the Mission, but we did think that it would be good fun for ourselves as well! There is no harm in that, is there? You have said lots of times that you love cheerful givers, and it must be better to do a thing willingly than grumbling all the time. Do people who get up bazaars never think of the fun, and the dresses, and the meeting with their friends, but only just of the charity for which they are working? Oh, mother, I don't believe they do! I've heard you say yourself —"

"Nan, Nan, Nan! I object to be quoted! It is dreadful to have an audience of six girls swallowing every word, and bringing them up in judgment on the first convenient opportunity!" Mrs Rendell showed her pretty teeth in a smile of amusement, and returned to the subject in hand with suspicious haste. "Well, you are honest, at any rate, and so long as you keep the idea of helping others to the fore, and don't allow it to be crowded out by the thought of your own enjoyment, I don't see anything to object to in your scheme. No; I don't give my consent yet! You must think it over quietly for a week, and be quite sure of your own minds. A sale would involve more work than you think; for you will have to give up time and money and do the thing thoroughly, if you once take it in hand. I will promise nothing to-night; for I wonder how many times you have come to me brimming over with enthusiasm about some new plan, and how often it has collapsed like a bubble in a couple of days! You are such changeable children!"

"Oh, Mummy, come! Call things by their nice names," pleaded Nan. "It's not fickleness—it's fertility of imagination; it's not a collapse—it's only a fresh beginning! But we really mean it this time, and you mean to say 'Yes,' too. I know you do; so nothing now remains but to talk it over with Kitty in the morning."

"Ah, yes! Until Kitty has been consulted nothing can be called certain," said Mrs Rendell, smiling again; and as she spoke she lifted her head in a listening gesture, and pushed her stool from the fire. She had heard the opening of a door, and knew that her husband had finished his after-dinner cigar and was on his way to the drawing-room; and the next moment he appeared on the threshold, looked round the group by the fire, and threw himself in a chair by Nan's side.

"Well, Mops!" The big hand descended on the girl's head, and ruffled the locks which had been so carefully put in order, while she turned up her face with a beaming smile, for there was a special bond of union between herself and her father, and they aided and abetted each other in mischief like a couple of merry children. "Well, Mops, how goes it? What pranks have you been up to to-day?"

"Oh, father, none at all. I've behaved beautifully—just like a real, grown-up lady! In the morning I pursued my avocations, and in the afternoon I went out calling, with light kid gloves and a card-case. Every one was out but old Mrs Reed, and you would have loved it if you could have heard us talk! We discussed the weather in all its branches. Cold—dampy-cold—dry cold; warm—close-warm—breezy warm; hot, thundery hot, scorching. She told me which of each she liked best, and which her poor dear mother had liked best; and I lingered on and on, hoping they would bring in tea, until at last I yawned so much that I was obliged to come away unfed. Then I had cold tea and scraps in the schoolroom, and we discussed charitable agencies."

"Oh, Nan, Nan, this will never do! You are getting altogether too civilised. I shall have no playmate left at this rate," cried her father, laughing. "Can't you be satisfied with two grown-up daughters, mother, and leave Mops to me for a few years longer?"

Mrs Rendell tried to look shocked, a task which she found somewhat difficult when her husband was the offender; but if her eyes betrayed her, the elevated brows and pursed-up lips made a valiant show of disapproval.

"At eighteen? She is past eighteen, remember. You don't expect a girl of eighteen to run about in short skirts, with her hair down her back?"

"She would look much nicer!" sighed Mr Rendell, looking regretfully first at the long white skirt, and then at the coiled-up tresses. "They grow up so quickly, Edith; I live in terror of having no children left—nothing but fashionable young ladies. One must give in to custom to a certain extent, I suppose, but I warn you frankly that Chrissie shall be the exception. It would break my heart to see Chrissie properly grown up. Chrissie shall always wear her hair down her back!"

Christabel screwed up her eyes at him across the fireplace with a smile of indulgent affection. He was so young, this dear old father! so ridiculously young, that his vagaries could not be treated with the severity they deserved. It was truest wisdom to take no notice, and lead the conversation to wiser topics.

"Any news in the great world to-day, father?" she inquired airily. "Any nice little bits of gossip to tell us? We look forward to hearing your news, you know, as part of the day's excitement."

"My news, indeed! Gossip, she calls it. If you had to provide for half a dozen daughters, Miss Christabel, you wouldn't find much time to spend in 'gossip.' I go to town to work, and leave it to you at home to run round collecting the news of the neighbourhood. I know nothing. I hear nothing. Men don't trouble themselves with gossip."

Seven long-drawn gasps of incredulity greeted this utterance; seven pairs of eyes rolled involuntarily to the ceiling; seven heads wagged in accusation.

"Oh, oh, oh! Who goes on 'Change and is told the latest jokes? Who goes to a *café* after lunch and smokes with his cronies? Who has afternoon tea, and talks again? Who travels every day with the same men in the train, and hears everything, every—single—tiny—weeny snap of news that has happened within ten miles around?"

"Don't know, I'm sure. I don't!"

"Oh, oh! Who told us about Evan Bruce, and about Mabel's engagement, and the robbery at the Priory, and—and—"

"For pity's sake, stop talking all at once! Take it in turns. Speak in pairs if you must, but not in a perfect orchestra. I didn't know I had been the first to hear any of those thrilling incidents, but it was quite an exception if I did. We generally read reviews, or talk business. I've no news for you to-night, at any rate."

"You always say so at first, dear. You're so forgetful. Think again. Frank Brightwen, now—he told you something?"

"Gold Reef shares gone up two per cent. Market closed firm, with a tendency to rise."

"I shall buy some at once. I like things that are going to rise. Be sensible now, for I shall have to go to bed in ten minutes, and I do so want to be amused. Had Mr Keeling nothing interesting to relate?"

"Bad cold, and feared influenza. Details of his last attack. Prescriptions from all the other fellows, with accounts of their own experiences."

"Deah me, how appalling! Worse than a tea-party! I had no ideah men could be so dull. Nobody engaged? Nobody married? Nobody going to give a dance? No new people coming to live in the neighbourhood?"

"Ha!" Mr Rendell struck an attitude of remembrance, at which the watching faces brightened with smiles. "Yes, now I come to think of it, there was one little item of news. I forgot all about it; but you will be interested, no doubt. The Grange is sold!"

The expression of curiosity on his daughters' faces was exchanged for one of blank amazement. Even his wife gave a start of surprise, and turned towards him with eager inquiry.

"Let! Really let, Alfred? You don't mean it?"

"So I am told."

"We've been told so so often that one grows sceptical. Is it really and truly sold, and the deeds signed? I sha'n't believe it unless they are, for difficulties have cropped up so often at the last moment. Are you quite sure this time?"

"As sure as it is possible to be about anything in this wicked world. Braithwaite tells me it's an accomplished fact. The deeds are signed, and the workmen are to begin putting the house in order next week. You may take it as settled this time, for the man really means to come. He is a certain Ernest Vanburgh by name, and has been living abroad for some years."

"And is there a Mrs Vanburgh, and has he any children, and are they young or grown up?"

"Is he a dull sort of man, or will he be hospitable, and give dinners and parties and help to make the place lively?"

"Is he musical, father, because there's that lovely big room where we could have such charming musical evenings?"

Mr Rendell shrugged his shoulders with an air of resignation.

"How like a woman, or rather, I should say, how like half a dozen women put together! My dears, I know absolutely nothing about the man, except that he has bought the place. He is in a hurry to get settled, so you will probably find out all about him for yourselves before many weeks are over. It's no use asking questions. He was willing to pay down the money, and that was all that Braithwaite cared about. He may be a bachelor or a second Bluebeard, for all I know; but I suppose in either case he will still be better than nobody."

"Of course he will. Blank windows are so dull. Curtains are much more interesting. There's so much character in curtains. I can tell the sort of woman who lives in a house merely by looking at her curtains. It will be a new interest in life to have the Grange let again."

"And I have a Feeling that it will be an Epoch in our lives. I have a Feeling that our Fate and that of the new tenants will be inextricably woven together. It may be foolish, but these convictions are borne in upon me; I cannot help them!" cried Elsie, clasping her hands and opening her blue eyes to the fullest capacity, as she turned a gaze of mysterious raptness upon the group by the fireplace. "Perhaps in years to come we may look back upon this evening as a milestone marking out the past from the future, and realise—"

A burst of laughter put a stop to further sentimentalising, and Elsie retired within her shell, aggrieved and dignified; but for once she was right in her surmises, for her own fate and that of her sisters was indeed destined to be permanently affected by the coming of the new tenant of the Grange.

Chapter Four
Castles in the Air

The news that the Grange was sold was truly of great interest to the Rendell family, for the house faced their own on the opposite side of the road, and its uninhabited condition had been a standing grievance. That one of the handsomest houses of the neighbourhood should remain empty was a serious matter in a small community, and the younger girls listened with bated breath to the accounts of the gorgeous entertainments which had been given by the last tenant, hoping against hope that the time would soon come when the house would once more be thrown open, and the great oak-panelled rooms re-echo to the sound of music and laughter. Like their own house, a portion of the Grange abutted on to the high road, so that a row of windows lay immediately open to inspection; but two great wings stretched back to right and left, and the house was surrounded on three sides by beautiful and extensive grounds. The late owner had spent lavishly in beautifying the place, and had asked in return a sum so exorbitant, that though many would-be tenants had arrived to look over the house, one and all drew back when the nature of his demands was made known, and the Rendell girls were not the only people who had despaired of a settlement. But now at last a delightful certainty had been gained, the deeds were signed, and the long waiting was at an end!

The morning after the news had been received, Agatha and Christabel rushed to the porch-room directly after breakfast, and flattened their noses against the pane to watch for the first sign of their chosen companion, that same Kitty of whom mention has already been made, and who came daily to join the schoolroom party, instead of indulging in the luxury of a governess of her own. She came at last, a tall lamp-post of a girl, with blue serge skirt blowing back from long brown legs, a plaid Tam O'Shanter perched on the top of chestnut locks, and a bundle of books tucked beneath the arm of a corduroy jacket. Christabel banged an eager fist upon the window, and rushed downstairs in a whirl of excitement to meet her friend, and carry her off to the schoolroom.

"My deah, such news! You'll never guess! It's perfectly charming! You'll go wild when you hear it!"

Kitty sat down in a chair and gazed calmly around. Whether she would "go wild" or not when the news was unfolded remained to be seen; but in the meantime her composure showed not the slightest sign of being disturbed.

"Um!" she ejaculated, and began to divest herself of her outdoor garments, as if nothing more important engrossed her attention. She tugged at the fingers of her deerskin gloves, and let them fall indiscriminately at either side of her chair; she sent her cap flying across the room, wriggled out of her jacket, kicked her overshoes beneath the table, then folded her arms and seemed to feel that she had no further responsibility in the matter. The art of putting away outdoor clothes was one, indeed, which Miss Kitty seemed powerless to master. In vain her mother exhausted herself in objurgation, and grew alternately pitiful and angry; Kitty kissed her fervently and vowed amendment, but the next day there was the jacket as usual, hanging over a dining-room chair, and the other garments dropped in as many odd places about the house. This method of procedure was, no doubt, a saving of trouble in the first instance, but retribution followed when it came to starting out again after lunch, when Miss Kitty might have been seen plunging wildly about the room in search of a missing glove or tie, while groans of despair attended every movement.

"Where *can* it be? Wish my things could be left alone! Always stuck out of the way! Shall be late again now, and get bad marks. Not my fault. Horrid old servants! Wish they'd do their own work, and leave my things alone." So on, and so on, until at last the missing article was found, folded up in a magazine, or thrust beneath a fern-pot, when Kitty would seize it resentfully, and stalk down the garden-path on her long brown legs, puffing and fuming, and feeling herself the most ill-used of mortals. On the present occasion Elsie and Agatha entered the room as she finished undressing, and the former immediately set to work to gather together the scattered possessions and put them away, for she was tidier-in-general to the household, and could never by any possibility bring herself to sit down comfortably in a room where a picture hung awry, or a tablecloth dipped unevenly at the corner. The while she moved about she cast a pensive glance at the newcomer, and exclaimed regretfully—

"Kitty doesn't approve. I saw it in her face the moment I came into the room. I knew she wouldn't, and I don't know that I do, either. It's a great risk!"

"I haven't heard anything to approve of yet. Chrissie has been too excited to descend to details. You seem to have been very busy! I never heard of any news when I was here yesterday."

There was a tinge of displeasure in the voice in which the last sentence was spoken, and Agatha, the tenderhearted, was quick to note it, and to explain away the misconception.

"There was nothing to hear. It happened later. There are two things we want to tell you about. One is a piece of news from the outside, and the other is our own special affair; but of course it's not really settled, for, as mother said, until you had been consulted, nothing definite could be decided."

"Think not, indeed!" said Kitty shortly. She put her hand in her pocket and drew forth a pair of steel-rimmed spectacles, which she placed, not on the bridge, but on the extreme tip of her nose. Her curly hair was roughened over her shoulders, the brown ribbon bow stood up erect at the top of her head; her arms were folded in deliberate inelegance, and she gazed over the spectacles with an air of grandmotherly condescension, comically at variance with her appearance.

"Let me hear about it at once, or Miss Phelps will arrive, and I shall burst with curiosity in the middle of lessons. What is it that you want to do?"

Elsie, Agatha, and Christabel immediately proceeded to explain the situation in characteristic Rendell fashion, all speaking together, and continuing to speak, without being in the least disconcerted by the babble evoked. Elsie whined, Agatha gurgled, and Chrissie drawled, while the listener rolled her eyes from one to another, catching a phrase here, a phrase there, until at length some dawning of the situation began to make itself known.

"A sale of work! We are to slave away making pin-cushions from now until July, and then sell them to some one else! I understand that; but what is the idea of doing it? Who is going to get the money when it is made?"

"The poor and needy!"

"Thank you so much! Most considerate, I'm sure!"

"Kittay, be quiet! The Mission, of course; the Mission at Sale. We thought we ought to help, as it is in debt, and we do no good with our money as it is. We could collect enough to buy materials if we give up sweets for the next few months."

Kitty's face fell gloomily. "I've only three and fourpence in the world, and it's mother's birthday next month, and Aunt May's and granny's the month after that, and Agatha's next week."

"Don't count me! I'm as poor as Job myself, but my old yellow sash will wash and make into sachets, and I'll cut the crushed parts out of hair ribbons, and use the ends for needlebooks. If they are a tiny bit stained, I will embroider flowers over the spots. We shall manage the work somehow, never fear; and think of the tea and refreshments, and sails in the punts! We shall simply coin money over them. Lilias is going to do the punting."

"Naturally she is!" Kitty's eyes twinkled with humorous enjoyment. "Easy and profitable! Just the sort of work Lilias likes. Oh yes, I agree. I'd like to work and feel that I was reforming the world, and it will be great jokes. I know what I'll do. I'll take snap-shots at the company with my new Kodak, and take orders for copies. There's an idea for you! People are so vain that they always think they would like a photograph—until they see a proof! If they refuse, I shall try another plan. I will snap them unawares, and say, 'I have taken several photographs of you this afternoon at moments which, perhaps, you would prefer not to have immortalised. The negative is yours for two and six.' How do you think that would work as a source of income?"

"Better not let mother hear you talk like that, my child, or the Kodak will be forbidden once for all, and it is really a lovely idea! You could take the punt with the different people on board, and groups eating refreshments, and talking to each other on the lawn. My deah, you will amass fortunes! I'm jealous of you. I believe you will make far more than we shall with our tea."

"But of course if it's wet"—insinuated Elsie persistently, only to be frowned down by her companions, who were eager to impart the second and most exciting piece of intelligence.

"It won't be wet, Croaky! Don't say that again. That's one piece of news, then; now for the other! Three guesses, Kitty, for a really convulsing piece of local gossip."

"Maud is engaged?"

"Not yet! You can guess that again later on! This special piece of news is not about our family at all. Some one else! Guess again!"

"Some one I know well?"

"No!"

"Slightly?"

"No!"

"Not at all?"

"Yes!"

"Then how on earth can I possibly—"

"It isn't necessary to know the person. No one knows him yet, but we soon shall. He is coming to—to—can't you guess? Think of the empty houses near here!"

"The Grange!" cried Kit, and clapped her hands with delight. "Some one has bought the Grange! How sweet of him! Now we shall have something to look at. He is coming soon, you say—oh, what fun! We can watch the furniture unload, and the family arrive. Who are they, and how many may they be? Lots of girls, I hope—the right sort, with plenty of fun in them, and pony-carriages of their own, in which they can drive us about!"

"We don't know a single thing about them, and can't find out. The man is called Vanburgh, which is all right so far as it goes, but whether he is married or a bachelor—"

"Of course he is married! A bachelor would never dare to take a house like the Grange. It would be downright wicked! He is a married man, with a grey beard, and a fat wife, and four beauteous daughters. I see them now before me, as in a mirror!" Kitty shut her eyes behind the spectacles, and screwed up her face into a grimace which was meant to be vague and visionary, but fell a long way short of success. She was fond of indulging in flights of fancy, and her friends waited for her utterances with smiling delight.

"Yes, yes, I see them all! Véronique, the eldest, is a stately beauty, tall and slender, with lustrous Spanish eyes, and locks—"

"Black as the raven's wing." Chrissie's murmur seemed a fitting climax to the description, but the Visionary objected to be interrupted, and turning scornful eyes upon her, said icily—

"Quite the contrary. Bright as pure gold! She knows not the meaning of fear, and rides an Arab charger, who knows every movement of her mistress's hand. She is betrothed to the scion of a noble house, and will shortly be led to the hymeneal altar, when we shall attend as maids of honour, clad in the sheen of satin and glimmer of pearls. Gabriella, the second, is *mignonne* in stature, with a wee, winsome face—"

But at this point in the description Agatha spluttered with laughter, and Christabel rose from her seat, and began banging down books on the table with disdainful emphasis.

"I refuse to listen any longer to such uttah rubbish."—"Wee, winsome face," repeated Kitty loudly, determined to finish the sentence or perish in the attempt. "Eyes blue as the summer skies, and a skin of snow and roses. She has a timorous, shrinking nature, and prefers a milk-white charger to her sister's untamed steed. Evangeline, the third, has tawny locks and a dimpling smile, and makes up by charm of manner for what she lacks in regular beauty. Valentine, the fourth—"

But the characteristics of Miss Vanburgh number four were fated to remain in obscurity, for at that moment a step was heard approaching the schoolroom door, and the historian made a dash forward to collect her books, and place them on the table, before the entrance of Miss Roberts, the governess.

Chapter Five
An Unexpected Visitor

During the next few weeks the workmen took possession of the Grange, and each morning as Kit made her appearance in the schoolroom Christabel had some fresh item of intelligence to unfold.

"A blue paper is going up in the bedroom—pale, pale blue, with loops of roses tied with lovers' knots—s–imply sweet! ... Nothing but brown paper in the little room over the door—nasty, common brown paper like you use for parcels. Hideous! What can they be thinking of?"—and the girls would stare together through the windows, watching every movement of painters and paperers with breathless interest.

Later on a still more exciting period was reached, when vanloads of furniture arrived, and their contents were spread about on the roadway. Then the Rendell girls massed themselves in the porch-room, and while they manufactured needle-books, and scattered bran over the floor in the wholesale manufacture of pincushions, Lilias played the part of Sister Anne, sitting with idle hands, reporting progress to the workers, and sounding a bugle-note of warning when any object appeared which demanded attention. The numberless packing-cases were baffling to feminine curiosity, but the furniture itself was so unique that the most prosaic articles assumed a surprising interest. There were no modern designs to be seen here, no cream enamelled bedroom suites, no green wood chairs, nor cosy corners. Everything belonging to the house was of a sombre grandeur which belonged to another country than our own. Sideboards and cabinets of carved Indian wood blocked up the roadway, and made black patches against the oak-panelled walls; overmantels of the same dusky hue stretched up to the ceilings, and Oriental rugs of priceless value, but distressing shabbiness, were spread over the floors, while the lower windows were covered with screens of carved wood, such as are to be seen over the windows of Turkish harems.

Lilias, the worldly wise, was pleased to pronounce the equipments of the house as in "a style of quiet magnificence," but her sisters were less enthusiastic, and Nan screwed up her saucy nose in open disdain.

"Very grand and antique-y, and all that sort of thing, but my, how dull! Fancy sitting in that oak-panelled room, with those black ghosts reared up against the walls, and the light shut out by those carved screens. I should go stark, staring mad! Give me something bright and cheerful, and lots of sunshine. What worries me is that there is so little that is feminine and frivolous. I haven't seen a single thing as yet that looks suitable for a girl's room."

"But think of the cases! All those dozens and dozens of cases. You can never tell what may be inside them. They may be stored with—"

"Treasures of buhl and ormolu!" sighed Kit softly. "That's what they always say in books, though I haven't the slightest idea what it means. Wouldn't it be a terrific blow if there were no girls after all?"

But such a possibility the Rendells absolutely refused to admit. The prospect of finding friends of their own age in the deserted Grange had taken such firm hold of their imagination, that Véronique, Evangeline, and Ermyntrude had already become living companions who played a part in their lives, and whose tastes had to be seriously considered in arranging the future. They longed for the time to come when doubt would be put at an end; but the Vanburghs seemed in no hurry to appear, and meanwhile April was at hand, and, as was their custom, Mr and Mrs Rendell prepared to leave home on a short holiday, leaving the girls alone to battle with the terrors of spring-cleaning.

Mrs Rendell had strong ideas on the subject of domestic education, and would allow no extra help to be engaged for this yearly upheaval. It was timed to take place in the Easter holidays, and each girl was expected to take a special task in hand, and to bring it to a satisfactory conclusion. She herself frankly confessed that she had come to a time of life when she was thankful to be spared fatigue and discomfort; but her husband was not so willing to make the admission, and talked about his proposed absence in an impersonal fashion, which vastly amused his hearers.

"Mother has had to bear the burden of housekeeping for over twenty years, and I think it quite time that some of you took it off her shoulders. It is good training for girls to learn everything that has to be done in connection with a house, so for your sakes as well as hers I feel it a duty to take her away." So he spoke, and Nan rolled her eyes at him in mischievous fashion, poking forward her head until her face was but a few inches from his own.

"And—er, what about your own? You do not love the smell of soft soap, do you, dear? I remember last year—"

Her father waved his arms helplessly.

"Everything tasted of it! Soup, fish, puddings, everything one ate seemed saturated with soft soap; and there is something peculiarly depressing about a house with no carpets on the floors. I feel as if I were going to be sold up; and if there is one thing more aggravating than another, it is to be obliged to sit in a fresh room every day, and have all one's possessions stored carefully out of sight. Now, remember, whoever dusts the books in the library is only to take out a few at a time, and put them back—ex-actly where she found them!"

"Yes, father!"

"No servant is to touch them! I know what that means—every book piled on the floor, and stuffed back into the shelves just as they come! You girls are responsible, and must dust them yourselves."

"Mine own fair hands shall do the deed—in gloves, however, for I know those books of old, and shall smother myself in sheets before I begin. I don't object to a few days' charing for a change," said Nan briskly. "I love rushing about in an apron, using my muscles instead of my brain, gathering all the ornaments together, and washing them in a nice soapy bath—"

"And watching the water get dirty! Isn't it lovely?" gushed Agatha enthusiastically. "It isn't a bit interesting when they are only a little bit soiled. I like figures and things with lots of creases where the dust gets in, and you have to scrub away with a nail-brush, and the water gets black— perfectly black! It's lovely!"

Every one laughed, even Mrs Rendell, though she felt in duty bound to protest at the idea of anything being "black" in her well-kept house; and the girls proceeded to sing the joys of spring-cleaning with youthful fervour.

"What I like best are the picnic meals," said Chrissie. "We always have the same things for lunch—a round of cold salt beef and beetroot, and coffee, and bread and jam. It is all put on the table at once, and we all carve for ourselves, and march about the room with aprons on, and behave as badly as we like. Then we have tea about three, and cold meat again for dinner, and fruit instead of pudding, and are all so stiff that we can hardly move, and all fighting to have the first hot bath. The water gets cold after the second, so it's a great thing to be first, if you can."

"And there are such amusing *contretemps*!" said Maud, the good-natured. "There seems to be a special imp of mischief abroad at these times, for something is bound to go wrong. You can't guard against it, for it is always the last thing you could expect, and it happens at the worst moment, and in some extraordinary manner stops all the wheels of the machinery. It is really excruciatingly funny—"

"You don't think so at the time! When Agatha knocked a nail into the gas-pipe on Thursday afternoon, when the shops were closed, and all the men had gone off to a beanfeast, you didn't think it much of a joke then!" said Elsie darkly. "We tried leaving the nail in and smearing the hole with soap, but the gas came out in gusts, and we had to turn it off, and there were only two candles in the house. ... We sat all evening in the dark, and undressed together in one room, because we were obliged to give the servants one of the candles. It wasn't in the least funny, and you didn't think so either."

"Oh, I don't know! It gave us a rest, which we wanted badly, and it is amusing to think of afterwards. I've often thought of it, and laughed to myself,"—and Maud laughed again, the happy, kindly laugh which was the outward sign of a sweet-hearted nature.

Altogether it was a very cheerful little party of workers whom the parents left behind when the hour for departure arrived. It was a bright, inspiring spring morning, just one of the days when it is delightful to start off on the first holiday of the year, and Mr and Mrs Rendell looked fully appreciative of the fact. He was attired in a new suit, while his wife, not to be outdone, had provided herself with a pretty blue coat and skirt, and a flowered toque which was perhaps a trifle more summery than the season justified. After twenty-five years of married life, it was still a delight to this husband and wife to steal off for a holiday by themselves, and Mrs Rendell took the same delight in her husband's approval as when she had first become his wife. Every detail of her attire was daintily correct, and so pretty did she look, so trig and smart, that her six big daughters stared at her in admiration.

"Perfectly s–weet!" was Chrissie's verdict; then her eyes passed on to her handsome, stalwart father, and a twinkle of amusement showed in her eyes. "They both do! And so spick and span—everything new from head to foot. They might be a newly-married couple—a trifle elderly, but ve–ry well preserved! I shouldn't wonder if people thought they were. How would it be if we hid a little rice?—"

"Happy thought! A most delicate attention. Keep them talking for a few minutes while I pay a visit to the kitchen," cried Nan, deftly nipping up the roll of umbrellas, and disappearing from the hall, to return with the meekest of meek faces, and bid a fond adieu to the parents for whose confusion she had been planning.

When the carriage drove off, the conspiracy was divulged to the other girls, who fully appreciated the humour of the position, but were unanimously eager to disclaim responsibility.

"I'd give worlds to be there when they open the straps!" cried Agatha. "It will be too killingly funny. They will both jump and get red in the face—father from laughter, and mother from rage. Oh-oh, it's lovely; but I didn't do it, remember! I hadn't a suspicion of it until this minute!"

"I couldn't have allowed it, if you had consulted me, but I'm glad you didn't!" Maud declared. "It will be exciting hearing how it comes off. They won't need rugs or umbrellas in the train, but crossing the Channel mother is sure to feel chilly, as she will never sit in the cabin. Father will settle her comfortably in a chair on deck and proceed to unfasten the rugs. Every one will look on, for there is nothing else to do on board ship but stare at your companions. Then patter, patter, patter, down the rice will fall, and roll along the deck. I can see it all! And the more they blush, the younger they will look; and the angrier and more confused they are, the more natural it will seem. Oh, I do hope and trust it comes off on the steamer!"

"It would be even better in the train!" said Lilias wisely. "If they once get settled in the train to Paris, they would be stuck with the same people for five mortal hours, whether they liked it or not, and they would stare, and stare, and stare. Whatever father and mother said, it would make no difference, for they would think they were only pretending. Oh, Nan, I wouldn't be you! You will catch it!"

Nan shrugged her shoulders recklessly. "Time works wonders. If they were coming home to-morrow I should tremble; but after ten days' galumptious holiday it wouldn't be in human nature to come home and be cross with a poor, hard-working Cinderella. Besides, why should they be vexed? When I'm married you can use as much rice as you like. I don't mind if I scatter it broadcast wherever I go. I shall just smile back in the people's faces, and hang on to Adolphus for support. If I can afford a little amusement to my fellow-creatures, I shall not be so selfish as to object;

and I must say that for my own part I do adore finding out a bride and bridegroom, and staring at them with all my eyes."

"I shall never marry; but if I do I shall wear my oldest clothes on my honeymoon, and snap at my husband every time he opens his mouth. That's the way to manage!" said Christabel with an air, and the two elder girls exchanged smiles of amusement. Neither of them volunteered any information as to how she herself would behave in the circumstances, for the nearer such a possibility becomes, the less easy it is to discuss it in indifferent fashion. Lilias dropped her lids in smiling modesty, and Maud's eyes shone with a happy glow. She was twenty-three now, and for the last four years a secret hope had dwelt in her heart, and invested the future with charm. It had begun on a certain holiday time, when Jim for the second or third time had brought home his friend Ned Talbot for a visit, and Ned had caught his foot in a rabbit-hole, and sprained it so severely that he was a prisoner at Thurston House for weeks, instead of days. Lilias and Nan were away at school at that time, but Maud had finished her education, and shared with her mother the task of amusing the invalid. She read aloud to him; played on the piano; was demolished at Halma; and, above all, talked to him on one topic after another, growing ever more and more intimate, until at the end of the visit it had seemed as if there was no secret which was held back from Ned Talbot's knowledge. He had not said so much in return, but there was no sense of chill in his reserve. He was naturally silent, and a word from him meant more than many protestations from another. Maud knew that he enjoyed her society by a hundred indefinable signs; and when they bade each other good-bye, the glance of the dark eyes seemed to speak of a warmer interest than that of friendship. Since then four years had passed by, and twice a year at least Ned had contrived to pay a visit to Waybourne.

Now that the other girls were at home there were no longer opportunities for uninterrupted converse, for, as the eldest daughter of a large household, Maud was often compelled to busy herself with household duties, leaving the charge of entertainment to the younger girls; but she felt sure that Ned understood, and no trace of dissatisfaction clouded her gentle spirit. She calculated happily that four months had passed since his last appearance, and felt her cheeks flush as she remembered Jim's accounts of a recent prosperous change in his friend's business. A great step upward had been taken during the last year, and now, for the first time, Talbot was in a position to keep a wife! This being so, who could tell what might happen next? The hour to which she had looked forward to so long, when Ned would give her a right to love him and to be his helpmeet in life, might be close at hand. Oh, it was a good world, a beautiful world! Life was in its spring, and every opening bud and flower in the green world without seemed to typify the hope in her own heart!

THE NEXT FEW DAYS WITNESSED A RUSH OF INDUSTRY.

The next few days witnessed a perfect rush of industry. It was no light task to complete the cleaning of so large a house in ten days' time, but many hands make light work; and while the servants scrubbed and scoured, the girls performed the lighter duties, washing ornaments, polishing pictures, turning faded draperies, sewing on new lengths of fringe, until old bottles were, if not exactly converted into new, at least assured a fresh lease of juvenility. There was always a rush to get the work finished a day or two before the parents' return, for the time that was over was legally the girls' own, to be employed in whatsoever manner seemed most pleasing. Christabel stayed in bed to breakfast; Agatha ate apples and read novels all day long; Elsie made copious entries in her diary, and wore her hair in the picturesque confusion which she considered becoming, and felt it cruel of her mother to forbid; Nan worked in her studio, and came down to dinner in a flannel shirt; Lilias wore her best clothes, and went up to town to see and be seen; and Maud dreamt dreams at her ease, without the disturbing consciousness of work undone.

By the end of the week the carpets were cleaned and ready to put down, and it was decided that the drawing-room felting should be laid first of all, because in itself it was a more lengthy task than the mere laying of squares, and also because the after work of arranging pictures and china would be greater here than elsewhere. The three maids shut themselves in the room together for an hour or more, and at the end of the time adjourned in a body to the library, where the young mistresses were busy arranging books. They looked flushed and discouraged, and each of the three had her own comments to make upon the situation. Cook reported that "that there felting wouldn't come right nohow." Mary put her hand to her heart, and said her inside ached with dragging the tiresome thing; and bright-eyed Jane smiled cheerfully, and vowed that "she didn't believe it never would meet no more." The girls adjourned into the drawing-room to investigate the difficulty, and found the felting neatly fastened at three sides, but steadily refusing to come within inches of the fourth wall.

"Seems as if it's shrunk itself somehow in the cleaning," said cook dolefully; but Maud only laughed, and went forward to the rescue in her cheery, capable manner.

"Oh, nonsense, cook! If the cleaning did anything, it would stretch it and make it bigger. It is purposely made rather a tight fit, or it would go into wrinkles, which would never do. It only wants a little coaxing. Nan and Agatha, you have the strongest arms, go over there and pull as hard as you can, while Elsie and I push towards you."

No sooner said than done. Maud and Elsie went down on their knees, and travelled slowly across the floor, pushing infinitesimal creases before them, while the others pulled and strained to make the most of the advantage thus given. It was a lengthy business, and the crawling operation was repeated several times over before the first ring could be induced to catch over its nail; but when this was done hope began to revive, and the pushing and tugging was carried on with such vigour that presently the last fastening was secured, and the workers rested from their labours, weary, yet triumphant.

"My back!" groaned Elsie, straightening herself with a groan; "it's broken in two. I feel as if I could never stand erect again."

"My hands!" groaned Agatha, stretching out her arms, and slowly uncurling ten cramped-up fingers. "They ache. Whew! I never worked so hard in my life. I shall be more careful about spilling crumbs on this carpet in the future, now that I know what it means to have it cleaned. How you ever got it up I can't think. It must have been even more difficult than putting it down."

"Broke every nail I 'ave," said cook concisely. "It's not woman's work, and that's the truth. We 'ad ought to 'ave 'ad a man to do it that 'ad proper tools; but there, it's done, thank goodness, for another year, and it's the worst in the house. Them squares is no trouble."

"No; I think you can manage the squares yourselves; but first of all we will have the furniture brought in here. The house looks so forlorn with the hall blocked up, and if we get one room tidy, we shall feel that we are getting on," said Maud, who as yet had not risen from the floor, but sat with feet stretched out, gathering resolution to begin work afresh. She stretched out her hands and drew herself slowly along towards the farther side of the room; but scarcely had she moved a couple of feet when she gave an exclamation of dismay, and, stopping short, passed her hand over the surface of the felting.

"Whatever is this? Something sticking up through the felting! Sharp little points, here and there. Dozens of them all about! What can they be?"

The others hastened to the spot, and gazed with horror-stricken eyes at a number of minute molehills showing distinctly in the felting, and each one presenting a sharp point when investigated by the touch.

"It's nails!" croaked Elsie deeply; and at that cook gave a groan of dismay.

"It is, for sure! Them dratted tacks! Your Mar said we was to put in a tack here and there between the rings, and there was a saucerful just there. Somebody has knocked it over, I expect, and scattered them about the floor."

Maud looked round with a despairing glance. The accident had happened in the worst possible position, as such accidents are invariably supposed to do, the nails being spilt a couple of yards from the wall, in such a position that two sides of the carpet must be unfastened before they could be removed. She stared at her sisters, and they stared back in a long, sullen silence.

"We can't do it again, and we sha'n't!" said Nan recklessly. "Send for a man, and let him break his fingers for a change. I need mine for another purpose."

"Thursday afternoon, my dear. The shops are shut, and not a man to be had."

"Never saw anything like it. It always is Thursday afternoon! Put a table over the place then, and leave the tacks where they are. No one will see them."

"Oh, Nan, as if a table could stay in the same place for a year. Besides, the nails are bound to come out; if we don't take them away, they'll work little holes for themselves, and then what would mother say? There's no use shirking it. The carpet has to come up again, and we shall have to do it."

"It's too disgusting! All this time wasted, and now to find ourselves farther back than when we started. I could cry!" protested Elsie dolefully; and Maud gave a little flop of impatience.

"Oh, so could I—howl, if that would do any good; but it won't, so we might as well stop talking and set to work. Begin at once, Jane, please; we'll push, and make it as easy as possible."

The workers crawled wearily back to their posts, while the audience, in the shape of Lilias and Christabel, stood in the doorway and cheered them with derisive comments.

"Amusing *contretemps*, isn't it? Reminds one of Maud's ecstasies the other evening. Quite pleased, aren't you, Maudie, to have another illustration of the humours of house-cleaning?"

"Never mind, darlings, keep cool! You'll think it very funny in six months' time. If you work hard you'll finish by to-morrow morning!"

The glances cast upon the miscreants in reply to their witticisms were so threatening, that they ran back to the library to stifle their laughter; but five minutes had not elapsed before they were back again, gasping in consternation.

"A caller! Some one at the door! Can't see properly, but it's a man! A young man in a frock coat and a tall hat. What shall we do?"

"Send him away, of course. Jane, quick! put on a clean apron, and tell the gentleman that Mrs Rendell is away from home. If he asks for us—we are engaged. Sorry you can't ask him in, as the house is upset. He'll see that for himself," added Maud, in a resigned tone, as Jane hurried from the room. "The hall looks as if it were in the midst of a removal, and if he had had any sense he would have known from the look of the windows that we were not in a fit state to receive callers. Anyhow, he will have to go away now."

The visitor, however, refused to go away, for, to the consternation of the listeners, the parley at the front door was succeeded by the sound of footsteps picking their way through the piled-up furniture, and Jane's suggestion of "The library, sir," was apparently neglected, for the tramp came nearer and nearer to the drawing-room door. Six pairs of hands were raised to smooth six ruffled heads, Maud twitched down her sleeves, Lilias stood in an attitude of graceful attention, and the next moment the door was thrown open, and Ned Talbot's deep voice called out a greeting.

"May I come in? I refused to be turned away at the door. How does everybody do? You look very busy. I am going to stay and help you."

Chapter Six
Nan plays Helper

Alas for Maud! Had it been for this that she had lived in dreams since October last, planning afresh, and yet afresh, every detail of the next meeting with Ned? Had it been for this that she had mentally arranged background, occasion, opportunity, sending abroad mother, and sisters five, and seating herself in solitude to await Ned's arrival? Had it been for this that she had cherished her dainty new blouse, refusing to crush it beneath cloak or shawl, and appearing over and over again in the pink of a bygone age, so that it might appear in its first beauty for Ned's inspection? Oh, it was hard to have planned so well, and then to be discovered with ruffled hair, flushed cheeks, and unbecoming attire! Lilias was only the more picturesque for her working attire, and was even now shaking hands with the visitor, and welcoming him in pretty, winsome fashion, as the other girls shook down skirts and aprons, and took furtive peeps in the looking-glass.

"Mr Talbot. You! This is a surprise. It is delightful to see you again, but we are so upset! We are in the throes of spring-cleaning, as you perceive. Have you come from town? Agatha, Chrissie, bring in a few chairs! This is the only room that has a pretence of a carpet, but at any rate we can give you a chair to sit upon."

"But I don't want one. I have been sitting in the train, and would rather stand for a change, or, still better, help with some work. Please don't treat me as a visitor! What were you about when I came in? Laying a carpet? Six of you! It doesn't take six women to lay one carpet, surely!"

Nan groaned dismally.

"It does indeed, and then they can't do it! It's nasty, horrid, rough, heavy work, only fit for men, and not for our poor little fingers. We had just succeeded, with immense labour, in fastening it all round when we made the cheerful discovery that a boxful of nails are scattered over the floor beneath. You came in at the ghastly moment when it had dawned upon us that it had all to come up again!"

Nan waved her hand with a tragic movement towards the little heap of nails, then, making a sudden step forward, caught her foot in a loose piece of braid at the bottom of her skirt, and went rushing forward at a headlong run, to be caught in Ned Talbot's arms, and so rescued from destruction against a corner of the wall.

"Nan, I told you that that braid was torn! I told you to sew it up! I *told* you you'd trip and hurt yourself," cried Maud reproachfully; but the culprit only laid her hand over her heart, and gurgled in impenitent amusement.

"But I didn't, you see! I came off all right. It's only a little end—not worth talking about!"—and she took a couple of pins from the corner of her apron and began fastening up the offending loop, while her sister lifted her hands in disapproval.

"Pins? They won't hold! Better go upstairs and sew it at once. If you don't, I warn you, Nan,"—but Maud did not get any further in her prophecy, for Ned Talbot came over to her side, and looked down at her with kindly, anxious eyes.

"Maud, you look so tired! Don't trouble any more about the carpet; I'll manage it for you. What's the good of a great lumbering six-footer if he can't manage a little job like that! I'll have it up and down again before you can say 'Jack Robinson,' and then we will have our talk in comfort."

"It's more difficult than you think," said Maud dolefully; but Ned only laughed, then proceeded to take off his coat and go down on his knees to attack the obstinate rings. The workers took advantage of the opportunity to adjust hair-pins, and divest themselves of soiled aprons, while Lilias, having no such defects to remedy, developed sudden interest in the work on hand, and knelt down on the floor beside him, holding out first one implement and then another for his use. The softly-tinted face and cloudy golden hair looked lovelier than ever about the long white smock which she had adopted as her working costume, and poor Maud stared at her own heated reflection with increased disfavour, the while she whispered in Nan's ear—

"I suppose he expects to stay for the evening. So awkward! Can we ask him, do you think, when mother's away?"

"Mother would be very much annoyed if we sent away an old friend, who has stayed in the house dozens of times, without even offering him a meal; especially when he has travelled twenty miles to see us!"

"But, my dear, what have we got? I can't give him dinner. There's nothing in the house but cold meat."

"Cutlets and tinned fruit—the refuge of the destitute! Send Mary flying to the butcher's!"

"It's Thursday afternoon!"

Nan's groan of dismay brought Ned Talbot's head round in inquiry. The rings were giving way obediently in his strong grasp, and Lilias was clapping her hands at each fresh success, and chatting away in animated fashion. The sisters waited until the work was resumed, and then continued the whispered conference.

"It always *is* Thursday when we want anything. People should never be allowed to shut their shops. Cold meat it must be, then, and nothing else, I'm afraid. We might manage to manufacture a few made dishes from the tinned things in the store-room, but *entrées* and savouries seem out of place in the middle of spring-cleaning, and the dining-room is impassable—a perfect block."

"We might alter that if we put out the things that are needed for this room. We had better go and do it now, for we don't seem needed here any longer,"—and Maud cast a wistful look towards the two kneeling figures in the corner. She envied Lilias her position; but it never entered into her honest heart to mistrust her sister's loyalty, or to put a cynical construction upon this sudden show of industry. All the girls were fond of Ned; it was only natural that Lilias should want to help him. She held out her poor, roughened hands, and looked appealingly at Nan as they stood outside the drawing-room door.

"I might wash them, mightn't I, and put on a pair of cuffs, and a fresh tie? I won't change my blouse, of course; but he is a man, and wouldn't notice what I'd done—only perhaps that I looked a little bit nicer!"

Nan nodded silently, a lump rising in her throat at the sight of the wistful face. She was the only one of the sisters who had been told the secret of Maud's heart, and the bond between these two girls was very strong and tender. She watched Maud until she disappeared from sight, with her lips screwed tightly together, and her eyebrows meeting in an ominous frown across her forehead. She felt very fierce and formidable at that moment, and it was a positive relief to be able to vent some of her pent-up irritation in work, so for the next ten minutes she dragged and tugged at the piled-up furniture, making order out of confusion, and carrying the lighter drawing-room articles into the hall, in readiness to be put into their proper places. Then Maud reappeared, smartened up by those subtle touches which every woman knows how to bestow, and no man is able to understand, though the result is patent to his eyes; and after a second consultation on the subject of dinner, a return was made to the drawing-room, to see how the carpet-laying was progressing. Ned Talbot was still on his knees, but now he was fastening instead of unfastening the rings, while Lilias was exhibiting a cup full of sharp, jagged little nails. The dreaded task was almost accomplished, and that in less time than would have been possible with the united efforts of the feminine household.

"Done already?" cried the new-comers; and Agatha shook her mane with a melancholy air.

"It's s–imply wondrous! He just pulls, and the thing meets as easy as winking. It doesn't seem a bit difficult. And to think how we almost killed ourselves! It's humiliating!"

"Don't feel it so at all. If I am beaten at carpet-laying all my life, I'll never repine. It's a woman's duty to do nice things, and pleasant things, and pretty things, and leave the men to do the hard bits," said Elsie, standing on one leg to relieve the pain which had come from long kneeling, and looking with melancholy significance at her thin little arms. "Look at those compared to his! Nature never intended me—"

Ned fastened the last hook, and straightened his back with a sigh of satisfaction.

"Done! That's all right. I'm glad I came in time, for it's stiffish work. I am staying in town for a few days, and thought I would chance it this afternoon, and run down to see you for a few hours."

He looked at Maud as he spoke, and she hesitated uncertainly, thinking once again of her mother's absence, the disordered rooms, the prescribed contents of the larder.

"It was very good of you, and we are very pleased. Will you—er—will you be able to stop and dine?"

"Thank you very much. Your sister has already asked me. If it wouldn't be giving you too much trouble."

"Oh, no trouble! I mean, of course, we are very much upset, and I don't quite know what we can give you, but if you will stay we will do our best!"

"Now, Mr Talbot, listen to me!" interrupted Nan decisively. "There are two alternatives open to you, and you can take your choice. Would you rather sit here by yourself, looking at albums and illustrated books while Mary changes her dress, and cook flies into a temper preparing a proper dinner, and Jane helps to tidy the dining-room, and Maud ransacks the store—room, and Elsie polishes up silver, and Chrissie cuts flowers, and I—"

Ned Talbot threw up his hands in despair.

"Mercy! What next? Please stop, Nan. You make me feel the most shocking intruder. If I am to cause such an upset, the sooner I rush back to the station the better. What is the alternative? Tell it me at once. You said I had a choice!"

"The alternative," said Nan slowly, beaming upon him the while, in a friendly, encouraging fashion, "the alternative is what would happen to us if we were alone, and you had not arrived. Dinner in the schoolroom, with the library pictures ranged along the walls, and the books piled on the floor. No flowers—no fruit—no waiting—no evening dress. Everything on the table at once, and very little of that. Cold beef—very good cold beef! I'll answer for that, for we've had it two days already—potatoes in their jackets, perhaps one other vegetable..."

"Nan!" cried Maud protestingly; but Talbot gazed at her with a smile, shadowed only by a faint anxiety.

"Pickles?" he queried eagerly. "Put my mind at rest on that point before we go any further! Surely there are pickles?"

"Pickles, cer-tainly! As many as you like; but mostly onions, I am afraid, for we like the cauliflowery bits best, and poke about with the fork to get them out first. But there are lots of onions. Cold beef and pickles, then, and something plain and wholesome in the shape of a pudding, such as stewed prunes and rice; biscuits and cheese to follow; and a really good cup of coffee made by our own fair hands."

"It's a feast for the gods! Nothing I should like better. Don't you know, Nan, that nine out of ten Englishmen would rather be set down opposite a joint of meat than half a dozen kickshaws! It will be like old times to have a meal in the schoolroom, and if you will really let me stay, and treat me exactly like one of yourselves, I shall enjoy it more than a dozen dinner parties. You will promise faithfully to make no alteration whatever in the *menu*?"

"Certainly, if you wish it."

"And—er—you will not feel it necessary to dress on my behalf! I can make no change myself, so please don't confound me by your magnificence."

Lazy Nan consented readily enough, but once more the thought of the blue silk blouse sent a pang of disappointment to Maud's heart. She should not be able to wear it after all, and the long hoarding up had been in vain. She reflected on the disappointing nature of earthly hopes, with a melancholy which would have done credit to Elsie herself, as she took her way downstairs to interview cook on the subject of dinner. It is one thing to give a promise to make no difference in a *menu*, and another to keep that promise to the letter, as every housekeeper knows; and even if circumstances did not allow of any substantial addition to the meal, there were a dozen little contrivances by which it could be given an air of elegance and distinction. They took time to arrange, however, as all such contriving do, and cook was cross at being asked to undertake fresh duties, and wished to know what people wanted coming worriting about a house when a child in arms could see he wasn't wanted! Maud smiled at the reflection that, in this instance, the child would be vastly mistaken in his views, but did her best to soothe the offended dignitary; and finally matters were smoothed over by Mary being told off to help in the kitchen, while Maud herself undertook the arrangement of the table.

"Nan will help me," she told herself encouragingly, as she mounted the staircase and saw through the window a procession of girlish figures making their way down the garden path, escorting Ned to a survey of the daffodils and spring bulbs, for which Mr Rendell was famous among amateur gardeners. Lilias walked first, a dainty figure against the background of fresh green; slim little Elsie picked her way daintily over the gravel; Agatha followed, large and beaming; and Christabel majestically brought up the rear. Maud pressed her face against the window and watched with a spasm of envy. Oh, to be out, enjoying herself with the rest—to let everything take care of itself, and take her place by Ned's side! Too bad to be kept indoors when her opportunity had come at last, and the sun was shining, and all Nature seemed bright and gay! No one seemed to have thought of her, or of offering to help, except Nan—dear, good, thoughtless, and yet most thoughtful of Nans; and here she came, flying three steps at a time, upstairs to the rescue.

"Oh, you are here! I've been searching downstairs. Out you go! If there's anything to do indoors, I'll do it. Your place is in the garden."

"I've been in the kitchen, and cook was so cross that I told off Mary to help her. I promised to lay the table."

"I'll do it for you!"

Maud tried not to smile. Well she knew what would happen if the work were left in Nan's care. Crooked cloth, forks and spoons looking as if they had been tossed upon the table; as likely as not, no cruets nor water-bottles; and a general air of slipshod carelessness, which would more than defeat all her arrangements.

"I—er—think I ought to look after it myself," she said apologetically; "but please help me, dear! If we work together we'll get it done in no time, and then I can go out and enjoy myself with an easy mind."

"I want you to go now. If you think I can't manage alone, send in Chrissie. She's even more particular than you, and I'll do as she tells me like a lamb!" said Nan, not one whit offended at the implied slight on her own powers; but Maud shook her head.

"I couldn't! I never ask help in an ordinary way, and I couldn't do it to-day!"

"Too proud?"

"Much!"

"Good for you! I'd feel the same. Come on, then; let's set to work and get it over. He'll be wondering what you are doing. Where are the things?"

"Mary has taken up some already, and the rest are in the pantry. I'll tell you what I want, and you can carry up a trayful at a time while I set the cloth. I know exactly how I want everything laid, you see!"

"Don't apologise, my love. I know I'm no good at finnicky work, but I'll fetch and carry with the best. Knives—yes! Glass—yes! Plates—yes! Leave the plates till the last, and bring up the rest first. Yes'um! I understand! Knives and tumblers for seven. They shall be yours before you can say 'Jack Robinson.'"

"Not too quick, now!" cried Maud warningly; but Nan was off, leaping downstairs in a succession of daring bounds, swinging round corners at break-neck speed, and singing at the pitch of her voice, after the usual decorous and ladylike manner in which she was wont to descend to the lower regions.

Left to herself, Maud took a couple of steps towards the window, turned back resolutely, spread the cloth over the table, and went back at a run to peer behind the curtains and see what was going on in the garden. Chrissie and Agatha were strolling about arm in arm; Elsie walked apart, bowed in thought; Lilias flitted among the flower—beds, gesticulating with graceful *abandon* as she called Ned's attention to the choicest blooms. Maud could hear her pretty ecstasies as plainly as though she had been standing by her side.

"The little dears! Aren't they just *too* sweet? Don't you love the first spring flowers? They seem so full of hope and promise!"

She had heard it all before, every time that a visitor was taken round the garden; and just for a moment a wish passed through Maud's mind that her beautiful sister were not quite so fond of acting a part for the benefit of strangers! As a matter of fact, Lilias took less interest in the garden than any of the girls, yet she always gushed the most! The next moment she pulled herself up sharply, abashed to have cherished such uncharitable sentiments, and went on resolutely with the laying of the table. Spoons and forks had been neatly laid in their places before Nan's approaching footsteps could be heard ploughing upstairs to an accompaniment of jingling glass and steel. She had taken the warning to heart, apparently, for there was a noticeable pause between each footstep; but, alas! when the top of the stair was reached, there came a sudden and violent change in her procedure. Maud heard a gasp, and then, even as she started forward to investigate the cause, in rushed Nan, head foremost, the contents of the tray raining on the ground, while she stumbled helplessly forward, and finally collapsed on the floor in a nest of knives and broken glass, to lift up her voice in a wail of anguish.

"Oh, oh, oh! I caught my foot! That horrid braid tripped me up at the very last step, and sent me flying forward. What shall I do?"

"I told you,"—began Maud, but stopped abruptly, knowing by experience how trying it was to be reminded of past warnings. "Oh dear, the fright you gave me! To fall down with such a dangerous load. Nan, are you hurt?"

"I'm killed!" cried Nan, with a sniff. "Talk of your fright, indeed: I'm shaking all over. I'll run away and drown myself. Always make a mess of everything I do! What will mother say?"

"Don't worry about that, dear. You were trying to help, and being so good and kind, and half a dozen tumblers are not a deadly thing. That won't ruin us. It might have been far worse."

"It is!" sighed Nan. "Two water-bottles—the best ones, too. I thought they'd look so nice. Oh dear; oh dear; and just when I thought I was getting on so well! I came up so slowly, stopping at every step. You might have heard me—"

"I did; but you know, Nan, I said before—Never mind, it's done now, so it's no use groaning. You look so white, dear; I am afraid you have had a shock. Don't try to do anything more, but go to your room and take some sal volatile, and lie down until dinner."

But at that Nan rose to her feet with a laugh of derision.

"I! I act the fine lady, and go to bed for a fall? Not likely. I shall have to work harder than ever to make up for this. The knives might as well go in their places first, and then I'll go down and get something to brush up the glass. Don't you come: it's dangerous walking over here, and I can do it quite well."

"Nan, please leave it to me! I am sure you are hurt, though you won't acknowledge it. Sit down and rest, if it's only for five minutes."

But Nan would not be persuaded. She picked up the knives and hobbled round the table, laying them in their places and tossing her head with an air of triumph, oblivious of the fact that a drop of blood marked each stage of her progress, leaving a vivid stain on the fresh white cloth. A groan of dismay from Maud's lips aroused her attention, whereupon she flushed red with dismay, and stared down at her cut fingers with an air of shocked surprise.

It was really too aggravating, and even placid Maud felt aroused to irritation; but it is difficult to upbraid an offender who is herself overcome with penitence, and who lavishes such violent reproaches upon her own head, as Nan now proceeded to do.

"Oh, mussey me, I thought they felt queer! They are cut all over. Lockjaw, I suppose. I shall never be able to speak distinctly any more, but have to push all my food between my teeth, like poor Jane Smith. Oh, Maud, Maud, I wanted to help, and I've only made things worse than before! I always do. Do please scold and get cross. Don't look so wretched. Abuse me as I deserve!"

"What's the good?" sighed Maud dismally. "You didn't mean to do it, and it's done, and can't be undone. Come to my room and I'll bandage your hands. I'm not afraid of lockjaw, but you can't go about any longer like that. Then we must get a clean cloth, and begin again."

Poor Maud! She set her lips and went through the new duties without shirking or skimping, resolutely avoiding a look into the garden. There was no chance now of being able to join Ned before dinner, and as soon as the meal was over he would be obliged to hurry off to catch the last train. After all the longing and expectation, it seemed as though she were to meet with nothing but disappointment.

Chapter Seven
Doubt and Dread

Maud had just time to change her working attire for a dress which was suitable for the evening, though not sufficiently dressy to break the compact which had been made with the visitor, before the gong sounded, and she returned to the schoolroom to join the other members of the party. Ned was standing beside the fireplace, and greeted her with a pleasant smile as she entered.

"You didn't come out and join us in the garden," he said; and when she replied with a vague murmur, "Ah, well," he added lightly, "perhaps you were just as wise. There is a decided nip in the air still, and if you get out of the sun, you are apt to feel chilled."

Maud's eyes opened with a quick glance of surprise, but she made no remark. The words had chilled her as no east wind could have done. Did Ned really believe that she would have stayed indoors and sacrificed an hour of his society for fear of a slight discomfort? If he thought this, he was indeed unconscious of the true nature of her feelings towards him; and though Maud was the last girl in the world to wear her heart on her sleeve, she had been happy to believe that she and Ned understood each other, and could count on a mutual affection. She did not know which hurt the more, the suggestion of her own indifference or the unruffled serenity with which it was made. As she sat opposite Ned at dinner, she studied his face, to see if she could find there a reflection of the depression which was stealing over her own heart, but looked in vain. Truth compelled her to admit that she had never seen him brighter, more radiant, more full of life and animation. She tried her best to throw off the cloud on her own spirits and to enter into the conversation, but the effort was not a success. The hands of the clock on the mantelpiece held her in fascinated attention. Every stroke seemed, to sound the knell of the bright hopes with which she had looked forward to this meeting, every stroke brought the parting nearer.

If Maud did not speak, the other girls more than made up for her silence, talking all together in true Rendell fashion, and telling the news of the last few months in their usual breathlessly eager fashion. Until now, conversation had had no chance of becoming general, and each one had some personal items of information to offer which appeared to her to be of absorbing interest. Lilias had paid a visit to an old school friend, where she had had many pleasing adventures, which she related in characteristic manner. Her sisters often discussed what it was which gave to Lilias's stories such a suggestive and flattering atmosphere. It must have been something peculiar in the way in which they were told; for though she never said such a thing in so many words, the hearers were yet impressed by the fact that she had played a leading part, had been surfeited with admiration, and positively oppressed by the attentions which she had received! This evening was no exception to the rule; for as she spoke the listeners saw before them a picture of her own lovely figure moving like a queen through the scenes which she described, her humble vassals following in her wake. Lilias must be cleverer than most people supposed, Nan told herself sagely, as she watched the face of the visitor, to see how he was impressed by the recitals. Impossible to say! Ned stared fixedly at his plate, and made no remark. He very seldom looked at Lilias at all, Nan noticed. If it was not too absurd, she would have thought that he really avoided looking in her direction, while at every point in the conversation his eyes turned towards Maud, as if asking her sympathy in his enjoyment. Nan's spirit rose with a bound, and she burst into the conversation once more, talking every one down by her high, clear tones.

"Mr Talbot, do you realise that I've growed up since you saw me last? I've said good-bye to childish things, and blossomed into a society dame. I'm a lady growed. Didn't you notice it?"

Ned's eyes gleamed upon her with the deep, kindly glow which Maud knew and loved to see.

"I didn't, Nan; I'm sorry. I thought you looked exactly the same!"

"Never noticed my long skirts, or my done-up hair?"

"No!" Ned looked surprised, and tilted slightly back in his chair to obtain a better view of Nan's head. It was really rather puzzling to decide whether her curly mop was intended to be up or down; and the burst of laughter which followed showed how perfectly his uncertainty was appreciated. Nan made a grimace intended to express reckless indifference, and waved her bandaged hand in the air.

"Well, it *is* up! Don't pay any attention to those silly things. I ought to know best, for I've three separate hair-pins sticking into my scalp at the present moment. Jim took me to my first dance when he was at home for Christmas. It was s-imply lovely! I was awfully nervous, for I generally manage to make an idiot of myself if I get a chance; but I got on finely. I fell down full length as I was entering the room, but that was only because the floor was so beautifully polished. I danced every single dance—all waltzes, and the most ex-quisite music. I was introduced to an awfully nice man. He had ears like windmills, and the biggest mouth I ever saw; but he could dance! We went on, and on, and on, as long as the music lasted, and never stopped once; and when it came to an end I was as red as a lobster. It was simply lovely!"

Elsie smiled in an elderly and forbearing manner.

"More than you were, I expect. I can just imagine how you looked, with your hair all wild, and a crimson face above your white dress. You never think about your appearance, Nan."

"Hope I never may. I haven't one to think about, and that's a blessing! It would be so boring to be pretty, and to have to worry about clothes and complexion. I'm thankful there's none of that nonsense about me," cried Nan, beaming; and every one of the listeners thought how pretty she looked at that moment, as she tossed her saucy head and smiled her dimpling smile; but they would not for the world have said so, and spoilt the charm of her unaffected self-depreciation. Christabel seized the opportunity, and took up the thread of conversation before any one else had time to come forward.

"Mr Talbot, I've been waiting to ask you a question. Do you know anybody called Vanburgh? The Grange is let at last, and the gentleman's name is Vanburgh. We are simply aching to get to know something about them. The furniture has arrived, but nobody is in the house yet, except the servants. We made up our minds that there would be a family of daughters, but we begin to have qualms." Chrissie was obviously pleased with the effect of that last expressive word, and repeated it once more with artistic relish. "Qualms, yes! Decided qualms. The furniture is so massive. We can't see anything at all that would suit a girl's room."

"I can't give you any help on that point, Chrissie. You can judge better than I; but Vanburgh is an uncommon name, so we ought to be able to find out something about them. Do you happen to know where they have been living till now?"

"Here, and there, and everywhere; wandering over the face of the globe! A great deal of the furniture comes from India and Egypt; and one of the workmen came over to ask cook for some hot water one day, and said he believed the master had been travelling abroad. I wanted cook to pump him to find out more, but she said mother had forbidden her to gossip about the neighbours. Such a nuisance! I love gossiping about my neighbours. I remember when I was a little girl, how I used to adore being in the drawing-room when callers came and discussed the affairs of the village. I knew I should be sent away if I appeared to listen, so I used to sit and pretend to play with a doll or a book, while my ears were fairly sticking out of my head with curiosity."

"You little hypocrite! I wouldn't have believed you could have been so deceitful. But do tell us if you know anything of the Vanburghs, Mr Talbot. Did you ever meet any one of the name?"

"I met a man once—a fellow about my own age. He was at Oxford with me, but not at the same college. I saw very little of him."

"That could not be the father, of course. He would have to be a son, and we never arranged for boys. What sort of man was he?"

"Humph!"

"I beg your pardon."

"Humph!"

"What does that mean? What sort of man is supposed to be represented by 'Humph!' may we ask?"

Silence! Ned Talbot screwed up his lips and shook his head with determined obstinacy. The girls stared at him in silence for a good two minutes. Then Maud spoke again.

"Do you decline to say anything but 'Humph' on the subject, Ned?"

"Absolutely!"

"How very interesting!" Nan clasped her hands in delight. "How mysterious! How gloomy! How frightfully suspicious! I'm sure there's something very dreadful about him, and in that case he will be even more interesting than the girls."

"Nan!"

"I can't help it. We know so many estimable people that it would be delightful to meet somebody bloodthirsty, for a change. Everything in Waybourne is so painfully commonplace that we are simply spoiling for a mystery, as the Americans would say. Now, Mr Talbot won't commit himself to a definite charge, but his silence is more impressive than words. I'm sure there's a mystery: something too gruesome and terrible to be divulged."

"You leap to conclusions, Nan. Perhaps I had better state at once that there is nothing at all mysterious about the man I mentioned—nothing of the kind, I assure you."

"Nor bloodthirsty?"

"Nor in the faintest shadow of a degree bloodthirsty."

"Nor thrilling, nor gloomy, nor terrible?"

"The farthest possible remove from such qualities."

Nan groaned with disappointment.

"What a blow! Another nonentity! I hope, then, that your Vanburgh has nothing to do with ours, for he sounds terribly uninteresting. Never mind; when you come down to see us in the summer, we shall have solved the mystery for ourselves; and you will be obliged to come down for our sale, you know. Have you heard anything about our sale?"

"I—er—yes; I heard something,"—began Ned hesitatingly. He half turned his head towards Lilias, and then once more stared down at his plate, while she continued for him, in her sweet flute-like voice—

"Oh yes; I told him about it. He has promised to come and help me when I get tired. I can't manage the punt all alone!"

Once again was noticed the subtle suggestiveness of Lilias's manner; but this time it was her pleasure to pose as a martyr—a poor, fragile martyr, to whom had been deputed a hard and ungrateful task, while her companions played in the sunshine. Nothing could be said against an unspoken accusation, especially in the presence of a stranger; but the sisters exchanged meaning glances across the table, and Nan stamped *so* violently upon Elsie's foot that that melancholy young person writhed on her seat. The best safeguard to the feelings of the family was to change the subject, which Chrissie at once proceeded to do.

"But sha'n't we see you again before midsummer?" she inquired eagerly. "Is this really the only visit you are going to pay us this time? Three skimpy hours! You generally come and stay over a Sunday at least. Can't you come again before you go north? Mother and father will be home on Thursday."

Ned Talbot flushed suddenly, and bit his lips under his moustache. He was evidently struggling with a spasm of nervousness; and Maud noticed as much, and wondered as to its meaning, even as she blessed Christabel in her heart for her welcome suggestion. Surely, surely Ned would not refuse!

"You are very kind," he said slowly. "I had thought of asking if I might come. I am anxious to talk to Mrs Rendell. If it would not be inconvenient to have me from Saturday till Monday so soon after her return, I should very much like to come." He looked inquiringly at Maud as he spoke, and she smiled a happy assent.

"I am quite sure it will be convenient; but I'll tell-mother the moment she returns, and she will write to you herself. You will probably hear on Friday."

"Thank you; I hope I may. This afternoon has been all too short, and I have not had time for anything. Not even a glance of 'Kittay.' It's absurd to pretend to have been to Waybourne when one has not seen 'Kittay'; isn't it, Christabel?"

Chrissie dropped her eyelids, and twisted her lip with an expression of supreme disdain.

"I do not say 'Kittay'; I say 'Kittee.' You are too sillay. Whatevah I say you mock me in this ridiculous mannah. I sha'n't speak to you at all next time."

Talbot made a gesture as of one heaping ashes on his head, and then, glancing at the clock, rose hurriedly from the table.

"I must go! Just time to catch the train. I had no idea it was getting so late. That comes of enjoying myself so much. I have had a jolly afternoon. Don't know when I have had such a good time." He held out his hand to Maud, and she took it, trying hard to smile as brightly as himself, but it was a difficult task. She would rather he had been less bright, less complacent. She could have been happier if he had gone away with a shadow of her own depression upon his brow. Poor Maud! she turned back from the door with an aching heart. The schoolroom seemed on a sudden unbearably grey and gloomy. Her former peace had given place to an aching doubt.

Chapter Eight
The Vanburghs Arrive

The next day, when Kitty arrived at Thurston House, she was informed of Ned Talbot's visit, and promptly remarked that it was a "mean shame" — the shame consisting in the fact of the visit having been so timed that she herself had been deprived of the pleasure of seeing one who was honoured by her special approval. All interest in Ned and his doings was soon wiped away, however, by a piece of intelligence so exciting that the listeners could only gasp, and hold on to their chairs for support.

It was Maud who brought the news to the schoolroom. She had been in the kitchen interviewing the cook, and had received it straight from the lips of that authority.

"Children, children!" she cried breathlessly, "the Vanburghs have arrived! They came late last night, cook says. She saw the table laid for breakfast this morning, and the postman said he had taken some letters to the house."

"Arrived!" The girls stared at one another in mingled excitement and disgust. "And we never saw them! How simply disgusting, when we have been sitting staring out of this window for the last three weeks! Late at night! What sneaks! Why couldn't they come in the daylight, in a decent, honest fashion? They might be ashamed of themselves! How many are there, and what are they like?"

But Maud knew nothing beyond the mere fact of the arrival, and the schoolroom party were obliged to control their curiosity as best they might until lessons were over, and they were free to station themselves once more in their place of observation. If the Vanburgh family had ventured out of the house about noon, they would have been slightly disconcerted to see the row of heads in the window opposite, all craning forward to watch their slightest movement, and bobbing behind the curtains when they imagined themselves observed. But, alas! they did not come out. The nailed door remained closely shut, and the disappointed watchers tried to console themselves by inventing satisfactory reasons for their non-appearance.

"They are busy, you see. There is so much to unpack. Gabrielle is hanging her ball-dresses in the wardrobe and covering them over with muslin curtains."

"She wouldn't unpack for herself, silly! They have a French maid who does all that sort of thing for them!"

"I know they have; but Gabrielle is so particular! She can't bear any one to touch her dresses but herself; besides, Thérèse has enough to do attending to the other young ladies. Evangeline has a bad sick headache. She is lying down in that room where the curtains are drawn. Travelling always does make her ill!"

"Ermyntrude is arranging her treasures. Her bedroom looks out on the garden, and she is nailing up pictures, and draping the mantelpiece. She has piles and piles of photographs to arrange. They will keep her busy all day. It's ridiculous to suppose that they would go out the very first morning after their arrival. You know how it is with us when we come home after a few weeks' holiday! There are a thousand things to be done."

The girls unanimously agreed in this decision. Nevertheless, the hope that one of the four Miss Vanburghs might appear at the windows kept them glued to their own posts until it was time to start for the daily walk.

The conversation turned exclusively on the subject of the new neighbours, as the little procession of girls and governess filed dejectedly down the street, and great ingenuity was exhibited in expressing disappointment in the language which was the order of the day.

"C'est un horrible shame," sighed Kitty sadly. "C'est tout bien pour vous, parce que vous êtes toujours ici; mais moi, je suis chez moi, et si elles sortez quand je ne suis pas ici, je serais *mad*!"

"J'expect qu'elles sorteraient quand nous sommes tous loin. C'est toujours le fashion!" sighed Chrissie, acutely conscious that her French was superior to that of her friend, but politely ignoring the fact. "Je demanderai à ma mère—er—er—(how do you say 'pay calls'?)—à faire une visite, aussitôt que possible."

"Moi aussi," assented Kitty. "Et puis vous savez, elle peut dit: 'J'espère, Madame Vanburgh, que vos mademoiselles seraient très grand amies avec mes filles. Voulez vous permittez qu'elles venez à thé mercredi prochaine?'"

"Oui, et puis elles nous inviteraient en retourn." Christabel tossed her mane over her shoulders and smiled in anticipation. She made up her mind then and there to decorate her bedroom with her most treasured nick-nacks on the afternoon of the Vanburghs' visit, and to keep her new hair ribbon unused for the occasion.

But no Miss Vanburghs appeared! The next day passed, and the next, and still another, and still no sign of a feminine presence lightened the dark windows of the Grange. The solemn butler flitted to and fro; the figure of a white-haired man could be dimly discerned, stretched upon a sofa, in the oak-panelled apartment immediately facing the porch-room of Thurston House; but that was all that the most unremitting scrutiny could discover. Nan shivered at an attic window for an hour on end, with no more exciting result than a glimpse of a tablecloth and a row of silver dishes; and the great nailed door remained persistently closed.

And then the blow fell!

There were no Miss Vanburghs! There was not even a Mrs Vanburgh! Could it be believed there was no woman in the family—no one but an old invalid gentleman, who spent his days on a sofa, or in a wheeled chair being slowly driven about the garden? A solitary man as tenant of the Grange! The finest house in the neighbourhood monopolised by an invalid! The ball-room, the billiard-room, the music-room, given over to the possession of one who would never use them; the stables unused; the gardens deserted! The Rendell girls could not believe it. It was too horrible to be true. Ermyntrude, Evangeline, and Gabrielle had no existence. The happy dreams which had been woven about them could never be fulfilled. It was indeed a cruel and crushing disappointment.

"What can he want with a house like that, the selfish, horrid creature?" demanded Agatha, nigh to tears. "If he is an invalid, what is the use of having a house big enough to hold a regiment of soldiers? There are hundreds of villas where he might have been as ill as he liked, without monopolising our only Grange! What is to become of us, if all the best houses in the country are sold to hermits, and invalids, and white-haired old patriarchs, with not a single child to boast of! Selfish! Inconsiderate!"

"I'm sorry his back is bad; but he had no business to come here," agreed Chrissie firmly. "We don't want invalids. We want a nice, big, lively family, with plenty of money and hospitable hearts. Oh dear! I'm lonely without Gabrielle. I'd taken such a fancy to her! This is worse than if the place had never been sold at all."

"But still, you know the old man may be nice!" Kitty suggested hopefully. "Wouldn't it be lovely if he took a fancy to us, and made us all his heirs? A million each! I'd buy a pony-cart and a phonograph—a friend of father has a phonograph at his home, and it's such fun listening to it. The cornet-solo is fine, and there's a cylinder of a baby crying which sounds just like a dog barking. The poor little soul was quite good, but its parents thought it would be nice to preserve its howls; so they pinched it and made it cry. Mean, I call it! Imagine her feelings when she is grown up, and this wretched thing is wound up to amuse strangers. So degrading! Parents ought to consider their children's feelings. I read an awful story once of a girl who was looking over old magazines with some friends, and she came upon a photograph of herself as an advertisement of Infants' Food! If that had happened to me, I should disown my parents and leave the country. Mr Vanburgh hasn't any children of his own, but he may like us all the more for that. It would be an interest in life for him to make us happy, and we should reward him by our devotion. It sounds like a book, and perhaps it may turn out for the best, after all. I believe it will!"

"Don't be so horribly resigned! I hate people who are resigned when I am miserable!" said Chrissie sharply. "I want some nice girls, and I don't care a rap about phonographs—silly, squeaky things! There was one on the parade at the seaside last year, and it irritated me beyond words! Besides, I don't think it's at all nice to make up to a person just because he is rich, and might leave you some money. I wouldn't do it. It's toadying; and if there is one thing I detest above anothah, it is—"

"I never said I would 'make up' to him. I never hinted at such a thing. We were not supposed to dream that he would leave us anything until he was dead, and then we would be overcome with surprise. I should hope I detest toadying as much as you! Toady, indeed!" and Kitty tossed her head and curled her lip in disdain. Both girls were upset by the sudden overthrow of their hopes, and therefore inclined to take offence more readily than usual. Christabel retired to the window in dignified displeasure, while Kitty wriggled into the corduroy jacket, stuck the Tam O'Shanter on her head at a rakish angle, and hitched her books under her arm in preparation to depart. Agatha's expressive frowns and smiles were of no avail towards a reconciliation, and the parting took place in forced and chilly manner.

"Good by-ee!"

"Good by-ee!"

Then the door banged, and Kitty went stalking home, to drown her woes in afternoon tea, and to have her ruffled feathers smoothed down by her mother's kindly sympathy.

Mrs Maitland regarded the disappointment from a personal standpoint, for the discovery that there was no Mrs Vanburgh was almost as great a blow to her as the absence of daughters had been to the schoolroom party. She agreed with Kitty that it was most officious of a solitary male to monopolise the Grange, and bemoaned the loss to the neighbourhood in a manner tragic enough to satisfy even her daughter's requirements.

"Oh dear! oh dear! and I was looking to her for so many subscriptions! I had put her down for two five-pound notes, and half a dozen guineas. I meant her to take half my stall at the hospital bazaar, and to be the secretary of the Mission. How useful I had made that woman, to be sure! and now she has vanished into thin air before my eyes. I'm terribly disappointed, Kit; but we must make the best of it. Poor, lonely old man! He will be bored to death in that silent house. Lies on his back, you say, and is wheeled about in a chair? That means paralysis, I suppose, or very bad rheumatism. It's sad to be old, and ill, and lonely." Mrs Maitland stared thoughtfully before her, cup in hand, and her eyes grew suddenly moist. She was thinking how blessedly well off she was in her cheery, sunny little home, with husband and child to love her, and good health to enable her to do her work, and to find pleasure in the doing; and the picture of the strange old man lying on his couch in the dim oak-panelled halls seemed by comparison gloomier than ever.

"We'll help him, Kit!" she said briskly. "We'll help him, you and I! We'll make his life brighter for him, and cheer him in every way we know!"

But, as it turned out, Mr Vanburgh was not anxious to be cheered, and Mrs Maitland found it more difficult than she expected to put her good resolves into practice.

Chapter Nine
Ned's Mission

On Thursday evening, Mr and Mrs Rendell returned home from their Continental trip. The house was spick and span, the girls were blooming in pretty evening dresses, and the travellers themselves looked immensely benefited by their holiday, so that the kissings and huggings of welcome were exchanged under the happiest conditions.

Nan was thankful to feel that no shade of displeasure lurked behind the tenderness of her mother's greeting, and before the evening was over actually screwed up courage to put a question concerning the discovery of the scattered rice.

The explanation was disappointingly simple. Mr and Mrs Rendell exchanged a smiling glance, and appeared much amused by the girls' discomfiture.

"Well, my dear, we had the carriage to ourselves as far as Dover, and your mother suggested in her thoughtful way that it would be wise to get some wraps ready, as it was often very cold on the pier. Obedient as ever, I unstrapped the bundle, and discovered your nice little plot. We lifted the cushions, poured all the loose rice on the seats, shook the cloaks out of the window, put down the cushions again, and had everything clear and tidy in ten minutes' time! It was a nice little diversion, which came just as we had finished reading our papers. Most thoughtful of you to provide it for us!"

"And you had no stray pieces left? None that caught in your clothes, and shook out afterwards?"

"I had a cloth brush in my bag, and I used it well. I am sorry to distress you; but we were not once mistaken for Edwin and Angelina. It was a brilliant inspiration on your part, and I sympathise with your disappointment. I said at once, 'This is Nan's doing!' and wished I was near, to pay you out for your audacity. I hope your other pranks afforded you more satisfaction. I expect you have been up to all manner of mischief while we were away!"

"I've been most industrious, father, and good, and docile. Ask Maud if I haven't. I had a few accidents: they *will* occur, you know! Trays, for instance, jumping out of my hand, and smashing the glass. It's a mercy I was not killed."

"Glass? What glass?" queried Mrs Rendell quickly; and Nan smiled back at her with infantile candour.

"Better tell her the first evening, when she can't find it in her heart to be cross," she had decided diplomatically; and there was certainly no nervousness apparent in the manner in which she made her confession.

"Oh, only some tumblers. Not so many. Seven or eight, perhaps. They were not the best ones; none of the best set were broken except two little water-bottles. Such a mercy, wasn't it?" She affected not to hear Mrs Rendell's groan of dismay, and spread out her scarred hands with an air of thanksgiving. "As for me, I can't imagine how I escaped. There were knives on the tray, and they fell in showers round me—literal showers—and dug into my hands! The blood—oh-oh!" Nan rolled her eyes to the ceiling, and shuddered dramatically. "Ask Maud! She wanted me to go to bed, but I struggled on. We were particularly busy that night, and wanted to help the servants."

"Ned Talbot was here. He appeared suddenly, when we were laying carpets, and went down on his knees to help us. He seemed to expect to stay to dinner, so we gave him a scramble meal, and he left by the 8:30 train," explained Maud hurriedly. She, like Nan, had decided to give her own special piece of news on the evening of her parents' return; but though she appeared to be looking in an opposite direction, she was acutely conscious of her mother's searching glances.

"In-deed!" Mrs Rendell said slowly. "He is staying in town, then, I suppose? Is he to make a long visit? Shall we see him again this time?"

"He said of his own accord, mother, that he would like to come from Saturday until Monday if it would not inconvenience you so soon after your return. I promised to give you the message, and said you would probably write yourself."

"He said he wanted particularly to speak to you and father. I wonder what about! He doesn't generally care to be with you as much as with us; but he said it as if he meant it—he really did. I can't imagine what he wants!" said Agatha the tactless, blurting out her thoughts as usual, and beaming round the company, unconscious of the consternation which her words had caused.

Maud flushed crimson. Elsie and Nan blushed in sympathy for her confusion, and Chrissie from sheer rage and irritation, and longing to take the big, blind blunderer by the shoulder and administer a good shaking.

Only Lilias remained cool and self-possessed, and came to the rescue with a change of subject, for which her sisters blessed her in their hearts.

No further reference was made to Ned Talbot that evening, nor was any letter forwarded to his London address; but next day, as Maud passed the morning-room on some domestic errand, a voice called her by name, and she entered, to find her mother seated before an open desk.

"I am writing to Ned Talbot," she said, "and I wanted to consult you before finishing. I think the time has come for plain speaking, Maud. Am I to tell this young fellow that we shall be pleased to see him or no? It has been easy to see that he has had a special attraction in this house for some years past; and now that his position is established, he may have made up his mind to state his wishes. I have little doubt what they will be, nor, I think, have you, so it lies with you to decide the question."

Maud laid down her bundle, and grasped the sides of the table to steady her trembling hands.

"Mother, I don't know—I'm not certain! I have only thought at times that perhaps—perhaps he cared—"

"Of course, dear. I understand that. He could not show his feelings too plainly while he was unprepared to speak. That is all right, I'm sure. What you have to consider is your own attitude. If you do not care for him, or do not wish to be hurried into a decision, we will postpone this visit until a future occasion. He himself doubted whether I could receive him so soon after our return, so that I can easily make an excuse. On the other hand, Maud, if you would like to see him—"

She paused significantly, and looked full into Maud's eyes. For a long silent minute that gaze continued, the mother sitting with raised head, the girl standing before her, flushed and shy, yet showing no sign of shrinking before her scrutiny.

"Yes, mother, I would. I'd rather you let him come!"

A quiver passed over Mrs Rendell's face, and her eyes dropped. No mother in the world can hear that her daughter's heart has gone beyond her keeping, without feeling a pang of pain mingling with the joy; and this was a peculiarly tender mother, despite her little airs of severity. There were a few minutes when she dared not trust herself to speak, then she held out her hand and drew the girl to her side.

"Bless you, my daughter! My good girl—my dear, kind helper. I'll miss you sorely; but I am glad of anything that makes for your happiness, now and always. You know that, don't you, darling?"

Maud put down her head and shed a few tears of happiness and excitement, which had in them no trace of bitterness. When the time arrived for leaving home, that would doubtless be a real trouble; but at present she could not realise the wrench, while her mother's certainty concerning Ned's love was the best medicine possible for the doubts which had been so distressing since the occasion of his last visit. In ten minutes' time she returned to her work, with no stain of tear-marks to tell of her recent emotion, but with a quiet illumination in her face which satisfied the mother that this attachment to Ned Talbot was no mere girlish fancy, but the deep faithful love which endures for a lifetime.

The important letter was posted, and the invitation which it contained accepted by telegram within an hour of its arrival, and half Friday night Maud lay with wide, bright eyes staring through the darkness, too excited, too happy, to sleep.

Ned arrived on Saturday afternoon. It was a glorious spring day, the sun shining so powerfully that for the first time in the year afternoon tea was carried out to the summer-house, while the family gathered around on various garden stools and chairs. They were hardly seated when Ned came walking across the lawn, a tall, handsome figure, in a spring-like suit, his dark face lit up with a smile of pleasure. Maud looked at him, aglow with love and pride; but as he drew nearer she busied herself with the teacups, and had only a casual word of welcome to offer. It would not do to appear too glad, she told herself; and when there were so many, an individual greeting was hardly noticed, nor was there any opportunity for *tête-à-tête* conversation.

When the tea-things had been carried away, however, and the girls began to wander about the garden in twos and threes, Maud found Ned by her side, waiting for her, and allowing the others to walk on ahead. She looked up with a questioning glance, and met a smile of frank affection.

"Well, have you finished your duties, and got five minutes' leisure for once? Come along, and have a walk with me. I never met such a girl for being busy all day long. Don't think I have ever seen you sitting with idle hands. You remember Jim's old nickname, 'Maud of all work'? A capital title! But he would have missed it badly if he had not had you to wait upon him. I used to tell him I envied him such a sister!"

Maud smiled vaguely and turned her head aside. It was all very kind, very flattering, very friendly, yet somehow it failed to satisfy; and even as she listened the old ache of uncertainty came back to her heart. It was difficult to say why, unless perhaps it was that Ned's manner was a little too friendly to be welcome. In the old days he had not been so much at his ease;

they had talked merrily enough together while the others were present, but so soon as they had been left alone a constraint had been wont to fall upon them,—a silence, awkward, embarrassing, yet in some inexplicable way more eloquent than words. Maud thought of the past with a quick catching of breath, and through the whole of that afternoon and evening the vague depression deepened, and refused to be argued away. Ned, it was true, took advantage of every opportunity of being near her, yet the time had been when he had seemed shy of approaching; and she preferred the shyness to this open friendliness. He talked to her more than to any one of her sisters, yes! in frank, cheery words with unlowered voice, as a brother might talk to a sister, or a son to his mother. He looked at her with kindly affection, and the look chilled her heart. Once again Maud passed a sleepless night, but the darkness was no longer illumined by rosy dreams, but black with fear and dread.

Sunday was a glorious day, and Maud felt it another drop in her cup to be obliged to wear winter clothes instead of blossoming out in the pretty spring costume which she had hoped to possess. The dressmaker had proved faithless, like the rest of her kind, and, being unable to finish two dresses by the promised time, had followed her usual custom and sent home the one destined for the younger sister; for, in spite of her gentle manners, Lilias had "a way with her" which carried infinitely more weight than Maud's good-natured placidity.

The sisters were standing in the hall providing themselves with hymn-books from the pile laid out on the top of the oak bench, when Lilias came tripping downstairs in her pale grey draperies, a very incarnation of the beautiful spring morning. Maud looked at her with ungrudging admiration, then turned instinctively to see how Ned in his turn was affected by the charming vision. She saw him flash one quick glance at Lilias, and immediately turn on his heel and walk to the other end of the hall, and throughout the walk to church she puzzled over the meaning of such behaviour. Why should the sight of Lilias in her fresh beauty disturb Ned's equanimity? Was it possible he had taken a dislike to her, or felt a masculine disdain for her innocent vanity? Maud honestly hoped not; for, though she desired above all things to possess Ned's love for herself, it would be still necessary for her happiness that he should accept as his own her five beloved sisters.

The day passed without any important developments. Maud went off to teach her Sunday-school class in the afternoon, trying hard to conquer the spasm of envy which overcame her at the sight of Lilias seated in the garden hammock, swinging herself to and fro on the tips of her little shoes, while Ned mounted guard by her side, and Agatha and Chrissie paced lazily up and down. Maud was devoted to her "boys," but on this occasion there was no denying that it was an effort to tear herself from home, and she would gladly have welcomed a holiday. Her path led through the garden, and as she approached the gate the hope flitted through her mind that Ned might offer to accompany her on her walk. It would be an opportunity for a quiet *tête-à-tête*, which was rarely to be gained in the midst of such a large family; and if Mrs Rendell's surmises were correct, surely—surely! But Ned did not even rise from his seat beside the hammock: he only waved his hand and nodded an unclouded farewell. The twelve mischievous little boys behaved with unprecedented decorum that afternoon; for, in spite of their elfish ways, they were devoted to Maud, and the ringleader sent round an imperative message to the effect that "Teacher was bad, and must not be worried."

NED SEEMED SUDDENLY TO TAKE HIS COURAGE IN BOTH HANDS.

It was characteristic of Maud also that she did not allow the lesson to suffer because of her own depression, but rather put into it more than the usual earnestness. She had always felt a heavy sense of responsibility in taking this class, and every week, as she looked at the eager young faces, she was thrilled with a fresh longing to help them to grow up into strong, upright men, who would be a power for good in the world, — "gentlemen of Christ," as the grand old phrase has it. When they were indifferent or callous, after the manner of boys, she strengthened herself against disappointment by remembering how words committed to memory in her own careless youth remained indelibly printed on the brain, to be a strength and solace in after years. The hymns and chapters were learnt as lessons now, but in time to come their true meaning would be revealed; and she loved to combat the suspicion that the Bible was a dull, uninteresting book, by relating the histories of its heroes in a manner most calculated to arouse schoolboy enthusiasm. Brave, lovable David, with his chosen friend Jonathan, the type of princehood; the gloomy but majestic figure of Saul, trustful Abraham, and fearless Daniel. It was a joy to make them live in the boys' imagination, and see the bright interest on the listening faces!

When Mrs Rendell said good-night to her daughter, she was especially tender in her manner, for she vaguely felt that all was not going well, and took herself to task for having forced a confidence. Could it be be that she had taken too much for granted? that her motherly pride had given her an exaggerated idea of Ned Talbot's feelings? He had shown no anxiety to speak to her in private, and at one time it seemed as if he would go back to town without touching on any but impersonal topics; but on Monday morning, after wandering restlessly about the house for some time after breakfast, Ned seemed suddenly to take his courage in both hands, and, coming up to his hostess as she sat writing notes, begged the favour of a few minutes' private conversation.

Mrs Rendell looked up sharply, met an embarrassed yet steadfast glance, and felt a throb of relief.

"Certainly!" she said. "In ten minutes from now I shall have finished my household arrangements, and will meet you in the summer-house. Go into the garden and enjoy a smoke until I come."

Ned walked away obediently, and Mrs Rendell thrust the half-finished note under her desk, too agitated to complete it. She had shown no signs of surprise to the young man himself, but her heart was beating quickly, and she bundled away her writing materials in a haphazard fashion very unlike her usual methodical ways. Her first thought was for Maud, and most of the ten minutes of Ned's waiting were taken up in interviewing the girl, and deputing to her a dozen little shopping commissions which would keep her occupied in the village for an hour to come.

"I am going to have a talk with Ned in the summer-house. You will find us there when you return. Come straight to me, and tell me how you have succeeded."

These were her last instructions, and when she had given them she turned sharply aside, lest her face should betray the meaning that lay behind her words.

Ned was waiting for her with an evident nervousness mingling with his usual kindly courtesy. He made no attempt to open the conversation with meaningless commonplaces, and, after they were both seated, several moments passed in silence. Then suddenly the two pairs of eyes met; the young fellow flushed and paled, and laid a hand on his hostess's chair with a boy-like pleading gesture.

"Oh, Mrs Rendell," he cried, "I have a great favour to ask you!"

Chapter Ten
A Tragic Surprise

Half an hour later, Nan Rendell let herself out of the front door, and ran hurriedly down the steps. Her sailor hat was perched uncertainly on the top of her heavy braids, the buttons of her jacket were unfastened, and she drew on her gloves as she walked, as if she had been in too much haste to finish dressing before leaving the house. Several acquaintances saluted her as they passed, but she rushed along unconscious of their greetings, and presently arrived at the point in the high road where houses stopped and the little township began. The shops which Mrs Rendell patronised were indiscriminately situated on either side of the road, which no doubt accounted for Nan's erratic dives to and fro. She peered her head round the corner of the draper's door, dashed across the road and craned through the grocer's window, stood on tip-toe to investigate the interior of the post office, then ran back once more, to interview the fishmonger, and ask if Miss Rendell had yet called to leave the morning order. It was in the confectioner's that Maud was run to earth at last. She was coming out of the doorway counting her change into her purse, when suddenly Nan's face confronted her, and she started back in surprise.

"You?"

"Yes, it's me. I've been looking for you everywhere."

"But I thought your were going to work? I left you hard at it. Got a headache?"

"Fer-ightful!" said Nan; and her looks justified the word, for her cheeks were pale, and her eyes looked worn and strained. "I couldn't work any longer. I thought a little walk would do me good, so came out to meet you."

"But—er,"—Maud hesitated uncertainly. She did not wish to appear inconsiderate towards her beloved Nan, but, remembering her mother's instruction, she could not bring herself to stay away from home longer than was necessary. She looked at her sister appealingly, and slid a hand through her arm.

"But—I've finished my shopping, dear, and mother said I was to go straight back. Wouldn't it do just as well to sit in the garden? You would get the air without fatigue, and I'd make you so cosy in the deck chair. You know, Nan, I—I want to go back!"

Nan turned her head aside, and spoke in a queer, muffled tone.

"Very well; but we'll go round the back way. It's only five minutes longer, and it's quiet. I don't want to meet any one. You'll do that to oblige me, won't you, Maud, as you have finished your shopping?"

Of course she would. Maud gave a little grip to her sister's arm, and turned willingly enough up the side street which led off the high road. As in all small towns, the change from town to country came surprisingly quickly. Three minutes' walk took the sisters into a pretty lane running parallel with the High Street, and commanding a sweeping view over the countryside. Here were no houses, only an avenue of beeches, with here and there a seat in a position of welcome shade. Maud often returned home by this quieter route, and seated herself on one of the benches to make up her accounts and enjoy the view at one and the same time. It was a favourite spot; but after this morning she could never pass it without a shrinking of the heart, a sickly remembrance of misery. At the first seat Nan slackened her pace insinuatingly, while Maud marched ahead, intentionally obtuse; but at the second a hand was laid on her arm, and such a trembling voice besought her to stop, that she forgot herself in sympathetic alarm.

"Nan, you *do* look ill! As white as a sheet. Lean forward and put your head on your knee, as low as you can get it! That is the best thing to do if you feel faint. Sit still for a minute, and then we will make another dash for home. You ought to lie down!"

But Nan sat bolt upright, clasping her fingers in nervous misery.

"I'm not faint. I'm thinking of you, not myself!—Maud darling; it's been a mistake—we were all mistaken; but you are so good, you will be brave for our sakes, if not your own. It would break our hearts to see you suffer."

She stopped short with a little sob of agitation, and Maud stared at her with wondering eyes.

"Suffer! I? Why should I suffer?" Then the colour rushed in a sudden wave to her cheeks, and her voice broke in the single, stifled inquiry, "Ned?"

"Yes. It is Lilias! He has asked mother for Lilias. She came upstairs and sent me out to meet you, so that you might not hear it suddenly. She thought you would rather have it so."

"How kind of her! That was good of you both!" said Maud calmly. Her heart had stopped for a moment, and was now beating away at extraordinary speed; a singing noise was in her ears: it was as if some one had dealt her a violent blow, and she was as yet too stunned to realise its nature. She turned her head aside, and *gazed* vaguely up and down. A nursemaid wheeled a perambulator on the opposite pavement, while a little white-robed figure trotted at her side, tossing a ball in the air. Maud watched her movements with fascinated gaze. It seemed as though some tremendous issue depended on whether the ball was caught in those tiny, uncertain fingers.

"Ned wants to marry Lilias, does he?" Her voice sounded strange and far away, and she noted as much, and pondered on the peculiarity. "They will make a handsome couple. Lilias is so fair. She will look well beside him."

"Maud, don't! For pity's sake don't take it like that!"

The tears were raining down Nan's cheeks, and she seized her sister's hand in a passionate grasp.

"I know all about it. I am almost as wretched as you are. Don't pretend to me. Say what you feel to me, at least, and it will help you to bear it."

"But I don't feel anything," said Maud dully. "It seems like a dream. Lilias! He loves Lilias, and not me; he never loved me at all! He has been thinking of Lilias all this time. It's—very—strange! I think what I feel most is shame for my own conceit. I have been deceiving myself all along, and that is a miserable thought! You should not sympathise with me, Nan: you should scold me, and tell me to be ashamed of myself."

She spoke in the same dull, strangled note, and Nan continued to cry and clasp her hand in distress.

"I could never do that, or be anything but proud of you, darling! It was no conceit at all on your part, for we all thought the same. He always seemed to prefer being with you, and to be so shy and constrained with Lilias. I suppose that was a sign, but we did not recognise it. Even mother was sure it was you: every one was, except Lilias."

Maud gave a quick glance upward.

"Did Lilias guess? Did she know that this was coming?"

"I have not seen her; but from what mother said, I imagine she did."

"And she will—she cares for him too?"

"Yes!"

It was a very low little yes, almost a whisper, but at the sound of it Maud shrank as at a blow, and her face became drawn with pain. For the first time a realisation of what the news meant, broke upon her, and she cried aloud in a voice sharp with misery—

"They will be engaged; they will be married; and I shall have to stay at home and look on! I shall have to take part, and pretend that I don't care. Oh, I can't—I can't do it! If it had been some one at a distance, some one I need never have seen, I could have borne it; but my own sister, living in the same house together all day long—that is too bitter! I'd rather die than face it!"

"Then I'll die too!" cried Nan hotly. "Whether Ned cares for you or not, you are all the world to me. You don't know how I love you, Maud! It would have broken my heart if you had married and gone away, and I never want to marry myself, if you and I can live together. No man could make up for you. I hate them all! Wretches! Nothing but misery wherever they come. I'll never fall in love, and you'll get over this in a few months, and we will look forward to having our own little house, and growing old together,—won't we, darling?"

"Yes, we will," assented Maud meekly. She looked at her sister and tried hard to smile; but the prospect seemed so dull—oh, so heart-breakingly dull!—after the rosy dreams of the past, that what was meant as comfort proved, after all, the last strain which was to break down her composure.

She threw up her hands to her face, and rocked to and fro in an abandonment of distress.

"Oh—oh, the days, and weeks, and months! They will be so long; I can't realise it yet, but I know how I shall suffer. Oh, Nan, isn't it hard, after being so happy—after feeling so sure? I never had a doubt all these years except just this last week, and then I thought it was my own foolish imagining;—and now to have it end like this! I can't believe it! Are you sure, are you quite sure? It seems like a hideous mistake!"

Nan shook her head, and her face hardened.

"There's no mistake on my part, but there's one on his, and a big one too. He'll find it out, that's one comfort! He'll suffer for it! If he thinks Lilias is going to be the sort of wife he needs, he'll find out his mistake. He thinks himself well off because he has a few hundreds a year, and is as proud as a king because he has a house of his own in a dull little country town. Lilias's ideas of poverty and his of wealth will come to much the same thing. She hates the country, and flies off to town at the least excuse. Ned is quiet and book-wormy; and she wants some one who is fond of life, and likes gadding about. They don't suit each other in any one way that I can see, and before a year is over they will have found it out for themselves. Then he will be sorry!"

Maud cut her short with uplifted hand.

"Don't, Nan; you make it worse! You mean to be kind, but it doesn't comfort me to think that he will be disappointed. I love him, you see; and I can't change in a moment because I discover that he doesn't care for me. I want him to be happy. It would make me more miserable than ever if I thought it was a mistake. You are too hard on Lilias. She is very sweet and amiable, and if she really loves him she will not mind little things like that. We never spoke about him together, she and I, and she has only done what I did myself. No one is to blame—no one! It was my own foolish mistake, and I must bear the consequences."

"You are an angel, and too good to live!" cried Nan, with a gulp. "I blame everybody, and myself worst of all. Prided myself on being sharp-sighted, and couldn't save you from a blow like this! ... Maud, you don't want to go home? You would rather not see him this morning? Mother said she would give no definite answer before talking to father, but would let him see Lilias for half an hour, and then pack him off by the midday train. She was going to tell him that under the circumstances she would prefer that he did not stay to lunch, so there would seem nothing strange about it if you and I were not back before he left."

"No," agreed Maud softly. She drew her watch from her belt and looked at the hour. "Perhaps you are right, Nan. It would be better not to try my strength too much this morning. In a day or two I shall have gained a little courage, but this morning I—I've had rather a shock, and feel weak and nervous. We will sit here and wait until he is gone."

"Wouldn't you rather come for a walk? The time seems so long when you are sitting still. A nice brisk walk through the woods!" suggested Nan insinuatingly; but Maud drew back with a quiver of pain.

"No, no! Not this morning! I should remember it always. Every step of the path would bring back this wretched day in the future, and I do so love the woods. Let me keep them free from association, at least. It will be bad enough to dread this road, as I always shall after this."

"Just as you like, dear, just as you like; but what will you do? You can't sit still and think all the time!"

"I'll make up my accounts," said Maud simply; and, despite her sister's cry of protest, she insisted on doing as she said. Pencil and note-book came out of her pocket, and one item after another of the morning's shopping was jotted down, and the result compared with the change in the housekeeping purse.

How could she do it? Nan tried to imagine how she herself would have acted in similar circumstances, and felt her heart beat fast at the possibility. Rage, storm, despair; drown herself in the nearest stream; lie down beneath the express train; bid farewell to the world, and retire into a nunnery. All these alternatives seemed natural and easy; she could imagine taking refuge in any one of them. But to go on with ordinary, everyday work, to take up the "next duty" and perform it in quiet, conscientious fashion—that was impossible!—the last thing in the world that she could bring herself to do.

She did not realise that the bent of a lifetime is not reversed in a moment, and that even the pangs of slighted love must be borne according to the temperament of the sufferer. Dear, placid, domesticated Maud found her best medicine in the "trivial round, the common task."

Nan, looking over her shoulder, saw that the little rows of figures were as neat and accurate as ever, and caught a sigh of satisfaction when they were added together, and the change in the housekeeping purse was proved correct. Even in the midst of her distress, Maud was conscious of a distinct sense of satisfaction in balancing her accounts to a penny.

Chapter Eleven
The First Engagement

The remaining hours of that day were the most painful which Maud had ever known. The sisters returned to find the household in a state of wild excitement, for such secrets seemed to leak out in the air, so that the very servants suspected the truth, and walked about the house with curious smiles. The housemaid confided to the cook that the missis had come in from the garden all of a tremble; had replied, "Yes! No! Certainly!" when asked for instructions, and had then sent Miss Lilias to see Mr Talbot in the drawing-room all by her very own self. What did that mean, she would like to know? And cook shook her head, and said it wasn't for nothing she had fallen up the cellar stairs the week before; and a very good thing too, if one of them did go off! When there were six of them waiting for their turns, the elders ought to hurry up and make room. Mary, the waitress, shed tears over her silver in the pantry, because there was a look about the back of Mr Talbot's head that reminded her of her young man, who had gone abroad to prepare a home; and all three flattened their noses against the window when Ned departed, in the hope of witnessing a tender and affecting farewell. They were disappointed, however, for Lilias did not leave the drawing-room, and only Mrs Rendell accompanied the young man to the door. She had put on her bonnet, and followed him slowly down the road, for ordinary duties must be attended to, even on the exciting occasion of the first engagement in the family, and on this particular morning there happened to be a committee meeting at the vicarage, which she felt bound to attend.

When Maud returned, therefore, only her sisters were at home to receive her, and she had barely entered the house before Agatha rushed forward, flushed and beaming, and drew her forcibly into the drawing-room.

"Maud, Maud, such news! Such excitement! Have you heard? Did Nan tell you? Isn't it lovely? The first engagement! Oh, how I have longed to have a wedding in the family, and now it's really coming off! It's too good to be true! Ned Talbot, too! Such a scrumptious brother! I always hoped he'd ask one of us, but I thought it was you. Funny, wasn't it? I said to Chrissie—"

"It was very bold and interfering of you to say anything of the sort, then; what business have you meddling with other people's love affairs?" interrupted Elsie sharply; and Maud glanced at her, and turned away quickly to avoid a look of sympathetic understanding. Elsie was old beyond her years, and had been quick to understand the true position of affairs; but Maud hardly knew which was more painful—Agatha's tactless speeches, or the other's undisguised commiseration. It was a relief to turn to Lilias and meet her lovely eyes, guilelessly free from any feeling but her own happiness. Lilias had little natural insight, and was, besides, so wrapped up in her own interests, that she was as blind as a bat to what was passing around. She came forward, smiling and blushing, and Maud kissed her, as was expected, and murmured words of congratulation, feeling meantime that this very unconsciousness would be her greatest assistance in the difficult time to come.

"I've heard all about it, Lilias. I hope you will be very happy. It is really all settled, and you are engaged?"

"Yes—no! Not formally, I mean. Mother won't consent to anything definite until she has consulted with father; but, of course, we,"—Lilias dimpled and smiled seraphically over the unaccustomed word—"we feel that it is settled. We are quite sure of ourselves, at least."

"Then I'd get married as soon as you could if I were you, in case you changed," said Agatha darkly. "You do change most awfully, Lilias, you know. When you bought your last hat you said it was a 'simple love,' and the next month you pulled it all to pieces. And you used to adore Fanny Newby, and now you go out of the side door when you see her coming. Get married in summer and have a rose wedding, and we'll all be bridesmaids. I pine to be a bridesmaid, with everything new from head to foot, and no nasty old clothes to wear out. That's the worst of being number five! I never have everything new at once. There's always a hat, or a jacket, or a blouse that has to be finished off. Let's sit down and talk about it now! There's half an hour before lunch, and it's impossible to do any work. Maud, sit down and take off your hat, and let's be comfy!"

"No, she can't. I want her! I don't care who is going to be married; I'm ill, and I want Maud to nurse me. My head is smashing. I believe it's sunstroke, for I sat out yesterday without a hat. I shall go crazy in a moment if somebody doesn't do something!" cried Nan loudly; and her sisters stared in dismay at her flushed, heated face. It was so evident that she was in pain that even Agatha submitted to a postponement of the longed-for "talk," and the conclave broke up for the time being, the sisters separating, to go off in various directions: Lilias to be petted and cross-questioned by the two schoolgirls; Elsie to indite a melancholy entry in her diary, beginning, "Yet another example of the strange intermingling of joy and pain": and Maud to lead Nan to her own room, and devote herself to the work of nursing, at which she was so clever. Perhaps Nan's head was really aching, perhaps the morning's excitement had brought on an attack of neuralgia, but whatever her ailment, she certainly made the worst of it, groaning and rolling her eyes to the ceiling as one in mortal agony; for she was wise enough to realise that nothing would take Maud so much out of herself as the necessity of waiting upon another.

When Mrs Rendell entered the room, and recognised the odours of eau-de-Cologne, menthol, and sal volatile, her first thought was of poor brokenhearted Maud; but, behold! it was Maud who was playing doctor, and buxom Nan who lay prone upon the bed.

A few inquiries and expressions of sympathy were spoken, and then a gesture bade Maud follow into another room. She went, shrinking from the ordeal, yet longing to have it over, and for a few minutes mother and daughter gazed at one another in silence. The girl's face was grave and set, but self-composed in comparison with that of Mrs Rendell, which was quivering with distress.

"My dear child! What can I say to you? I can never forgive myself for my part in this disappointment. I should not have spoken as I did the other day, but I thought at the time that it was the right thing to do, and I had no doubts on the subject. What can I do to help you, dear, through this difficult time?"

"Speak as little as possible about it, mother, please," said Maud softly. She pressed her lips together, wincing with pain, and Mrs Rendell's eyes flashed a look of approval in reply.

Of Spartan bravery herself, it delighted her to see her daughter bracing herself up to bear her trouble without useless outcry and repining.

"I quite agree, darling," she said warmly. "After to-day we will never mention the subject; but there are one or two things which must be said first. To begin with, Ned has no suspicion of our mistake. I took care of that; and it may help you to know that, after all, we were not so very far from the truth. He spoke quite openly, and it seems that for the first two or three years you were the attraction! He said he had been sincerely attached to you, but that he saw you regarded him simply as a friend. Then Lilias came home, with her more demonstrative ways; he turned to her for comfort, and now,"—She stopped with a little eloquent gesture, while Maud gave a groan of pain.

"Oh, mother, that is hard—to think that it came so near, and that I spoiled my life by my own mistake! I suppose my very anxiety not to show how much I cared made me seem stiff and constrained; but I never meant him to take it in that way. It makes it worse than ever, and yet I'm glad too. It's a comfort to feel it was not all imagination."

"I thought you would feel it so; that is why I told you. But you must not talk of your life being spoiled, dear. These are early days, and I hope there are many, many blessings which still remain open to you. It is a great mistake to think that marriage is the only gate to happiness. A single woman may have a most full and useful life."

"Yes, mother!" assented Maud dutifully. Poor Maud! her heart died down within her as she spoke, and her thoughts flew away to old Mary Robins in her lodging, and Miss Evans in her stuffy little cottage, and she wondered if it were really, really possible that she—Maud Rendell—could ever grow like them, and feel satisfied with the duties and pleasures which constituted their lives! "Full and useful!" It sounded estimable enough; but her young heart hungered for happiness also, and at the moment that seemed lost for ever. The downcast face was so pitiful that the tears came into Mrs Rendell's eyes as she watched it.

"Don't think of the future, dear," she said fondly. "Take each day as it comes, and try to bear it bravely, and I'll help you in every way I can. Ned will come down pretty often, for I must consider Lilias as well as you, and we cannot consent to have a formal engagement until they know each other more intimately than at present; but it will not be so hard as you expect. You must be at home sometimes, for the last thing we want to do is to arouse suspicion; but I will arrange that you have as many changes as possible; and in any way that I can help I am at your service, dear, if you will only let me know!"

"Thank you, mother," said Maud again, and made a little involuntary movement towards the door, whereupon Mrs Rendell dismissed her, after a lingering embrace. She saw that it was misery to the girl to discuss her disappointment, and realised that it would be the truest kindness to allow the subject to drop. It was only natural that Maud should find it easier to talk to a friend of her own age, and Nan would be able to help more than any one else in these first painful days. Later on her own turn would come; and all day long the mother's mind was busy weaving plans by which Maud could be shielded from suffering, and her life made bright and interesting during the months ahead.

Lessons came off badly that afternoon, for the girls were too much absorbed in the excitement of the prospective wedding to be able to fix their attention on the problems of arithmetic and geography. When the great problem of the hour was to decide the number of bridesmaids and what kind of frocks they should wear, how could they be expected to feel any interest in discovering how many yards of paper it would take to cover the walls of a problematical chamber, or in describing the eccentricities of the Gulf Stream? Miss Roberts realised the impossibility of the situation, and shortened the hours in considerate fashion; and no sooner had she taken her departure than the three girls rushed to the porch-room, surrounded Lilias in a whirlwind of excitement, and dragged her to a chair in their midst.

"At last we can talk! Such a pity Nan is ill, and won't let Maud leave the room; but we can have it all over again with them to-morrow. Talk! I feel as if I could talk for ever! Oh, Lilias, how do you feel? If I were engaged, I don't know what would happen to me! I should go stark, staring mad with excitement."

"How nice for him! You would have another person to consider then, remember," said Lilias prettily. "I am not at all inclined to go mad, though I am certainly very much excited. It is difficult to describe my feelings. I can't realise it yet, and feel all—"

"Jumbled up!" suggested Agatha sympathetically. "Of course you do. I should myself. Oh, Lil, do have them in yellow! I've been thinking about it all the afternoon, and I think yellow would be sw–eet! With bouquets of daffodils! Very few people have yellow, and it would be so uncommon, and make us look much paler too. I shall have a face like a beetroot with excitement; I know I shall."

"I daresay! And how should I look, I'd like to know?" queried Christabel loftily. "Sea green, my dear. I'm sallow enough as it is, but imagine my appearance in a yellow dress! I should present a shocking spectacle! Nothing is so nice as pink: it suits every one, and is so bright and pretty. Pink silk dresses, with Leghorn hats."

Elsie grimaced in disapproving fashion.

"So commonplace! Every one has pink. We must have something altogether unique and striking. No use deciding now, for we will change our minds a dozen times before the time arrives. When are you to be married, Lilias? What is the date?"

"My dear, I've no notion! I am not even properly engaged yet, so how could we begin talking about marriage? I believe we are to be put on probation for some months, so it will certainly not be this year at any rate."

"What a bore! I'm longing to stay with you in your own house. It's my idea of happiness to go and stay with you girls when you are married.

You will ask us all in turns, won't you? I'd like to come with Chrissie; and then, if you and Ned get too affectionate, we can amuse ourselves in another room. It will be lovely having no grown-up person in the house. Oh, well, of course, you are grown-up, if it comes to that, but only young grown-up, and that makes all the difference. You won't make us do things because they are 'good for us'—send us a walk when we don't feel inclined, for instance, or to bed early, or make us eat 'good plain food.' When I come to stay with you, I should like never to go out unless I have something special to do, and to have tea for lunch, and nice rich cake, and laze about from morning till night, just as I felt disposed."

"And you'll ask people to meet us, won't you, Lil, and take us about, and give us all your old gloves and ribbons? Marie Elder's sister is engaged, and he won't let her wear any gloves that are the l—east little bit soiled; so Marie gets them all. I hope Ned will be fussy about your things, too. What shall you call your house? I hope it's a nice one. Florrie Elder is going to have a blue drawing-room, and Marie is working her a cushion of the most ex-quisite ribbon-work you ever did see. Florrie says she would quarrel with her nearest and dearest if he dared to lean against it. If you like, I'll ask her for the pattern, and do one for you. It wouldn't matter having them the same, when you live so far apart."

"What will Jim say? Ned and he vowed that they would be bachelors all their lives, and live together when they were old. Now he will be obliged to marry himself, in revenge. How I shall detest the girl! She won't be half nice enough for him, and he will like her better than us, and that will be horribly exasperating. I don't envy her when he brings her to see us, that's all! Six sisters all glaring at her in a row, and saying to themselves, 'I don't like her nose!' 'I don't like her eyes!' 'What a hat!' 'However could he fall in love with her!' And mother all icy kind, and father smirking behind his moustache. That's what will happen to you one of these days, Lilias, when you go north, 'on view,' to Ned's people."

Lilias rolled her eyes, and affected to tear her hair in despair.

"Oh, don't! I pray you, don't! I shall die with nervousness. Poor little me! His parents are reserved and undemonstrative, like most North-country people, he says, but are very tender-hearted at bottom. That means, I suppose, that they would be stiff and polite all the time I was there, and begin slowly to unbend just as I was coming away. Frederica, the girl, goes in for higher education, and doesn't care a bit about going about with other girls. I know they will be disappointed with me. Ned is so silly, and he is sure to tell them."—She stopped, sweetly simpering, and the hearers had little difficulty in guessing what it was that Ned would tell his people. He would say that his *fiancée* was the loveliest girl in the world; that she had hair like spun gold, a complexion of milk and roses, and eyes soft and dewy as a violet. Then Lilias would arrive in person, and his people would think that he had not said half enough. Each of the three hearers had a vision of Lilias advancing to meet the new relatives with lifted eyes, and a smile that would melt a heart of stone; each one saw in imagination the sudden thaw on the watching faces, and beheld Lilias installed forthwith as the pride and darling of the household. They smiled at one another in furtive amusement, but discreetly avoided putting their thoughts into words, for Lilias fished so transparently for compliments, that it had become an unspoken law never on any condition to encourage her by giving the desired assurance.

Agatha turned aside to hide her amusement, and, the next moment, gave a jump of astonishment.

"Keep still! Don't move! For your lives don't look out of the window! Sit where you are, and go on talking. My dears, he is watching us! The Vanburgh! I distinctly saw him lean forward and stare across. He is in the room directly opposite, and he dodged back the moment I looked. Fancy his being as much interested in us as we are in him! How exciting!"

"We must look very ridiculous, sitting here in a row, chattering and waving our hands as if we were mad. I don't wonder he stared, but I do want to stare back. Let us take it in turns to peep beneath our eyelashes, while the others go on talking," suggested Elsie; and the proposal was carried out forthwith, each girl watching till the coveted glimpse had been obtained, and informing her companions of her success by groans and exclamations.

"I see him, I do! He is staring across. He looks very ill. His hair is quite white. Poor old man, how dull he must be!"

When it came to Chrissie's turn she stared across with undisguised curiosity, and refused to accept her sisters' reproaches when the white head was hurriedly withdrawn from view.

"I was the last! You had all had your turns, so I have not deprived you of anything," she maintained. "I only meant to smile at him in a kind, neighbourly fashion. He will look out again in a few minutes, never fear!"

But Mr Vanburgh's face appeared no more at the window, and it seemed as if the knowledge that he had been observed had been so unwelcome as to put an end to his scrutiny. The girls could only comfort themselves with the remembrance that their mother had promised to call at the Grange during the next few weeks, when, no doubt, first-hand information would be forthcoming about its occupant.

Chapter Twelve
Not at Home!

After due consultation, Mr and Mrs Rendell decided to sanction a private engagement between Lilias and Ned Talbot for a year to come, with the understanding that if the young people remained of the same mind, no objection would then be put in the way of their speedy marriage; and as they would be allowed to correspond, and to meet as often as opportunity offered, the decision was received with satisfaction by the lovers. Lilias complacently settled to be married in fifteen months' time, and was resigned to a probation sweetened by the receipt of constant letters, presents, and adulation; while Ned, with characteristic honesty, confessed in his own heart that he had no very deep acquaintance with his beloved's character, and that he could not be better employed than in the study of the same. Lilias's exquisite girlish beauty had so dazzled his senses, that he had been shy and ill at ease in her presence, and their conversations together had been of the lightest, most impersonal nature. It would be an entrancing occupation to discover all the hidden charms possessed by this sweetest of created beings; for, like most young men, Ned was convinced that a lovely body must needs be an index to a lovely mind, and that beauty of face was but a reflection from the soul within. Every month that passed would draw Lilias and himself more closely together, as each came to know and understand the depths of the other's nature. So Ned told himself happily, as he came down to Thurston House for his first visit in the new character, a week after the all-important interview.

Lilias met him at the door, and led him into the drawing-room, all fragrant with spring flowers and plants. She looked like a flower herself, with her soft pink and white colouring, and to the last day of his life Ned Talbot could never inhale the fragrance of a narcissus or a hyacinth without a spasm of painful remembrance. It brought back so vividly the intoxicating joy of that meeting. They talked together in lover-like fashion, Lilias alternately shy and reticent, and queening it over him with absurd little airs of authority, at which he laughed with a lover's delight, until presently a tap came to the door, and Agatha's face peeped round the corner to announce that tea had been taken out to the garden, and to ask if the lovers would rather come out, or, have it sent to them indoors.

"Here, please," said Lilias.

"Oh, we'll come out certainly," cried Ned in the same moment, and then turned to her with a smile of apology.

"If you don't mind, dear! I want to see Maud. She was out when I left the other day, you remember, and I can't feel that I am really received into the family until Maud has given me her blessing."

"Just as you wish, of course. It does seem a pity to stay indoors when the weather is so glorious!" assented Lilias readily. Though inwardly annoyed that she should have appeared more anxious than Ned for an extension of their *tête-à-tête*, she was far too proud to show her vexation. Nothing could have appeared more ready or more natural than the manner in which she rose from her seat and slipped her hand through Agatha's arm; but even while she smiled and chatted she was registering a vow to punish Mr Ned on the first opportunity.

Out in the garden Maud sat, busying herself with the teacups and nerving herself to face the dreaded moment, as footsteps approached nearer and nearer her seat.

"Maud!" cried Ned, and gripped her hand with affectionate fervour, "I was longing to see you. It seemed too bad going away without a word from you the other day. We have so much to say to one another!"

"Yes, indeed; but meantime I must pour out the tea! Are you going to make yourself useful and hand round the cups?" replied a laughing, self-possessed voice, which Maud hardly recognised as her own. It was easier to play a part than she had expected: the looking forward had been worse than the reality; and, as she met her mother's smile and Nan's approving glance, she even began to feel a dreary pride in her own composure. Lilias had seated herself between two of her sisters, an intentional revenge for the slight which she considered herself to have received, and Ned was therefore left free to devote himself to his old friend.

"Of course you saw—you knew what was coming," he whispered confidentially, when the general conversation made it possible to exchange a quiet remark. "I realised that I gave myself away by my awkwardness and stupidity whenever she was present, but I was powerless to prevent it. And you were so good to me, Maud, always doing your best to help and make things easy. I can never be grateful enough for your friendship. I am so thankful to feel that you are at home still. It seems an assurance of safety; for you'll look after her, and see that she gets into no danger through all this long year of waiting."

He looked at her appealingly, and she gave a forced little laugh.

"Oh yes, I'll ward off the beasts of prey. There are so many, you know, roving about this sleepy place. She will meet so many dangers!"

"Don't laugh at me! I can't help being anxious. She is so young and child-like, and there are dangers everywhere. Illness, accident, infection. I shall think of them when I am far away, and worry myself to death. But you are a bulwark of strength, Maud, and if you will take her in charge—"

Maud laughed again. It seemed so ridiculous to think of any of her sisters promising to take Lilias in charge! Lilias, the most cool-headed, independent, and self-confident member of the family. She was infinitely more capable of taking care of the whole family than the family was of influencing her movements; but Ned could not be expected to realise as much, and he was obviously wounded by the absence of expected sympathy.

An exclamation from Christabel, calling attention to Kitty Maitland's figure crossing the lawn, came as a welcome interruption, and Ned took the opportunity to cross to a seat on the other side of the group, while Maud watched his departure with mingled relief and concern.

"He thinks I am hard and prosaic, and is disappointed in me. Well, better so! He won't confide his rhapsodies in my ear any more, and that would be really more than I could bear. The old days are over, and he must look elsewhere for sympathy."

Meantime Kitty had seated herself on the grass, and was proceeding to account for her appearance.

"Please I hope you don't object to my coming back so soon! Mummy has gone with father to call on Mr Vanburgh, and I walked with them to the Grange, and came in here to wait until she comes out. She put on all her new things, and looks a perfect duck. I expect he will like her awfully, and I told her to introduce my name into the conversation as often as possible. 'My daughter likes this'; 'My daughter likes that'; 'As my little girl says to me';— that sort of thing, don't you know, just to attract his attention. Perhaps he will tell her to bring me with her next time she calls, or even ask me to tea by myself. He may have nieces or grandchildren who will come to stay, and then it would be useful to know a girl in the neighbourhood. I think he is certain to ask me—"

"Mother!" interrupted Chrissie shrilly; and her voice was so sharp with distress that every one stopped talking, to listen to what she had to say. "Mother, Mrs Maitland has gone to see Mr Vanburgh before you! I asked you to go! I had set my heart on your being the first caller; and now it's too late, and you can only be second. I told you so! I *said* how it would be!"

Mrs Rendell lifted her brows with the little surprised air of reproof which Chrissie knew so well.

"I regret to have disappointed you, my dear," she replied, with elaborate politeness; "but I fear I should hardly have been the first caller, even if I had gone the day after my return, and I have been too much occupied this week to pay outside visits. I am sure you will be delighted to hear Mrs Maitland's report, and will not grudge Kitty the pleasure, if she makes Mr Vanburgh's acquaintance before yourself."

Chrissie collapsed into silence; but, veiled by her thickly-flowing hair, she grimaced to herself and scowled at her friend, who was regarding her with that air of enjoyment which it is impossible not to feel when a companion receives a nice little snub for her pains!

Agatha and Elsie had already begun to invent forecasts of the news which Mrs Maitland would have to tell, when, to the amazement of all, who should appear round the corner of the house but that lady herself! She carried her card-case in her hand, and waved her hand in greeting; but, for once in their lives, the girls were too much overcome with surprise to respond.

Back already, when she had barely had time to go up to the door and retrace her steps! What did it mean? Not at home? But Mr Vanburgh was always at home. According to report, his farthest expedition was into the garden, where surely he would be able to receive a visitor on a bright spring afternoon. Surprise held them dumb, until Mrs Maitland had reached speaking distance, when, with one accord, they deafened her with inquiries, to which she did her best to reply after the first greetings were over.

"How do you do, Mrs Rendell? Good afternoon, Mr Talbot. I am one of the privileged *few* who have been told your secret, and I wish you every happiness, and dear Lilias also. I tell every engaged couple I meet that I hope they may only be as happy as I am. My dear children, don't pull me to pieces; this is my very best dress! I'll tell you all about it in a minute. I am so glad to have this opportunity of seeing you all together, for I was longing to come over. May I sit here? Well, then, to begin at the beginning..."

She put her card-case on her lap, and clasped her hands together in preparation, and the girls watched her with approving eyes, for Mrs Maitland was a most satisfactory story-teller. She began at the beginning—the very smallest possible beginning—instead of halfway through the narrative, as other grown-up people had a habit of doing, and went straight through to the end, noticing every detail, and describing it in racy, picturesque language.

"Well, we went up to the door and rang the bell. It is not an ordinary everyday bell, but a quaint, wrought-iron handle, hanging on a chain from a sort of signpost arrangement, and I could hear it pealing away in most melodious fashion inside the house. The curtain inside the glass panels of the door was caught slightly back, and I could get a peep into the vestibule. The oak has been left untouched, and there are palms on either side sunk into great pots of copper with snakes and dragons and all kinds of uncanny animals standing out in relief. I was still peering through when the inner door was thrown open, and the butler appeared, upon which I straightened myself at once, and tried to look stately and dignified. I had just one minute to take in the inner hall, so cannot tell you much about it, except that it is a perfect museum of wonderful and beautiful things—pieces of tapestry hung on the walls, carved oak cabinets full of curios, a figure of a knight in armour, and curious Eastern-looking lamps burning dimly in the distance; but the butler looked so very solemn and imposing that I dared not stare as much as I should have liked. 'Is Mr Vanburgh at home?' I asked; and he inclined his head in a gracious bow. 'He is at home, madam, but is not receiving visitors.' I drew out my cards, and said, 'I am sorry to miss seeing him. I hope he is not more unwell than usual to-day?' He bowed again, like a mechanical figure, and said, 'Mr Vanburgh charges me to say, madam, that as he is unable to return visits, he must deprive himself of the pleasure of receiving them while in Waybourne.' I never felt so small in my life. Dismissed on the doorstep, and sent away like a child! I don't know how I looked, or what I said. My one idea was to get out of the man's sight as quickly as possible; and the door had no sooner closed on him than I began dreading Kit's disappointment. It was a most trying experience! Father has gone for a walk, and I came in to break the news to you!"

She looked appealingly at Kitty as she finished, and met a glance of blackest gloom. This was indeed a blow. Not only were there no Miss Vanburghs, but the only Vanburgh who was left refused to open his door to visitors!

"Piteous!" cried Chrissie; and Agatha struck her hands together in despair.

"There ought to be a law about it—a law to prevent hermits from buying the best houses in a neighbourhood. Does he mean to say that he will see nobody?" she cried. "Perhaps he didn't know who you were, Mrs Maitland. He takes an interest in us, we know, for we have *seen* him staring across. Perhaps if he had known you belonged to Kitty, it might have been different. Mother, you will go all the same, won't you? You won't give up without trying?"

Mrs Rendell shrugged her shoulders.

"I am not particularly anxious to be turned away from the door, and I see no reason why I should be treated better than Mrs Maitland. The servant is evidently entrusted with a general message. I think the best thing will be to send father across on Saturday afternoon, to see if the rule applies to ladies only. If Mr Vanburgh really wants to be quiet, we can't force ourselves upon him. I am sorry the Grange is not let to more interesting people, but we must make the best of it. It has evidently been chosen as a museum in which to store a collection of art treasures, and, after all, you must remember it is no more closed to us now than it has been for years past."

"Dear me, no! We can live without the Grange, I hope. Let the poor old dear shut himself up if he likes. He will be the loser, not we!" cried Mrs Maitland, laughing. That was the worst of grown-up people! They were so aggravatingly reasonable and resigned!

Chapter Thirteen
Diogenes at the Window

After a storm comes a calm. As in Nature, so in the affairs of human life, and the Rendells found another example of the truth of the old adage in the month following Lilias's engagement. Nothing seemed to happen; even the interest which had been taken in the new occupant of the Grange died away after Mr Rendell's failure to gain admission, and one day jog—trotted away after another in monotonous fashion.

They were dreary days to Maud, but at the end of even the longest and dreariest she acknowledged to herself that the battle was not so hopeless as she had expected. The trouble was there, the difficult moments arose, the quick stabs of pain following happy memories, but she herself was strengthened to bear them in a manner which she could not have believed possible. Maud was one of the sweet, open characters who are religious by nature; but though she had asked for God's help every night of her life, she had never been conscious of its presence in such abundance as in this hour of trial. It almost awed her at times to realise her own strength, and this testing of the power of faith was a ray of light shining out of the darkness. Passages from the Bible which she had known all her life became suddenly instinct with new and wonderful meaning; the words of Christ went straight home to her sore heart and comforted it as no earthly power could do. The new communion had a joy and a sweetness which she had never known before, and her character grew daily stronger and deeper under the influence of sorrow nobly borne. Her mother's tenderness, moreover, manifested itself in a hundred little schemes for her distraction, and Nan's demonstrative affection heartened her for the fight. The world was not all lost because Ned had chosen another; and, so far from neglecting her old duties, Maud worked away more industriously than ever, finding her best medicine in a busy, occupied life.

Ned Talbot had gone back to the North, whence he could not return for two months to come, and Lilias settled down contentedly to play the interesting part of the *fiancée*. She did not fret for her lover, but seemed abundantly content to receive his letters, and pen lengthy answers; and though the date of her marriage was so far ahead, she began at once to make preparations for her future home. One rainy afternoon she shut herself in her bedroom, and rearranged all her belongings, leaving the lowest drawer in the wardrobe empty, and covered with fresh white paper. Then she wrote something at her desk, lingered outside the door for a minute, and finally rejoined her sisters, with a mischievous smile curving the corners of her pretty lips.

Presently Chrissie ran upstairs on some trifling errand, and came to a stand-still on the landing, uttering sharp cries of surprise; then Agatha followed to discover the cause of the excitement, and guffawed with laughter, when Nan and Elsie jumped from their chairs and ran helter-skelter in pursuit. They found the two younger girls leaning up against the wall, staring at the door of Lilias's room, on the centre of which was tacked a square of paper, neatly lined and lettered:—

Notice!

To All Whom It May Concern

Miss Lilias Rendell desires to inform her friends and the public generally that she has just opened a Bottom Drawer, and that every description of household goods, useful and ornamental, will be gratefully accepted towards the furnishing of her future home.

NB—Carved oak articles especially welcome!

"That's one for me!" cried Nan, grimacing. "What is your especial fancy, my love—a side-board or a dining-room table? Don't be bashful, pray! Aim at the sky, and you may succeed in hitting the tree. I shouldn't wonder if I rose to a milking-stool, if you asked me nicely."

"And I'll work you a kettle-holder, sweet one, as soon as the sale is over, and Chrissie a—"

"Twine bag," said Chrissie, simpering; "but until July you might as well give up the idea, Lilias. Every moment we have, we must use for sale-work, and every penny we can save in to the bargain. We can't attend to you just yet."

"I thought perhaps you might start me with a few contributions from the things you have made," said modest Lilias. "The drawer looks lonesome with nothing in it, and I've made it so tidy! It would be a comfortable home for that little blue cushion, and the mats with the roses. And you would never miss them!"

"Wouldn't we just? The very best things we have! It is a pity your modesty doesn't equal your taste. I should miss the smallest thing we have made; and whenever I get low-spirited, I turn them all out of the box and gloat over the collection—eleven pin-cushions, three sets of mats, a table centre, three work-bags, two handkerchief sachets, six babies' shoes, and a nice wool shawl! It's not bad for a start, and there are lots of things on hand, besides Nan's carving and brass-work. It would be like tearing my heart out of my body to give anything away, and I don't think it would be at all a nice idea to start your collection by stealing from the poor!"

Lilias looked appalled at the suggestion, but all the same she was not too much shocked to seize on the chance of future spoils.

"Agatha, how can you? I am the last person in the world to think of such a thing. I suggested the sale, remember; you would not have had it at all but for me; but how could a little thing like a pin-cushion be called a theft? However, it's all right; don't give them me at present if you would rather not. After the sale there are sure to be some things left, and then— You would not mind giving them to me then, I suppose?"

"Certainly not. At least I am quite willing if the others are," said Agatha, looking round inquiringly; upon which Nan and Elsie nodded assent, and Chrissie bargained, "Unless I am engaged myself by that time, when, of course, they must be equally divided,"—a contingency so remote that Lilias congratulated herself on a good morning's work, and felt that so far as pin-cushions were concerned the future held no further anxiety.

Work for the sale had, indeed, been carried forward with great zest; and now that the days were lengthening, there was a good two hours after tea, when Kitty could join the party in the porch-room, and stitch away at some dainty task while carrying on that breathless stream of conversation which never seemed to run short, despite the daily meetings. Nan brought down her carving, and worked at a little table of her own; Elsie cut and planned with delicate, accurate fingers; and the three younger girls sewed away in characteristic fashion: Agatha bending double over the seam; Christabel, erect and stately, drawing her thread to its full length with leisurely, dignified movements; and Kitty, with her spectacles on the tip of her nose, peering over them from time to time in grandmotherly concern at the frivolity of her companions.

Nothing more had been discovered about "Diogenes," as Mr Vanburgh had been nicknamed since his refusal to receive visitors; but on fine days his couch was wheeled close to the window, and as he lay looking out, it was inevitable that the movements of the girls in the sunny porch-room immediately opposite should attract his wandering attention. When they glanced across in their turn, he politely turned aside, and appeared engrossed in his book; but no sooner were they at work again than the tired eyes would be lifted once more, to dwell with wistful interest on the bright young faces. One afternoon in especial, as Nan sat bending over her carving, the conviction strengthened that she was observed. She peered under her eyelashes, smiled mischievously to herself, and suddenly leapt from her seat in a manner most startling to the nerves of her sisters. She hopped on one foot and waved her arms in the air; she swooped down on Chrissie's work and threw it wildly to the ceiling; she thrust her face into Elsie's and went off into a peal of maniacal laughter, which sent that nervous young person flying to the farthest corner. She seized a bundle of ribbons and danced an impromptu skirt dance, flourishing them to and fro, while he onlookers scuttled together like rabbits, and felt that their lives trembled in the balance. Finally, after succeeding in turning the room topsy-turvy, and raising the most powerful doubts as to her own sanity, Miss Nan tottered out on to the landing and collapsed in a breathless heap on the lowest stair, while her sisters looked on askance from a discreet distance.

"H–have some sal volatile! I'll get it from my room. Never mind, dear, you'll be better soon!" stuttered Elsie fearfully; but at that the crazy creature laughed afresh, though in a more restrained and natural fashion.

"Oh no; I am not mad! I did it for a purpose, my dear, as you shall hear. That poor old Diogenes was lying on his couch, looking across with such a dull, pathetic face, and I felt so sorry that the poor dear had nothing more exciting to amuse him. He must be precious dull when he takes so much interest in girls like us, and I felt grieved to think how little fun we had given him, sitting sewing day after day like so many machines. I says to myself, says I, 'It is in your power, Margaret Rendell, to infuse some brightness into the lot of this poor lonely sufferer, and you are going to do it! He shall have some excitement before the day is over, bless him!' Therefore, as you perceived, I executed a new and original war-dance for his benefit, and sent you all attitudinising about the room. That's the reason of this thusness, and Diogenes is now, no doubt, full of agitation, believing that one so young and fair has suddenly lost her wits, and imagining you all occupied in binding me to the bedpost till help arrives!"

"I don't know how he feels, but I feel extremely ill!" grumbled Elsie, her sympathy suddenly changed to resentment. "Sticking your face into mine and laughing in that crazy fashion. Never do it again! My heart is right up in my throat, and thumping like a steam-engine. I can't work any more. I am going to recover my equanimity in the garden!"

Poor Diogenes! It was baffling to curiosity that all the actors should have disappeared at the most exciting moment of the play; and the actors themselves were fully aware of the fact, and with child-like enjoyment determined to lengthen out the mystery. The porch-room was abandoned for the afternoon, and such sequestered nooks in the garden as were invisible from the Grange were chosen as resting-places, while Kitty willingly consented to walk an extra half-mile on her way home, so as to avoid going out by the front gate. Such a reversal of the usual comings and goings would, it was hoped, give the final touch to Mr Vanburgh's curiosity, and teach him a wholesome lesson on the folly of shutting himself up and holding no communication with the world. When Agatha suggested that the poor old dear might lie awake all night from agitation, Nan cold-bloodedly hoped that he would, since he, on his part, had been so cruel as to shut the doors of the Grange against his neighbours.

She would have been much surprised if she had known how, and for whom, those doors would first be opened!

Chapter Fourteen
A Visit of Ceremony

At the beginning of May the first returning ray of brightness came into Maud's life. A letter arrived from a friend of the family who had been living abroad for her daughter's education, and had now reached Paris, preparatory to returning to England in a month's time. It had been all work and no play for the girl during the winter, her mother wrote, and it had been long promised that the month in Paris should be entirely given over to pleasure-seeking. Mabel had drawn out a programme so lengthy and varied, that Mrs Nevins doubted whether she herself would have strength to go through it. One thing at least was certain, that the girl's enjoyment would be doubled by the presence of a companion of her own age, who would be able to share her ecstasies, as a tired-out, middle-aged woman could never do. Therefore, might Maud come? Could Maud be spared for a month to give Mabel the very great pleasure of her society? She should have every care, and be brought back to London early in June.

Mrs Rendell carried the letter up to Maud as she practised in her room, and handed it to her with a smile; and Maud flushed and paled, and laid her hand affectionately on her little mother's shoulder.

"Mummy! how much from you, and how much from Mrs Nevins? You have had something to do with this, I'm sure you have. The suggestion came from you in the first instance!"

"Pooh! What a child! Such notions as she takes!" cried Mrs Rendell laughingly. "How it comes about is little matter; you don't need to be told how truly delighted Mabel will be to have you. You can believe in that, at least. And Paris! You have always wanted to go to Paris, dear!"

"Yes, mother, I have. Oh yes, always!" Maud smiled bravely, trying hard to appear as pleased and elated as her mother expected. It was not the first, nor the second, nor the twentieth time that she had discovered schemes for her own benefit during the last few weeks. School friends had been invited on visits; books for which she had wished had opportunely arrived from town; concert tickets had been purchased with unprecedented frequency. Maud fully appreciated the kindly purpose of these attentions, and, to a certain extent, enjoyed the amusements provided; but she was conscious of a dreary regret that these long-wished-for pleasures should arrive at a time when it was impossible to throw herself into them with whole-hearted enjoyment. The regret was particularly keen at this moment, for to her, as to so many girls, the first trip abroad had been the dream of a lifetime, and a pang came with the realisation of how different from her expectations the realisation must be. The ache at her heart would cloud the brightness of the beautiful city,—she would look at everything, as it were, through a veil of crape. The tears rose to her eyes despite all her efforts, and she turned hastily aside, fearing that her mother might think her ungrateful for receiving the news in such churlish fashion. Mrs Rendell, however, affected to notice nothing unusual, and talked away in cheery accents, discussing various practical matters concerning the proposed visit, in which it was impossible not to feel an interest. Maud's tears dried gradually; she found herself suggesting amendments to the plans, and growing momentarily more interested and eager. She was to be entrusted with a sum of money with which to buy presents for her sisters, besides a well-filled purse for her own use. She and Mabel could choose their summer clothes together, amid the bewildering fascinations of Parisian fashions; and there was absolutely no limit in the amount of sight-seeing permissible. She could run the whole gamut, from the Louvre to the Catacombs, and get to know her Paris almost as well as she knew her London. What girl of twenty-three would not feel her woes assuaged by such a programme, especially in the company of a bosom friend to whom she had been devoted from childhood?

Mr and Mrs Rendell rejoiced to see Maud's brightening face, and to hear her voice raised to its old happy ring, as she busied herself with preparations for her journey; and Nan rejoiced as much as they, and racked her brains to discover how she could best assist in the same preparations.

"Let me do some sewing for you! Do let me help!" she pleaded, and proceeded to stitch up the seams entrusted to her with such unprecedented care and neatness, that Maud hid the garments at the bottom of her box, not having the heart to disclose that the seams were on the wrong side, and must needs be as laboriously unpicked! She upset a box of tooth-powder over a blue serge skirt; squeezed a bundle of boots on the top of a chiffon bodice, and went beaming downstairs, feeling that at last she had learned to be domesticated and to render efficient service!

Maud departed smiling and cheery, and all the members of the family drew a breath of relief as she drove off from the door. The secret consciousness of her suffering had been a cloud over their spirits for the past month, and now, as was only natural, a reaction set in, when restrained spirits found their vent.

Mr and Mrs Rendell went up to town for a couple of nights to attend a dinner-party and reception, and the girls discussed how they could best organise a little festivity on their own account. It was decided to hold the first picnic of the season, bicycling to a favourite spot in the woods, where primroses and bluebells were luxuriant, and to invite Mrs Maitland and Miss Phelps to drive up in a pony cart stored with provisions for an out-of-door tea. Everything was arranged—cakes were baked, sandwiches cut, cream and milk corked up in bottles, and a basket packed with every requisite—when, "of course," as Elsie had it, the rain descended in sheets, and the project was frustrated.

The usual scene of grumbling and ejaculating followed, before the girls could resign themselves to their fate. To settle down to practise and study seemed unbearably dreary after looking forward to such a charming excursion; but there was nothing else to be done, so they marched sulkily to their different occupations, and did not meet again until after four o'clock. Then the schoolroom party joined Lilias in the library, and were about to summon Nan from the attic, when Mary entered, bringing a card on a salver.

Some one had been brave enough to face the elements, and pay a call in the midst of a downpour of rain. Whom could it be? Lilias examined the card with curious eyes, and turned in surprise towards her sisters.

"Miss Thacker! Don't know her from Adam. Who in the world is Miss Thacker?"

"Oh—er—er—Wait a moment and I'll remember!" cried Agatha, ruffling her hair in reflection. "I've heard the name, I'm sure—I know! She's the creature who's come to Willow Cottage. She called once before, and mother said she could not for the life of her decide whether she was quite mad, or only three-quarters. What can she want?"

"Have to go and see, I suppose. Or stay, I'll bring her in here, to have some tea, and then you can help me to entertain her; but whatever you do, don't laugh! It's awfully bad form to make fun of a visitor." And Lilias left the room, to return followed by a tall female figure, which certainly approached perilously near the grotesque in appearance.

An old-fashioned poke bonnet and a gauze veil shaded a solemn white face, braids of red hair fell over the cheeks, horn-rimmed spectacles covered the eyes, while the absence of two front teeth gave a singularly blank and unpleasant expression to the mouth. A merino shawl was folded across the shoulders, and a venerable silk skirt dripped with rain upon the carpet. An extraordinary-looking figure indeed; and it would appear that eccentricity was not confined to appearance only, for the stranger returned the girls' salutations with wriggles of the body, and began at once to talk in a soft guttural voice, running her words together without any stops, and at such express train speed that every now and then she was obliged to stop short, and give a deep gasp of exhaustion.

"S–S–Sorry your mother is from mome me dears quite counted on finding her rat ome. Said to myself at lunch must go and see Mrs Rendell s'afternoon such a kind woman full of sympathy for rothers! Hurried out and thought as had come so far might come in and see Miss Rendell as servant said at tome and disengaged!"

The big mouth opened in a gasp for breath, which was heard throughout the room, and Lilias stammered out a dismayed assent.

"Certainly—of course. So glad you did. If I can do anything I shall be most pleased—"

"Of course, my dear. Your mother's daughter. Knew it by your face. Not tany tea, thank you, bad for digestion enjoyed bad health for many years and can only stay a minute. Called at four rouses already to-day with no result. Breaks your rart to see the callous sardness of the human race, every luxury and ease themselves and cold as sice to others. Wouldn't believe it unless you were present to see rebuffs si get. Ladies not a mile from this souse—could mention names but won't—pay pounds and pounds for gloves and dats and not talf-a-crown to spare for crying need, but said to myself all day, Mrs Rendell will help! I'll get ta welcome there!"

"Oh yes, I'm sure mother would be pleased," stammered Lilias, more and more puzzled to understand the drift of the strange woman's remarks. From the farther end of the room a little squeaky sound was heard, elaborately turned into a cough. Lilias grew hot with embarrassment, and Miss Thacker peered suspiciously over her spectacles as she produced a circular from her satchel and handed it over for inspection. It bore the heading "Waybourne Home for Incurables," and set forth a plea for help with which the girl was already familiar. She read it over, however, once and yet again, puzzling her head meantime as to what to do next. To refuse to give a donation was to class one's self at once among those whose "callous sardness" had been denounced, and Lilias's love of appreciation was so intense, that even before this unlovely stranger she could not bear to appear in an unfavourable light. She determined to delay the evil moment, and leave to her mother the unpleasant task of refusal; for it seemed in the last degree unlikely that Mrs Rendell would desire to supplement her ordinary subscription by a gift to an unauthorised collector.

"I am very sorry you should have had your walk in the rain," she said sweetly, "but, of course, in mother's absence I can make no promises. She will be home the day after to-morrow, if you could call again to see her."

She flattered herself that she had evaded the difficulty very cleverly, but Miss Thacker rounded on her in unexpected fashion.

"Shouldn't dream of asking you my love. Too much respect for your dear mother but wished to appeal to young and generous sarts like self and sisters! Any contribution however small! Every little helps. Most grateful I am sure, subscription or donation?"

"But—but," Lilias heard three separate gasps of dismay from the window, and realising that no help was forthcoming from that quarter, nerved herself to the unpleasant task.

"We should like to subscribe very much indeed, if we could, but we have only a small allowance, and at present are doing all we can to assist another charity. I fear that we cannot spare any more money—"

Miss Thacker peered at her solemnly through her spectacles, and shook her head from side to side.

"Ah, yes, my dear, can if you will! Every luxury and comfort, cup overflowing, only Will is lacking. Look into your rart and ask yourself what can I deny myself for rothers? Some worldly bauble, some article of adornment which you had planned to get, which you could do without, and reap pa rich reward. What is a hat, a dress, a fan, compared to the succour rof suffering garts?"

Now, as it happened, Lilias was bound for town the very next day to buy a supply of those fineries which her soul loved, so that this suggestion was so aptly timed as to strike her dumb with confusion. She could have gushed over the poor incurables for an hour on end; was ready to shed tears at a recital of their woes; but to give up a new hat in order to devote the money to their use, this was a flight of generosity to which Miss Lilias Rendell could never attain! She grew hot with anger at the inconsiderateness of the stranger in proposing such a sacrifice, hotter than ever at the thought of the three young sisters agape to hear her answer. Here was a pretty alternative, to consent and go without some detail of her summer outfit, or to refuse and be branded as vain and selfish? Lilias chose a middle course, and, extracting half a crown from her purse, handed it over with melancholy resignation.

"I shall be pleased to give you a small donation, but I would rather my name did not appear in your list. Put it down as from a friend."

"Or a Giver—a Cheerful Giver!" cried Miss Thacker, with an accent on the adjective which brought the blood into Lilias's cheeks. The wretched woman seemed to have fathomed her reluctance, and to be scoffing at her beneath a pretence of approval; but surely, now that she had got what she wanted, she would take her departure, and end this most trying scene. She made a little movement of dismissal, whereupon Miss Thacker glanced appealingly at the window.

"And our rother dear young friends," she was beginning, when suddenly she put her hands up to her face and made a curious spluttering noise, at sound of which the sisters started in dismay. She recovered herself at once, and continued her harangue with redoubled energy; but suspicion had been aroused, and could not easily be allayed. That laugh! It had been so like, so extraordinarily like; and yet that hair—that complexion—those missing teeth! It could not be! Chrissie drew nearer and nearer, staring at the stranger with searching scrutiny, met a direct glance of the eyes, and straightway flew upon her, wrenching off bonnet and veil, and twitching the horn-rimmed glasses from her nose. She squeaked and struggled, and fought the air with her woollen gloves, but it was of no avail: there she sat, discovered and exposed, with Nan's dark tresses streaming down behind the auburn front, Nan's dimpling smile breaking over the whitened face.

"Such callous sardness! Dragged my hair out by the roots! Is that the way you treat your visitors, my dear young friends?" she stuttered; but her dear young friends had no sympathy for her woes, and crowded round her, breathless with indignation.

"Wretched, miserable girl, so it was you all the time! What made you do it?"

"Wanted to amuse you on a wet day, and couldn't think of anything better. Did I do it well?"

"Abominably well! I could never have believed we should have been so deceived. How you managed to disguise your voice I can't think, and to make yourself look so awful. You are as white as a clown; and your teeth, Nan! What has become of your teeth?"

"Covered them with black sticking-plaster, that's all. Not even for your benefit, my dears, could I extract my two front molars. I smeared my face with cold cream, and then rubbed in flour. Sticky, but efficacious, and sucked a chocolate all the time, to make my voice thick. I'll swallow it now." Nan gulped, and rolled her eyes in expressive enjoyment. "When I was dressed, I stole downstairs, let myself out of the side gate, and rang at the bell as bold as brass. Mary did not recognise me, so I felt I was safe; but my one terror was lest you should go upstairs to call me down."

"And you found all the clothes in the dressing-up box! It is so long since we used it that I had almost forgotten the dear old things. The shawl and skirt I recognise, of course, but you have trimmed the bonnet yourself. I will say for you, my dear, that you made the most appalling old woman I have ever encountered."

"But I don't quite approve of making fun of anything so very, very sad as those dear incurables!" said Lilias solemnly. "Well, perhaps you didn't make fun of them exactly, but it was not quite a nice subject to choose for a practical joke. We ought to think of them tenderly.—By the by, I want that half-crown, Nan. Give it back to me!"

"N–ay!" drawled Nan, shaking her head, and speaking in broad, North-country dialect, "N–ay, lass! I'll none give it oop. It mun bide with me till I dee! I'll give you back good coin of the realm instead, but this precious piece is mine, and shall be pierced with a hole, and chained to my side, to commemorate the occasion. It will be good for you as well as for me. You can look at it, and remember how generous you were!"

"Humph!" said Lilias, and turned to the tea-table to pour out the long-delayed tea. It was too strong to drink; and when Mary appeared in response to the bell, it was a treat to see her stagger back at the sight of the dishevelled figure in the arm-chair, and to watch the smile of benign condescension with which Nan wrinkled up her face and inclined her red-brown head.

Mary was an old friend of the family, and on sufficiently intimate terms to express her opinion in terms unchequered by forms of politeness. She wished to be informed what Miss Nan would be up to next, and repeated with unction her own description of the "Hugliest old woman you ever set eyes on," as given to cook in the kitchen, ten minutes earlier. "We've been talking about you ever since, and wondering what you were after."

This was fame indeed! The girls shared in the reflected glory of Nan's performance, and only regretted that it had not been witnessed by a larger audience, while Chrissie, in especial, bewailed the absence of her *alter ego*.

"Kitty will never forgive us if she doesn't see you," she declared. "Oh, Nan, do go and call upon Mrs Maitland! Then Kitty would see you, and you might get some more money from her! It would be the most splendid fun. Oh, Nan, do! I'll love you for ever, if you will!"

Elsie and Agatha swelled the chorus by groans of appeal, and Nan visibly wavered. She could do nothing until she had had tea, she declared, but after that, if the rain grew less heavy, she would consider the matter; and hesitation being taken for assent, she was plied with cake and waited upon with obsequious attention. The elements seemed in favour of the scheme, for, by the time that tea was finished, the downpour was exchanged for a gentle drizzle, which could afford no excuse to a weather-proof creature like Nan Rendell. She was therefore shawled and bonneted once more, escorted to the front door by a giggling and excited quartette, and set off forthwith to tramp half a mile of muddy high road, half abashed at finding herself abroad in such a strange guise, altogether delighted at the madcap nature of the expedition.

The visit to Mrs Maitland was a huge success, for Kitty sat staring solemnly over her spectacles, while her mother had obviously much ado not to laugh outright at the eccentricities of her visitor. In the matter of donations she presented a firmer front than Lilias had done, but Nan would not allow herself to be foiled without a struggle. When Mrs Maitland said bravely, "I cannot see my way to giving anything more at present," she bridled as with indignation, and replied—

"But you must not consider yourself, you must consider Me! Here am I, tramping through mud and mire, drenched with rain, and chilled with cold; here rare you in your comfortable home, surrounded with luxury and dease, and you turn a deaf ear to the cause si plead, and let me toil in vain. No! I cannot gaze upon your good, kind face, and believe in such callous sardness ... The smallest trifle, if it be but half a crown—"

Well, it seemed a cheap price to pay to get rid of the terrible creature! Like Lilias, Mrs Maitland meekly handed over the desired coin, and rose to her feet with an air of determination.

"And now, if you will excuse me! I am rather busy, and—"

Nan bowed and smirked, then suddenly swooped across the room to where Kitty sat, her arms stretched wide in invitation.

"And will the dear child give me a sweet kiss before ri go?"

The consternation of the "dear child" and her mother can be imagined; but discovery came with the next moment, together with such shriekings of delight, such shakings and scoldings, such questionings and exclaimings, as were proper to the occasion. Nan returned home in high glee, chuckling over the success of the afternoon's escapade, and far from suspecting that the chief adventure still was to come. Such was the fact, however, and this is the way in which it happened.

She had passed along the high road in safety, meeting few inhabitants, owing to the inclemency of the weather, and looking forward with delight to the welcome which she would receive from her sisters. Presently Thurston House came in view, and, sure enough, there were four excited heads bobbing to and fro at the window, four broad beams of amusement to testify to the grotesqueness of her appearance. Nan lifted a solemn glance in return, and Chrissie, seized with a sudden demon of mischief, pointed a forefinger at the door opposite, and gesticulated violently in its direction. As plainly as words could speak, that forefinger said, "Call at the Grange! There's an adventure for you, if you like! Beard the lion in his den. I dare you to do it! You dare not go!"

It was done on the impulse of the moment, and on the impulse of the moment Nan turned and skipped obediently across the street. She never thought of possible consequences; her one idea was to horrify her sisters by pretending to carry out the suggestion, and the sight of their agitated faces pressed against the pane was sufficient encouragement to sustain her courage, as a pull at the bell sent a pealing chime through the house. The appearance of the old butler in the doorway did indeed evoke a thrill of nervousness, but then, what mattered? Visitors were never admitted, and she would certainly be dismissed, even as the others had been before her!

She quite prided herself upon the *sang-froid* with which she made the usual inquiry—

"Mr Vanburgh is at home, I presume? Will he be able to see me this afternoon?"

"Certainly, madam. Will you walk in? Mr Vanburgh is quite at liberty."

The horror of it seemed to take away all power of resistance. Did the man drag her in by force, or did she obey him of her own accord? Nan could not tell. The awful truth remained that the next moment she stood within the hall, and the door was shut behind her!

Chapter Fifteen
Diogenes at Home

"This way, please, ma'am. Will you come up-stairs?" said the butler; and Nan stumbled blindly forward, past the branching palms, the Indian cabinets, the knight in his glittering armour, past a hundred treasures, with never an eye to notice one of them, and a heart beating fast with agitation. The ascent seemed to last for a year, yet it would be over far too soon; the dreaded moment of introduction would arrive, and, in the name of all that was horrifying and perplexing, what should she do then? By what name should she be announced? What should she state as the object of her visit? What excuse could she offer for her intrusion?

"If I ever get out of this alive, I'll first pay out Miss Chrissie, and then turn over a new leaf for life! No more practical jokes for me!" said Nan to herself, and pulled her bonnet resolutely over her face. The butler had paused, and was looking at her inquiringly as he threw open the door of his master's room, and waited to announce her name. She croaked at him,—there is no other word to describe the inarticulate sound which issued from her lips,—then swept forward, and the man retired, no doubt thinking the stranger's manner on a par with her appearance.

Left to herself, Nan took a few steps forward and stopped abruptly, finding herself in a room which was at once the most beautiful and the most extraordinary which she had ever beheld. In every direction in which she turned her eyes, they were greeted by some quaint treasure, which had been brought from the ends of the earth to be stored against a background of tapestry and carved oak panel. It was like stepping back hundreds of years, and finding one's self in an old baronial castle; and the occupant of the room was in keeping with his surroundings. He lay on his couch, staring at her with sunken eyes, a picturesque-looking old man, with a complexion of bleached transparency; a white head, covered by a velvet skull-cap, and a wasted form, wrapped in a dressing—gown of embroidered Oriental silk. He looked both sad and suffering, and Nan recognised as much with a pang of regret for all the hard terms she had lavished upon his want of hospitality.

Yes, indeed! he looked too ill to receive visitors; too weary to be troubled with the commonplaces. What could she say to explain her own visit? What in the world should she find to talk about?

"Won't you sit down?" said a melodious voice. "Pray take a seat! I cannot wait upon you myself, as you see, but I can recommend that old saddle-bag. It is most comfortable." As he spoke, the invalid waved his hand towards a chair near his own, and Nan seated herself upon it in silence, glancing timidly in his face. This dumbness was appalling. She racked her brains to think of something to say, but no ideas were forthcoming; she could only twist her fingers in embarrassment, and wait another lead.

"It is most kind of you to come to see me on such a tempestuous afternoon," Mr Vanburgh continued politely. "I did not expect any callers. Ladies, as a rule, are not fond of venturing out in the rain, unless they have special business on hand."

Bravo! Here was a lead at last! What could be better than to follow up the suggestion of a business call? Nan asked herself eagerly. Mrs Maitland had regretted the loss of subscriptions upon which she had counted from the wealthy owner of the Grange: would it not be a good action if she could draw Mr Vanburgh's attention to the needs of the Incurables, and induce him to promise a subscription? She would not take the money, but leave the address of the secretary, to whom it could be forwarded. Oh, it was admirable—an admirable idea! The afternoon's escapade would lead to good after all. Nan's elastic spirits rose with a bound, and she smiled upon her companion with restored equanimity.

"I have a special business. I did not come merely to pay a call, but to ask your help for a cause in which I am much interested. I hoped that you might feel inclined to give a subscription, and can assure you that any sum which you may decide to give—"

To her dismay, the benevolent expression upon the watching face disappeared, as she spoke, to give place to one of suspicion and distrust. Mr Vanburgh moved himself on his pillows, so as to face her more fully, and stared at her fixedly, beneath frowning brows.

"You want a subscription! You have come here to beg—to ask for money?"

"But not for myself!" explained Nan eagerly. The scrutiny bent upon her was so searching that she felt bound to protest against a personal interest. "It was for a charity, a local hospital, which is in want of funds. It was thought—I thought that, as a newcomer to the neighbourhood, you might like to hear about the various organisations, and to give some support. There is a large poor population at Sale, a mile from here, and the committee is always short of funds. Many of the old residents have left, and the new ones don't—don't always." —Her remembrance of odd sentences heard at committee meetings came to a sudden end, and the voice trailed off in inarticulate murmurings.

"Do not always come forward in their place. Just so! And I am to understand that you are deputed by these various charities and organisations to plead their cause and collect subscriptions?"

Nan cleared her throat vigorously. It was the only way she could think of by which to gain time, and decide how to evade the question.

"They are most grateful for all they can get. The committee would send you an acknowledgment of your subscription. It would be better to send it direct, instead of giving it to me. I just wish to call your attention—to tell you particulars and enlist your interest—"

"Just so!" said Mr Vanburgh again; and Nan fancied that there was a slight softening in the watching eyes. "Just so. And for what special charity do you wish to plead to-day?"

"For the Home for Incurables!"

"Ah!" The word came with a hiss from between closed teeth. "Indeed! You choose your object well, madam! I congratulate you on your discretion. The cause is truly fitting."

She had made a false move this time, there was no doubt about it, for the old man's voice was sharp with displeasure; but blundering Nan could not even now imagine wherein lay the offence.

She gaped at him, with a stammering—

"Fitting! Why fitting? I don't understand what you mean!"

"Only that being incurable myself, I need your charity every whit as much as those for whom you come asking help—"

"Incurable! You won't get better! Never get better until you—"

"Die? Precisely! That is what it means. I shall spend my life upon this couch, or being wheeled about in a bath-chair, suffering torments of pain and weariness until death comes to set me free—the kindliest friend that could step inside my door!"

"Oh!" cried Nan sharply. "Oh!" The tears rushed to her eyes, and she trembled from head to foot. It was terrible to listen to those words, terrible to her youth and strength to hear death spoken of in those yearning tones;

her heart—Nan's big loving heart—went out in a rush of sympathy towards the lonely sufferer. She stretched her hand towards him, and cried brokenly, "I'm sorry! Oh, I'm sorry! We knew, of course, that you were ill, but we never thought it was as bad as that."

"We! Who are we?" Mr Vanburgh's fingers closed over her hand, and he held it firmly in his own, while he gazed at her with a gentleness of mien before which Nan's resolution died a sudden death.

"My—my sisters!" she stammered humbly. "Oh, Mr Vanburgh, forgive me. I'm Nan Rendell. I live in the house just across the road. I'm not an old woman at all, only a stupid girl dressed up. I never meant to come, but Chrissie dared me, and I thought I would come to the door and ring, to give her a fright. I never thought you would let me in. You had refused to see all other visitors. My father and mother called, and Mr and Mrs Maitland—"

"They did, and many others. It was very kind, but I felt too ill to receive them. With you, however, it was different, for I seemed to know you already. I had seen so much of your life through 'my study window'—"

"Saw me! Then you knew all the time who I was? You knew—"

"I did! Yes. It was very interesting. I wondered how long you could keep it up."

"But how—how?"

Mr Vanburgh smiled quietly.

"My couch is placed near the window, and during my long lonely days I devote a good deal of attention to the passers-by. About three o'clock this afternoon I observed a black robed figure steal out of your side gate and approach the front door. I saw her admitted by the servant. I saw her go out once again, and, like her sisters, kept watch for her return."

"And you saw Chrissie point across to your door, and heard my ring?"

"I did. And rang myself, to give orders that you should be admitted. That is the true and authentic account of the mystery. It is not so mysterious after all, is it?"

"It's very embarrassing!" Nan was suddenly overcome by a consciousness of how ridiculous she must have appeared in her assumed character, and collapsed into feeble laughter, "What *must* you think of me?"

"To tell the truth, I prefer your ordinary appearance. It is difficult to recognise you in this attire. Would you think it a liberty if I asked you to resume your ordinary guise? Please!" and he waved his hand with an appeal which had in it an element of authority, despite all its courtesy. Nan felt very small, very much like a mischievous child who has spilt the ink-bottle, and is sent upstairs to be washed and tidied; but, all the same, she was not sorry to remove the ugly trappings, and appear in her true guise once more. Bonnet, veil, spectacles, and cloak came off in succession; her dark hair curled in little rings round her forehead, and the round young throat rose like a pillar above the quaintly-cut bodice. If Lilias had been in her sister's place, she would have reflected that her antique costume was appropriate to her surroundings, but such thoughts as these never occurred to honest Nan. She was merely concerned to see that the last remains of powder were wiped away, and, being satisfied on this point, smiled at Mr Vanburgh in friendly fashion.

"That's better!" he said cheerfully. "I begin to recognise you again. I have seen you only from a distance so far, but I seem to know you very well. You are 'Nan,' you say, and you are what—number three, I suppose? The young lady who went away the other day is the elder sister, and after her comes the fair one with the golden locks."

"Lilias! Yes; she is the beauty of the family; I come next, and then Elsie, the little one, with big, dark eyes. We call her 'Mrs Gummidge,' because she is melancholy, and feels things 'more than others.' Then comes Agatha; you know Agatha! the great big girl with the huge feet and the rosy cheeks; and Christabel, the youngest—"

"Oh yes, I know Christabel!" said Mr Vanburgh, smiling, "and her friend who comes to lessons every day: the brown-legged stork, with the red cap and the curly locks. I like that child. She looks honest and straightforward! Who is she?"

"Why, that's Kitty!" replied Nan, in a voice of surprised reproof, for surely every one in Waybourne must know an important personage like Kitty! "Her name is really Gwendoline Maitland, but everybody calls her Kitty; and she was longing to know you, and made her mother come to call in her new spring clothes, with a promise to bring in her name at every turn of the conversation; and then, after all, you would not receive her!"

"That was very sad! I am afraid I must have appeared churlish; but, as a matter of fact, I came down to Waybourne to avoid old friends, rather than make new ones. I am too ill to be sociable. It is a trial to me, nowadays, to meet strangers."

"And yet—"

"And yet I wished to see you! That seems rather a contradiction, does it not? But I have always been fond of young people, and I seemed to have made your acquaintance in spite of myself. Perhaps you are hardly aware how plainly one can see into your sitting-room from here."

Nan smiled and bent forward to look across the street, in response to a wave of the invalid's hand.

The porch-room was exactly opposite, and the three-sided windows did indeed allow an extraordinarily clear view of the interior. The girls had always believed themselves out of range of vision when they were seated at the table; but at this moment Nan could distinctly discern four anxious faces scanning the opposite house, catch Agatha's craning movements, and Lilias's waving hands. The sight provoked an irresistible chuckle of amusement, and Mr Vanburgh's eyes turned towards her in wistful scrutiny.

"You seem very merry together, you young people. Life is full of happiness to you!"

"Oh, we have our trials!" said Nan quickly. "We are awfully happy together; but still, of course, it isn't all as we should wish. Each one of us has a grievance, and could talk about it for hours at a time, if we had a chance. Sometimes we have dreadful fits of dumps. Elsie has them chronically, but the rest of us are up and down. I'm generally up myself; but still, I have my moments!"

"I should think they are very rare! Would it be indiscreet to ask what is your peculiar cross?"

Nan pondered with raised brows and an expression which grew more and more uncertain.

"It's rather difficult to say straight off, isn't it? There *is* something, I know, but I forget what it is. I am always making stupid mistakes for one thing, and that is so awkward, now that I am supposed to be grown up. I'm eighteen, so I ought to know better. I went out to my first dinner-party this winter, and the most awful thing happened. A stupid male creature took me in, with a collar about a foot high, and such an affected drawl that I could hardly understand a word he said. However, I talked away and tried to be pleasant. I have a habit of waving my hands when I talk; we all have— perhaps you have noticed it! I was telling a story, and came to a point where it seemed necessary to lift my hand suddenly, to give emphasis to what I was saying. Well, I did it, and at that crucial moment if the waiter didn't go and hand a sauce-bowl over my partner's shoulder! My hand met the bowl, and ... Maud was sitting opposite, and she said that never in all her life had she seen anything so appalling! The bowl flew up in the air, turned a somersault, and the sauce rained down in showers upon his knees! He had his serviette spread open, of course, but still it was bad enough. There was silence all round the table. He sat stock still, staring at his hands, all brown and dripping; then he said, in a very small, exhausted voice, 'I think I had bettaw—go up-sta-ahs!'"

Mr Vanburgh lay back against his cushions and pressed his hands to his mouth. His shoulders heaved, and a curious muffled sound emerged from his lips. He tried to strangle it, tried to frown, to choke the inclination in his throat, but it was of no avail: laugh he must, and laugh he did, his slight form shaking with merriment, the tears rising in the tired eyes and streaming down his cheeks. Nan laughed afresh at the comical spectacle, and as she looked a door behind the couch was pushed gently open, and a startled face peered round the corner. It was the face of the dark-skinned foreigner who was the invalid's attendant, and his master greeted him with affectionate freedom.

"Yes, Pedro! Yes! It is quite true! I was laughing! It is a long time since you have heard such a sound from my lips. No wonder you are startled. It is this young lady who has wrought the miracle."

The dark eyes rested on Nan's face with a glow of gratitude which made the girl's heart beat fast with pleasure. The eloquent Southern glance conveyed many meanings, but he said simply, "The signorina is welcome! I hope the signorina comes again!" and left the room in the same quiet, unobtrusive manner in which he had entered.

Chapter Sixteen
The Curtained Pictures

When Mrs Rendell returned home and heard of Nan's latest escapade, she was breathless with horror and consternation.

"I don't know what I am to do with you, child," she cried. "Every time I go away there is a fresh outbreak, and you seem to grow worse instead of better. It is useless to warn you!"

"Oh, mummy dear!" Nan's voice was full of protest, and she stared with reproachful eyes in her mother's face. "It's not fair to say that! I always do as you tell me. I never do what you have forbidden. You can't think of a single instance where I have played a trick the second time, when you have cautioned me against it!"

"But what is the good of that, when you immediately hit on something even worse?" queried her mother despairingly. "What sane woman would ever dream of forbidding a girl of eighteen to walk about the streets in disguise, and go begging for subscriptions at strange houses? It takes away my breath, even to think of it! All sorts of things might have happened!"

"But only nice things did happen, dear! I always fall on my feet, you know, and Mr Vanburgh is an old love. He sent his respects to you, and hoped you and father would do him the favour of paying a second call, as he would much like to make the acquaintance of my parents! It was the first time in my life that I had heard you spoken of as adjuncts of my noble self, and I can tell you I felt proud. Really and truly, it was a blessing I went, for you can't think how he enjoyed seeing me. I said good-bye three times over before he would let me go, and I told him every single thing about our family!"

"I've no doubt you did!" Mrs Rendell groaned aloud, and stared helplessly at the ceiling. "Please add to your list of prohibitions for the future, my dear, that you are forbidden to go outside the door in an assumed costume; and do try to behave like a reasonable creature, instead of a harebrained schoolboy! I can't make any promise about calling again until I see what father says."

Nan was comfortably secure that her father would do as he was told, and had little difficulty in persuading the good man that, above all things in the world, he desired to make the acquaintance of his neighbour. There was little fear that the visit would be deferred too long; for with five daughters vying with each other to introduce the subject on every possible opportunity, and to discuss times and seasons at breakfast, lunch, and dinner, it speedily became an object to get the call paid as soon as possible.

On the very next Saturday afternoon, therefore, Mrs Rendell attired herself in calling array, was carefully surveyed by a critical audience, pronounced to be a "credit to the family," and despatched to the Grange, with a score of divergent instructions as to what to do, what to say, and, above all, how to lay the foundation-stone of a future intimacy.

Perhaps, if the truth were known, Mrs Rendell was scarcely less excited than her daughters at the prospect of being admitted into the presence of the mysterious stranger; but if this were so, she was doomed to disappointment, for the invalid seemed too weary and dispirited to enter into conversation, and it was only by a most apparent effort that he roused himself to reply to her remarks. Mrs Rendell would have felt repelled by his coldness of manner, had it not been for one redeeming point—his unaffected interest in her children! The wan face brightened into a smile at the mention of Nan's name, and he begged that the girl might be allowed to come over to see him "often—as often as possible," in a tone of unmistakable sincerity. Mrs Rendell assented graciously; and, mindful of the reproaches which would be hurled at her head if she returned without doing her best for every member of the family, suggested that perhaps Mr Vanburgh would like to make the acquaintance of the other girls also! He hesitated for a moment, but looked gratified by the suggestion.

"If they would not find it too dull. I am fond of young people, but am always afraid of boring them by my company. Our lives lie so far apart. Perhaps they would come over at different times, and let me make their acquaintance by degrees. The two younger ones especially—your own daughter and the little girl who is her friend."

On the score of this distinction, Christabel and Kitty were the first couple to take advantage of the invitation and cross the road to interview Diogenes in his den. They confided in each other that they were "simply dying of fright," but contrived to conceal their expiring condition beneath haughty and dignified exteriors. The manner in which Chrissie requested the old butler to inform his master of their advent would have done credit to a princess of the blood, while Kitty stalked upstairs behind her with majestic gravity. Outside the dreaded door, however, it was impossible to resist exchanging a grimace of agitation, and it was another instance of the contrariety of men that the butler should turn his head at that inopportune moment, and discover them so employed. Chrissie grew red with mortification, and Kitty spluttered with laughter; so, after all, it was in the guise of two blushing, giggling schoolgirls that they made Mr Vanburgh's acquaintance, instead of that of self-possessed women of the world, as they had fondly hoped would be the case. He looked from one to the other as they sat before him—big, bonnie, well-grown girls, with flaming locks and fresh complexions, and there was a great wistfulness in his gaze. The girls felt it; and though the meaning thereof was a mystery, they understood that here was an understanding, sympathetic soul, and immediately lost their feeling of shyness.

In ten minutes' time they had confided to him their dream of the "Select Academy," and he had promised to recommend the school to his friends, with a seriousness which was balm to their vanity. Nothing is more annoying to mature women of fourteen than to be treated as if they were children; and when Mr Vanburgh discussed at length various points of management on which the future partners were at variance, and gave valuable suggestions on architectural designs, Christabel screwed up her eyes at him with her most approving smile, and reflected that seldom, if ever, had she met a grown-up person with so much common sense! Tea was brought in for the girls' benefit, and Kitty poured it out, spilling the milk over the cloth, and covering the wet spot with the muffin dish with admirable presence of mind. She felt so much at home that she helped herself to cake a second time without being asked, drank three cups of tea, and only refrained from a fourth because the pot was drained. After tea, conversation turned on hobbies, and it being discovered that one girl had a mania for miniature jugs, and the other for foreign post-cards, the Italian servant was summoned, and received instructions in his own tongue, which resulted in an addition being made to each collection: Kitty returned home hugging "a little d–arling" jug of Italian pottery, while Chrissie exhibited a Chinese post-card, and pictures of Mongolian belles printed on transparent rice paper. The glories of the interview lost nothing from their descriptions; and Lilias and Elsie sighed continuously until the time came for their own visit.

In each heart the thought lay concealed that if Mr Vanburgh had been so kind to the other girls, he must of a surety extend a still greater favour to herself. The mirror assured Lilias that she was a sight to "make an old man young"; while Elsie shook her head over the reflection that only those who have suffered themselves can sympathise with the woes of others. But, alas! disappointment awaited them; for, strange to relate, the invalid found

Lilias's fragile charms less attractive to his eye than the healthful vivacity of her sisters; while condolence was so distasteful to his ears, that he fairly scowled down Elsie's plaintive assurances of sympathy. As a matter of fact, it was brightness and amusement of which the recluse was in need; and as the last visitors were the least humorous members of the family, it followed that their presence was least welcome. Awkward silence recurred at intervals; and when the girls rose to say good-bye, no request was made for a further visit, though a message was sent to Nan, begging her to come by herself on the first convenient occasion. Elsie made a public announcement in the schoolroom that evening that she washed her hands of Mr Vanburgh, finding in him a cold and unresponsive soul; but Lilias was not so easily discouraged. It rankled in her mind that she had failed where others had succeeded, and she determined to break down Mr Vanburgh's prejudice and win the post of favourite, cost what it might. She had not had a fair chance when Elsie was present. The members of one's own family are apt to betray surprise at injudicious moments, to check one's innocent rhapsodies by counter-assertions, and even to quote words used on previous occasions, as a proof that conduct does not coincide with theory. There were a dozen pretty little speeches she had been longing to make, but it was impossible to deliver them when Elsie was sitting there, listening with all her ears, ready to repeat them to a schoolroom audience, or even commit them to the surer testimony of her diary. Some day she would make excuse to go alone, and then—! Lilias nodded her head in assured self-confidence, and watched Nan's air of proprietorship with a smile, convinced that her own triumph was at hand. She was beginning to realise that a declared understanding was less exciting than an incipient love affair; the thirst for fresh conquest was upon her, and in default of any more interesting prey, she determined to turn her attention to Mr Vanburgh, and raked her silly little head to devise schemes for subjection.

Honest Nan had no scheme at all, nothing but the kindliest desire to cheer a lonely old man, and was so entirely her bright merry self at the second interview, that again, and yet again, the sound of laughter broke the silence of the room. She discovered that the old man had a keen sense of humour, though it had long lain dormant; and as it seemed to please him to hear her chat away in unconstrained fashion, chat she did, with such an accompaniment of sparkling eyes, waving hands, and sunny smiles, as was a positive tonic to behold. She told stories of her own adventures or misadventures, which Mr Vanburgh capped by remembrances of his own boyhood; they compared notes as to their mutual sensations at critical moments, and so sympathetic did they appear, that the girl was forced into an expression of astonishment.

"You remember so well! Most old people seem to forget how it feels to be young, especially people who have not had any children of their own. How have you managed to remember all these things?"

The old man looked at her quietly. The smile left his face, and the lines round his lips and eyes seemed to deepen in sudden, mysterious fashion. Nan divined that she had touched a hidden wound, and waited anxiously for his reply. It was a long time in coming, and then it was altogether a surprise. Mr Vanburgh touched the bell which lay near at hand, and spoke a word of direction to the Italian, who appeared at the summons.

"Take this young lady into the study and show her—my pictures!" he said slowly; and Nan followed Pedro out of the room in perplexity of spirit. The man's dark eyes studied her face critically, but no words were said until the room was reached, and they stood together before a curtained alcove.

"It is his sorrow, the sorrow of his life," murmured the soft voice plaintively, as the curtain was drawn back, and Nan gazed with awed eyes upon four portraits hung against a fluting of crimson cloth. The rich frames, the carved table beneath, with its bank of white flowers, gave the alcove the appearance of a shrine; and a shrine it was indeed, dedicated to the memory of a lost happiness.

The first portrait was of a man, the second of a woman, with a beautiful and gentle face, which bore so strange a likeness to those of a boy and a girl on either side that it was easy to trace the relationship between them.

The girl bade fair to become as lovely as her mother; the boy was a magnificent fellow, with waving locks, thrown back from a noble brow, and such an air of pride and candour in the carriage of the head and the flash of the eyes as would have filled a parent's heart with pride to behold. Nan's eyes passed by the other two portraits to dwell on this with wondering admiration; and something in the appearance of the beautiful young lad seemed strangely familiar. Family likeness is a marvellous thing, revealing itself in the most unexpected fashions; and though at first sight no two people could have been more unlike than this incarnation of youth and strength, and the bleached and weary invalid in the next room, it was certainly of Mr Vanburgh, and no other, that Nan was reminded at this moment. The shape of the eyes was the same, the curve of the lips, the growth of the hair on the forehead. She looked back at the first picture, and gave a start of recognition. She had not realised it at first, but yes! that handsome, happy, self-confident face had once belonged to Mr Vanburgh himself; it was his own portrait at which she looked. Nan wheeled round to the servant with an agitated question:

"It is himself! But why is he here? They are dead, these others, but he—"

"He also is dead, signorina," the man replied, and bent his head as if in obeisance before the picture. "He died with those he loved. Something lived on, perhaps, but not my master. He lies buried with them—his wife— his son—his daughter. All that he had. Ah, what a tragedy! One day all happiness and love; the next it is done, it is over, his heart is broken! We were out yachting together, and my master and I have gone on shore on business—to make purchases, to buy provisions. We should join them again next day; and meantime they went a little cruise to pass the time—an excursion to a bay which the signora wished to visit. It was all calm when they started, but those are treacherous seas; a squall sprang up, and they were driven on the rocks. The gale lasted two days, and at the end pieces of wood were washed ashore from the wreck. There was nothing else— no, nothing! We were like madmen both, searching about, and waiting, always waiting, year after year. ... They might have been picked up, and landed at some far-away port; they might for a time have lost their minds and been unable to remember. Such things have been; and why not again? But at last hope died away, and strength with it. He took no rest, no care for himself, and so the illness came which ends as you see. Then I took him away, for the living must come before the dead, and I had my duty to him to remember. We have wandered over the world, signorina, in search of health and peace, but they come not with money. Everything else,"—he waved his hand round the exquisite room, with its paintings, its carvings, its china, its treasures of ancient art—"everything else, but not these. So at last we came home, to rest—and die!"

Nan trembled and was silent. She had no words in which to express her passion of pity, but the Italian understood, with the quick insight of his race, and flashed a grateful glance upon her.

"It is not every one to whom he shows these pictures. They are covered with a curtain, so that they are hidden from the stranger; but every morning we come together, he and I, and put fresh flowers. It is a great sign of his favour to the signorina that he should have sent her here. He has opened his heart to her as is not usual with him, and she can help him if she will."

"Oh, I will! I will! I long to help him," murmured Nan brokenly. She stood gazing at the pictures until the curtain dropped once more, and she found herself being escorted back to her seat.

Mr Vanburgh looked at her silently. It was not possible for him to be whiter than usual, but his lips were contracted in a nervous pressure, and a nerve was throbbing visibly at his temples. Nan stretched out her hand impetuously and laid it over his; the fingers were icy cold to her touch, and she rubbed them between her own with tender care.

"Thank you!" he whispered breathlessly, and looked at her with kindly eyes.

"You are a wise child. You understand how to console. Words are too weak. You judged too quickly, you see, in taking for granted that I had always been alone. Fifteen years ago—you saw their portraits?"

"Yes. They are all beautiful; and oh, the boy!"

"My son!" sighed the father softly. "Yes, if you could have seen my son. It was not only I, but every one who met him said the same thing: that they had never seen his equal. All that I did was for him, to prepare for the time when he should succeed me. He was so strong, so full of life; it seemed impossible that he could die."

"Mr Vanburgh, how did you bear it? How can people go through such trials and live? To lose everything at once, and live on, and keep one's reason—I can't understand it. You must be very good!"

The old man smiled sadly.

"No, child, I am not good. I had my time of madness and rebellion, and my old self died, never to revive again; but I have kept my faith in God. I could not afford to lose that, as well as everything else. He has taken from me all that made life beautiful—first my dear ones, and then the strength which might have made it possible to find fresh interests; but such discipline must be for some great end, and I am growing nearer and nearer to the time when I shall know the reason. There is an explanation ready for me, and I am waiting to hear it. You will never have a trouble sent to you in life, child, without the strength to bear it; and the greater the trial the greater may be the reward. Even in this life I have had compensations; when the sun of prosperity is shining we do not realise our need of God, but when the clouds gather, we turn homewards like tired children, and the help never fails. In my loneliness I have learned to know Christ, and the peace which is His gift to those who trust Him!"

He shut his eyes and remained silent for a long time, while Nan studied the emaciated face with anxious gaze; but when he looked up again he was calm and collected, almost smiling.

"My little friend, I have shown you my Holy of Holies, but we will never speak of it again. You know my sorrow, and we will understand each other without words. I have learned to be thankful for the unexpected blessings which come into my life, of which your companionship is one. You will always be welcome when you can spare an hour to sit with a lonely old man; and I am glad to have made the acquaintance of some young people for another reason. My nephew, my heir,"—he drew his brows together with a frown of pain,—"is coming next month to pay me a visit. He will be with me for some time, and if you will be kind enough to extend your friendship to him I shall be grateful!"

"We will! We will! But oh, I wish he were a girl! Are you sure you have no girl nieces that you want to invite as well?"

"More girls?" Mr Vanburgh smiled faintly. "I should have thought you had enough, with five sisters of your own. A boy would surely be more change, though, as far as that, Gervase is more than a boy now. It is three years since he left Oxford, and he is quite a man of the world by this time."

Nan groaned deeply.

"I know them! I know them well, and I detest them! Really old men are quite sensible and humble, but the young ones put on as many airs as if they owned the world, and didn't think much of it at that. I like schoolboys immensely—mischievous, grubby little schoolboys, who keep white mice in their bedrooms, and are full of pranks and jokes; but no young men for me, thank you! Jim, our brother, is the only really nice one I know, and even he thinks that the world was made for his convenience. No one dares to contradict him; and it is the most maddening thing in the world to argue with him, for he never even takes the trouble to answer, but simply chuckles in condescending fashion, and chucks you under the chin. We know another very nice man, too—Ned Talbot; but for a clever man who has taken degrees and scholarships and appointments above everybody else, you wouldn't believe how stupid and blundering he is. As blind as a bat. He—but never mind! I didn't mean to speak about him, only to say that if your nephew is coming down at all, do have him in June instead of next month! Jim is coming home then, and Ned will be here, and we have all sorts of plans in the air. It would be nicer for him when there would be some men to take him about, and he would have a really good time. Don't you think he could come in June?"

"He could probably arrange to stay on a little longer. He will be with me for some considerable time, as there is a great deal of business which we must do together. I will tell him what you say when I write, and impress upon him that June is a period of special attraction!"

"And then he will be at our sale!" said Nan gleefully to herself; and the same thought occurred to each of her sisters, when this latest piece of news was unfolded.

"How lovely!" gushed Agatha. "Now he can buy my shaving-case! Father said it was a useless bauble; but a rich young man can afford baubles, and I feel sure he would like the look of it upon his dressing-table. I'll mark it 'Sold,' and say I kept it specially for him."

"I don't believe he will come at all. Men detest bazaars; but if he does, we must make him buy far more than that," said Elsie firmly. "If we can't sell that veil-case, we will pretend it is for ties, and that no gentleman's wardrobe is complete without it. And we'll raise all the prices whenever he comes near!"

"I don't suppose he'll eat toffee, but he must hand round the tea and make himself useful. We can keep him busy at our stall," said Chrissie; while Lilias stared into space, and smiled in a soft, dreamy fashion. "After all," she said thoughtfully, "after all, I think he had better help me, instead of Ned! Ned knows quite a number of the people, and could make himself agreeable going about and talking; but this poor fellow will know nobody but us. Yes! yes! he shall be my assistant in the punt!"

Chapter Seventeen
A Budget of Letters

One bright May morning Mrs Rendell sat by her desk ostensibly busy with accounts, but in reality watching the movements of her daughter Lilias, who lounged on the window seat reading the letters which had just been delivered by the second post. Mrs Rendell herself had brought these letters into the room, and consequently knew full well who were her daughter's correspondents, and which envelope contained the separate effusions. The dainty grey, with its edging of white, came from Lilias's bosom friend, a certain Ella Duckworth, whose sayings and doings were so constantly quoted in the schoolroom that her very name had become the signal for groans of disapproval; the fat white packet bore the magic name of the *Bon Marché*, Paris, and contained patterns of material for the frock in which Lilias intended to array herself at the garden parties of the coming season; and the narrow envelope, with its bold, even writing, was a familiar object in the Rendell household, whose authorship required no explanation.

Mrs Rendell handed this letter to her daughter with a smiling remembrance of the days when such letters used to come to herself—of her eagerness and delight, her insatiable appetite for more. As she added up her weekly bills and balanced her accounts, soft little trills of laughter greeted her ears from the other end of the room, and she smiled again in enjoyment of her child's happiness, and lifted her head to regard the pretty picture. The sun shone on Lilias's fair head, transforming it into an aureole of gold; pink and white were the colours of her morning dress, pink and white was her face, and the blossom on the hawthorn tree which shaded the window seemed made on purpose to form a background to the charming figure. Mrs Rendell's eyes softened with motherly pride; but the next moment her brows contracted and her expression grew troubled, for there on the seat lay Ned Talbot's letter unopened, while Lilias smiled and dimpled in enjoyment of her friend's effusion. It seemed strange that a girl should show so little eagerness to read a lover's letter; but Mrs Rendell reflected that perhaps Lilias preferred to leave the greater treat to the last, and comforted herself thereby. When Ella's letter had been read, then of course Ned's would be even more eagerly devoured; but no! Lilias regretfully folded away the sheet in its envelope, regarded the two unopened envelopes with languid indecision, and finally selected the packet from Paris as more worthy of attention. If she had looked up at that *moment* and caught the flash in the watching eyes, Miss Lilias would have been on her guard; but, as it was, she complacently settled herself to the study of patterns, holding up the little squares of gauze to the light, laying them against her dress, and pleating them in her fingers with an absorption which rendered her unconscious of her surroundings. Five minutes passed, ten minutes, and still she turned from one novelty to another, unable to make a choice among so many temptations; and still her mother watched from her corner, the pencil stayed in her busy hands. The irritation had faded from Mrs Rendell's face, and given place to an expression of anxious tenderness; for Lilias's indifference to Ned's letter was but another strengthening of the growing conviction that the girl's feeling for her lover fell short of what it should rightly be. A dozen signs, too subtle to be put into words, but none the less eloquent, had attracted Mrs Rendell's attention within the last few weeks, and sent a chill to her heart. Above all things it was imperative that Lilias should love her future husband with all the strength of which she was capable, for Lilias's mother knew that no other power but love could develop a selfish nature, and make a noble woman out of a vain and thoughtless girl. Love has wrought this miracle before, and will again; and through all her grief for Maud's disappointment, Mrs Rendell had comforted herself by the reflection that Lilias was the one of all her children who was most in need of a softening influence, the one to whom the love of a good man might be most valuable. Dear, sweet Maud could not be selfish if she tried, but an early engagement might be the only means of saving Lilias from the injurious effect of flattering and worldly friends. So the mother had reasoned with herself; but her arguments would lose all their force if Lilias herself had no love in her heart for her future husband. A loveless marriage is a catastrophe for any girl, but for Lilias it would mean moral suicide: a deliberate settling down into a selfish, self-seeking life! Was it possible that she had accepted Ned for no higher motive than a love of excitement, and the puny triumph of making the first marriage in the family? Mrs Rendell would not judge the girl so harshly without unmistakable proof, but, her suspicions being aroused, she could not be content until she grasped the true position of affairs. A broken engagement was the last thing which she desired to have in her family, but better that, a thousand times over, than that two lives should be wrecked for ever!

She waited patiently until, at last, Lilias deigned to read her lover's letter, watching her face with scrutinising eyes. It was evident that something in the closely-written sheet did not commend itself to the girl's approval; for as she read the white forehead grew fretted with lines, and the lips took a sullen droop. The smiles faded away, and it was a very blank, dejected edition of Miss Lilias Rendell who looked up at last, to meet her mother's glance.

"Well, what is it, dear? You seem troubled. No bad news, I hope?"

"Oh no—nothing serious, at least. Ned seems worried. Things don't go smoothly in the new Works, and he has such high-flown ideas. It seems to me he makes troubles, by expecting every one else to be as quixotic as himself. He is not likely to find high-flown notions among ordinary business men!"

"And since when, my dear, have you become acquainted with the feelings of business men?" inquired Mrs Rendell sharply; then, in a softer tone, "My dear child, I implore you not to begin your engagement to Ned by discouraging his highest motives. Men, as a rule, are not overburdened with sentiment, and it is the duty of a wife to encourage all that is good and generous. You would be grieved, I am sure, to feel that your influence had a sordid or worldly direction!"

"Oh, mother!" protested Lilias, shocked beyond words at the possibility of such a charge, as we are all shocked when our secret thoughts are put into words, and we see them before us in all their naked hideousness. "Oh, mother, as if I could do anything so dreadful. Ned says I am his good angel; of course, of course, I want him to be good; but it is depressing, isn't it, when as soon as one gets engaged business begins to go wrong, and every letter brings news of some fresh worry or unpleasantness? It is enough to make one feel melancholy!"

"Yes, dear, it is, and I'm sorry for you. It is a disappointment to us all to hear that Ned is so unhappy in his new position, for it seemed to promise so well six months ago. Father is anxious to have a talk with him on the subject, and see if he can help to smooth the way, so the sooner he can come the better it will be. Does he make any suggestion in his letter as to the date that will suit him best?"

"Y—es!" said Lilias; and her face clouded once more. "He wants to come on the twentieth; and it is so awkward, for the Duckworths want me to go to them for that very week. They are having a tennis party, and their first day on the river, and several teas and dinners. It would be such a delightful week! I thought, perhaps, Ned might put off his visit until June. Maud would be home by that time, and they would both be sorry to miss each other if he came earlier."

Mrs Rendell looked at her with a mingling of exasperation and relief—relief that she should be so ignorant of Maud's feelings, exasperation that it should be possible for one sister to be so oblivious to the sufferings of another. She could not but realise also that Lilias would prefer a week of gaiety at Richmond to a visit from Ned Talbot; and her distress at the thought made her voice sound somewhat sharp as she replied—

"There is some one else to be considered besides yourself, my dear. You forget that your father and I would prefer to see Ned at once, and would not approve of postponing his visit. It is you, and not Maud, whom he comes to see; and you would surely not choose to spend the time in frivolity which might be given to helping and comforting the man you have promised to marry?"

"No—no, of course not, mother!" cried Lilias, shocked once more at the suggestion of her own selfishness. "I'll write at once, and say that the twentieth will suit us all." She gathered her letters together as she spoke, and rose to leave the room, holding her head well in the air, and keeping up an appearance of composure so long as she was in her mother's sight, but once outside the door the tears of disappointment rushed to her eyes, and she brought down her foot on the floor with a stamp of irritation. She felt jarred and disappointed, and thoroughly ill-used into the bargain. Only two months engaged, and already involved in trouble and anxiety, and expected to give up her own pleasure in order to condole with a dejected lover! She had imagined that it would be Ned's place to console her; and if his fears should prove well founded, surely it would be she who needed consolation in the prospect of a long, uncertain engagement. Lilias had known one or two girls who had waited year after year while their *fiancés* struggled against adverse circumstances, and she was by no means anxious to follow their example. They lost their beauty, and grew thin and pale; people spoke of them with expressions of commiseration; the subject of marriage was studiously avoided in their presence. Lilias grew hot at the thought that any one might possibly regard her in such a fashion. When she had become engaged to Ned Talbot, the future had appeared *couleur de rose*, and she had sunned herself in the prospect of increased importance at home, and the honour which would be paid to the beautiful young bride by her husband's friends and relatives. How miserable, how humiliating, if all these dreams came to naught, and she found herself bound to an unsuccessful man, with all her ambitions nipped in the bud!

Lilias's thoughts roamed back over the past, and a dull resentment against her *fiancé* grew in her mind; for did it not seem that he had always been unlucky, that the brief space of prosperity that had preceded her engagement had been the exception, not the rule, in his experiences? Old Mr Talbot had died while Ned was still at college, and the necessity of looking after the business for the benefit of the family had compelled the young fellow to sacrifice his own hopes of a profession, and settle down to a commercial life. Mr Talbot had owned "Works" of some kind; Lilias had the haziest idea of their purport. Ned manufactured "engines and things," she told her friends vaguely, and spent his days amidst clanking machinery, in an atmosphere impregnated with steam and oil. A dozen years before, "the Works" had been a profitable concern, but it had steadily declined in value, as more powerful firms monopolised the trade. Ned had struggled hard against the tide, but his term of management had been far from prosperous, and when, a year ago, his most formidable rival had come forward with an offer to take over the smaller firm, and instal him in the position of manager over the united businesses, he had been thankful to accept, and to believe that his anxieties were at an end. Six months—scarcely six months—and already he was beginning to feel uneasy, to suspect trouble ahead! Lilias tightened her lips, and her eyes gave out an impatient flash. It requires a noble nature to preserve unswerving confidence in a man through a period of reverse, and Lilias was not capable of the effort. It seemed to her that such a want of success must surely be Ned's own fault, and something startlingly like dislike sprang up in her heart, as she realised how closely she herself would be involved in his failure. Her mother had declared that it was her duty to encourage Ned in his quixotic scruples; but surely, surely, it was also Ned's duty to consider her interests, and to be ready to sacrifice his scruples, if they threatened injury to the future which she had agreed to share!

Lilias was as angry as it was in her nature to be, but her love of approval made her unwilling to exhibit herself in so unamiable a mood, and she rushed upstairs to the porch room to recover her composure before joining her sisters in the garden. The worst of belonging to a large family, however, is that it is exceedingly difficult to secure privacy, and, as fate would have it, who should be seated in the porch room but Nan herself, the very last member of the household whom Lilias would have wished to meet in the circumstances. Her flushed face and tearful eyes could not escape attention, but while Maud would have been tactfully silent, Elsie sympathetic, Agatha gushing, and Christabel apparently unconscious, Nan must needs stare with all her eyes, whistle like a schoolboy, and exclaim inelegantly—

"Halloa! What's up? What in the world are you in a rage about now?"

"Now," indeed! As if she were in the habit of flying into rages every ten minutes of the day! As if it were not universally acknowledged that she had the sweetest temper in the family! Lilias felt more irritated than ever, and would have enjoyed nothing so much as taking the big blundering creature by the shoulders and giving her a good shaking. She controlled herself, however, and answered with a gallant attempt at pathos—

"Rage is hardly the word, Nan. I am very, very miserable. You don't understand, and I am not at liberty to explain the reason. I am in trouble—horrible trouble!"

"Humph!" quoth Nan sceptically. "Doesn't seem to have a chastening effect upon you. It affects us all differently, I suppose. I should have said you were in a savage rage, if you'd asked me!"

"But I didn't ask you, you see, and it is very wrong of you to judge. If I could tell you the truth, you would realise your mistake, but I must keep my own counsel."

"Of course, of course! Don't tell me, I beseech you; I can't keep a secret if I'm paid for it," said Nan calmly, and with an absence of curiosity altogether maddening to the listener. There was nothing Lilias wanted more than to be coaxed to tell her trouble and pose as a suffering martyr, for her sister's benefit. She flounced out of the room in high dudgeon, and Nan stopped her work and looked after her with thoughtful eyes.

"This is the beginning," she said tragically to herself—"the beginning of the end!"

Chapter Eighteen
Ned in Trouble

When Ned Talbot arrived a fortnight later, his face showed that his anxiety had been no imaginary thing. He looked, indeed, so worn and aged, that his friends were shocked to see him, and tears of commiseration rose in Lilias's pretty eyes. The consciousness that Ned looked to her for consolation roused a natural womanly tenderness in her heart, and nothing could have been sweeter than her behaviour on the day of his arrival. As for Ned himself, fresh from the grim northern town, with the everlasting clang of machinery sounding in his ears, it seemed a very foretaste of paradise to find himself in the fragrant southern garden, seated beneath the shade of the trees, with Lilias's lovely face smiling upon him. He told her as much in lover-like fashion, and she protested modestly, and smiled more angelically than ever for the rest of the evening, in order to live up to her reputation.

"We won't talk about disagreeable things to-night! We will just be happy!" she said coaxingly; and Ned assented, only too thankful to banish anxiety for a few hours, and to talk sweet nothings among the flowers. Lilias was the most delightful plaything in the world, and queened it over him with such amusing little airs of sovereignty, that he asked nothing better than to play the part of adoring slave. So the first evening passed happily enough; but the next day brought the lovers face to face with reality. When a great anxiety is tugging at a man's heart, it is not possible to banish it for more than a few hours at a time, and Ned yearned for his sweetheart's sympathy, and felt a corresponding chilling of heart when she persistently checked his confidences, and tried to continue the playful banter of the first interview. He could not respond, could not laugh and jest and pay compliments; the cloud of coming disaster seemed to blot out the sunshine, and the light words jarred upon his ears.

"It is no use, dear; I am sorry to be such a doleful companion, but I cannot pretend to be cheerful. You must bear with me, for my anxiety is on your account even more than my own," he told the girl tenderly. "I cannot bear to think of bringing anxiety upon you, when I had hoped instead to have shielded you from it all your life; but trouble is said to draw hearts more closely together, and if we stand shoulder to shoulder now we may find unexpected sweetness in the midst of our trial."

He looked at Lilias entreatingly, and she gave a forced little smile.

"I should like to know exactly what the trial is, Ned. You have said a good deal about being unhappy in your letters, but nothing really definite. I can understand that, after being your own master, it is trying to accept a subordinate position, and that many little things jar and fret you, just because it is a new thing to be under subjection. It is certain to be trying at first, but if you have patience—"

Ned stopped her with an exclamation, half amused, half irritated.

"Patience—patience! My dear girl, you don't understand of what you are talking! You surely don't imagine that it is about my own dignity that I am anxious! I should not allow any personal slight to disturb my equanimity, for I did not make this change without counting the cost."

"But it is so different when it comes to the test. However brave you have resolved to be, you cannot help being annoyed and fretted. I know! Oh, I know quite well," declared Lilias, with an elaborate forbearance which seemed to have an irritating effect upon the hearer. He drew in his lips, as if struggling against a hasty reply, and when he spoke it was in a tone of studied moderation.

"Come and sit down, dear, and let me thrash this out! It is your right to know exactly how matters stand, and I will try to explain them to you. What affects me affects you now, so I look to you to advise and counsel. No one can help me as you can; no one has so much right to speak; so let me begin at the beginning, and try to make all clear to your dear little mind. You know that at my father's death I had to give up my own dream of going into a profession, in order to carry on the Works for the benefit of the family. It had been decided that Frank, the second boy, should take this place, but he was still a youngster, and could not then have taken so responsible a post. It was a blow to me, for it was anything but the sphere which I should have chosen, and it was hard to have to give up all my own dreams—"

"It must have been! I can sympathise with you, for I know the feeling. Nothing tries me more than to have my plans upset, and it is constantly happening in a house like this, where there are so many others to consider. And it must have been bad for the business too, for you knew nothing about it, and had no experience—"

Ned coloured, and made an uneasy movement with his shoulders. As a matter of fact, his early days of authority had been accompanied by mistakes which he had been glad to forget, though he had mastered the details of the business in a surprisingly short space of time. It was not pleasant to hear a reminder of his inexperience from the lips of his *fiancée*, and he could not stife a reflection that it would have been kinder on her part to have spared him even so covert a reproach. He tried to hide all signs of annoyance, but there was an edge in his voice as he replied—

"I was inexperienced, no doubt, though perhaps not so much so as you imagine. All my life I had been accustomed to spend a great deal of time at the Works, and as I grew up my father had taken me into his confidence about his growing anxieties, for even in his days he was beginning to feel the strain of competing with the bigger firms. The day for small men is over, Lilias, and one by one the private manufacturers go under, ruined by the struggle to compete with the great firms who are backed by practically unlimited capital. It was a dying cause which I had to fight, and I became more and more convinced of the folly of holding on until everything was lost; and then, in the very nick of time, as it seemed, our most powerful rivals stepped forward and offered to take over our business and to give me the post of manager. There could be no doubt about accepting such an offer, and all my friends rejoiced with me in the belief that the lean days were over, and that a long lease of prosperity lay ahead."

"But why did they make you such an offer when your business was so bad as you say? I can understand that it was a capital thing for you, but where did they come in? They must have had an idea that it was for their advantage as well as for yours, or they would not have tried to get you," said Lilias, with a shrewdness that brought the smiles back to her lover's face.

"Why, what a cute little woman!" he cried fondly. "She grasps the position at once! Yes, of course, they made the offer for their own advantage, not mine, for, you see, dear, there were a certain number of good old-fashioned customers who still kept to us, and their business was well worth having, though not valuable enough to make our Works pay when the smaller orders dropped off. By taking over our connection they made a considerable addition to their profits, even allowing for the handsome salary given to me. Looking at the offer from a business point of view, I saw no reason to doubt its good faith, but six months' experience has raised some ugly doubts. More than once of late I have felt convinced—"

"Of what? What are your doubts? What do you believe they mean to do?"

Ned jumped to his feet, and stood facing the girl, with clenched hands and a face convulsed with emotion. His eyes flashed, the veins stood out upon his forehead.

"I believe that they mean to suck my brains,—to get all they can out of me,—experience, introductions, connections, to suck me dry as they would an orange, and then throw me on one side! I believe that the salary was a bait to bribe me to give up my independence, and that it did not matter to them that it was unusually large, since at the very moment of offering it they had determined that my lease of office should be of precious short duration. They cannot, for shame's sake, for their own reputation's sake, dismiss me already, but in a hundred ways they are bringing pressure to bear; in a hundred ways which you could not understand, they are making it impossible for me to go on,—forcing me into resignation—"

"Oh, hush, hush! Don't get excited. You frighten me when you are so fierce. I am sure you are mistaken. You are worn out after all these years of anxiety, and imagine what is not true. I am sure they do not want to get rid of you; and if they did, what does it matter, since you say yourself they dare not dismiss you? Come, be a good boy, and be happy with me, and forget all about this horrid old business. All men have worries, but they should try to forget them when they come home! I give you full notice that I shall forbid business to be mentioned in our house when we get one."

The glance which accompanied these words was meant to be irresistibly coaxing; but, so far from being sobered yet, Ned seemed goaded into fresh irritation.

"Worries! Worries! You call it by a contemptible little name like that, when I am face to face with ruin,—when our whole future is trembling in the balance? Don't you understand that there are things that a man may not do, and that orders may be put upon him which he cannot obey and preserve his self-respect? He may be forced to resign even when he would gladly work his fingers to the bone, if by any fair means he could keep his post?"

"Ah-ah!" cried Lilias, with a deep, indrawn breath, as if now, at last, she had come to the real pivot on which the question hung. "Ah, yes, Ned, I understand that if you once get the idea in that romantic head of yours that you are being coerced to do what is not according to your lights, there is an end of all peace until you are undeceived! We have known you so long, remember, and heard all about your college days from Jim. 'Don Quixote,' they called you, because you were always taking up high-flown notions of duty. It was delightful at Oxford, and such a good example to the other men; but in business—you can't keep it up in business, Ned! I am only a girl, but I hear people talk, and I know quite well how it is. It is impossible to make a living at all, if you are too particular what you do, and are always stopping to consider other people besides yourself. You say that you were beaten by the other firms when you were managing your father's Works, and now you will let yourself be beaten again, if you give way to these foolish prejudices and scruples."

'LILIAS! DON'T SPEAK LIKE THAT, DARLING!'

Lilias finished with a breathless gasp, and Ned stood looking down at her in silence. An expression of absolute horror had grown in his eyes as he listened to her words, and now he threw himself down on the chair beside her, and grasped her hands in appeal.

"Lilias! Lilias!—don't! Don't speak like that, darling! My little white girl, don't turn pleader against me! You are to be my helpmeet, my good angel, the inspiration of my life; don't begin by wishing me to do less than my best! I am not imagining difficulties—you know I am not—but even if I were, would it not be better to lose something for conscience' sake, than deliberately to sell myself for gain? I am in great perplexity, Lilias, and need all my courage. I beseech you not to discourage me!"

His words were, in effect, a repetition of Mrs Rendell's on the same subject, and now, as then, Lilias was shocked into a softer, more unselfish frame of mind. The ready tears started to her eyes, and her voice quivered with emotion.

"Indeed, indeed, I long to help you! I would not hinder you for the world. I was trying to reconcile you to your position—to save you, if possible, from worse trouble in the future. I know you will never consent to do what is wrong, but if you are firm and patient, all may still be well. It is worth trying, at least, for if you threw up this post what is to happen next? You would have nothing to do."

"I could always earn a salary of a few hundreds a year. If they have done nothing else, these last years have given me a thorough technical knowledge of my own business, and that has a marketable value nowadays. With the influence of the old name to back me up, I could find some firm ready to take me in and give me a subordinate post. If I had only myself to think of, I should not worry my head, for I have never had any ambition to be a rich man; and the mater has her private income—I need not be anxious about her. The change would fall heaviest on you, and it is of you I think. I meant to give you a home worthy of yourself, with every luxury and comfort, but that may not be possible now. Can you forgive me, dear, for bringing all this trouble upon you?"

He looked wistfully into the lovely face, and Lilias pressed her lips together, staring fixedly at the ground. At that moment she could not bring herself to say that she forgave him, or to express any complaisance at the thought of the future. Imagination ran riot, and she saw as in a picture a little house in a smoky manufacturing town, and shrank with distaste from its narrow walls and meagre furnishings. Yes, indeed! Ned might well declare that she was the greatest sufferer, and it was only right that he should pity her. If this breakdown had happened three months before, her parents would not have consented to her engagement, and it should have been his duty to be well assured of his position before involving another, as she was now involved. The swelling of resentment grew so strong, that, against her better judgment, it forced itself into speech.

"You seem fated to misfortune! It follows you wherever you go. But this cannot all have sprung up within the last two months. You must have known something about it in March,—in April,—before you spoke to me!"

From the flash in Ned's eyes she feared that he was about to make some hot reply, but he checked himself, and answered with gentle forbearance. Only, if she had had eyes to see it, the shadow had fallen deeper than ever over his face, and his shoulders bent, as if an additional burden had fallen upon them.

"No, Lilias, I knew nothing! I would never have proposed to you if I had not honestly believed in my good prospects. The difficulty has arisen since then; but don't be afraid, I shall not urge you to any sacrifices on my behalf. I will work hard, and you shall stay at home until I can give you all you desire. I will not ask you to share a poverty which you dread so much."

"I wouldn't mind it for myself. It is of you I think!" murmured Lilias sweetly. "I should love nothing so much as to help you, Ned, but I am such a useless little thing that I should only be a drag. If it had been Maud, it would have been different. Maud is cut out for a poor man's wife, and would be blissfully happy living on twopence-halfpenny a week, and making it go as far as half a crown, but I am so stupid. My money seems to fly away, and I could not be economical if my life depended on it."

Ned sighed, and looked round the garden with a wistful air.

"I wish Maud were at home!" he said. "She is always so good and helpful. It puts new strength in a man to hear her talk. The house does not seem like itself when Maud is away!"

Chapter Nineteen
Gervase Vanburgh

"Humph!" remarked Miss Nan to herself the next afternoon, as she watched the lovers pacing the garden walk, "Humph! unless my eyes deceive me, relationships are strained between our dear young friends. The atmosphere seems charged with—not electricity, but an amount of ice which is suitable neither to the season nor the occasion. Strikes me, I'd better be out of the way! I'll do an act of charity to another and a good turn to myself at one and the same time, and go and have tea with Diogenes!"

She spoke with a certainty of welcome, justified by the delight with which Mr Vanburgh invariably greeted her appearance, for she had discovered that nothing pleased him so much as to see her running in and out of the house, popping in for ten minutes' chat on her return from a walk, or livening a dull afternoon by taking her work across the road, and stitching by his couch. This latter attention had also brought about the happy results of interesting the invalid in the coming sale, and more than one of Nan's efforts was bought before it was completed, thereby affording that young lady a terrible temptation to scamp the work which remained. On the present occasion, however, she was in a lazy mood, and frowned sternly on her conscience, when it suggested that she should make use of the opportunity to finish a certain table centre. No, indeed, she decided, she would do nothing of the kind. Unwilling work was invariably a failure, and she felt no vocation to do anything more energetic than sit still and eat Mr Vanburgh's delicious cakes, and drink Mr Vanburgh's excellent tea.

She stood up then, and, as a preliminary step, regarded herself critically in the mirror, for among other things which had been borne in upon her concerning her new neighbour, one was that he was exceedingly fastidious about appearances, and as sharp as a needle to discover any discrepancies in her attire. He was too polite to put his criticisms into words, but his face spoke volumes, and certain historic occasions, when she had sat smarting beneath the consciousness of a missing button or a crooked tie, had made a lasting impression on the mind of the careless young woman. Nowadays, however fleeting might be her visit to the Grange, she never went without a careful examination of her appearance. A shop window answered the purpose of a mirror, if nothing better could be found, and one morning, as Agatha and Christabel walked along the village street, they had been reduced to a state of speechless amazement by discovering Nan twisting and turning before the wired windows of the Bank, with as much concern for her appearance as though she had been Lilias herself.

On the present occasion there were only a few stray locks to be pinned in order, and then the glass reflected a charming picture of happy girlhood. The piqué skirt was fresh and neat; the pink shirt belted in by a natty white band, and the dark hair curled softly round the fresh bright face. Nan stared at herself solemnly, contorting her face into the curious, strained expression with which nine women out of ten regard themselves in a mirror, twisted round, to be sure that her belt showed no unsightly gap, pulled her tie accurately into the middle of her collar, and finally fastened on a sailor hat, and ran gaily across the street. She did not go to the front door this time, for—unique and extraordinary sign of favour—to her, and to her alone, had been granted permission to use the garden gate, enter the house by the side door, and so make her way upstairs unannounced. Mr Vanburgh had been anxious to put every facility in his favourite's way, for only an invalid can appreciate the brightness which had come into his life since this merry-hearted girl had taken compassion upon his loneliness. To see her bonnie face peering in at the door, to hear her ringing laugh, and listen to her voice, was better than any tonic, and seemed to put fresh strength into his feeble body.

Up the stairs, then, Nan ran, and made straight for the study where the invalid spent his afternoons. The door was closed, but to wait to announce her arrival by a knock was a proceeding far too dignified for one of her impetuous nature; she merely turned the handle, thrust a mischievous face round the corner, and announced boldly, "I've come to tea!"

There was no answering exclamation of delight, and Nan had just discovered, with a gasp of surprise, that the couch was empty, when a tall, fair-haired man rose suddenly and confronted her.

"Oh," cried Nan, and stood agape with astonishment.

"I beg your pardon," drawled the stranger, and stared back out of a pair of handsome, sleepy eyes, "You—er—you expected to see Mr Vanburgh; I am sorry to say he is not very well—"

"Not well? Oh dear, I'm sorry! And are you the doctor?—Have you come from town?"

"Oh no!" The tall man smiled, as if, for some reason, the idea seemed quite preposterous to his mind. "I am not the doctor. I am Mr Vanburgh's nephew. I was coming to visit him shortly in any case, and as I heard that he was not well, I thought it better to come down and see for myself exactly how he was."

"Of course. I am so vexed that I did not know about it, but I have been so busy this week that I have not seen him since Sunday. He is really ill? In bed? Not able to get up?"

"He has kept in bed for two days, but is coming in presently to join me at tea, so I hope that you—er—you will fulfil the intention with which you came!" and the speaker smiled at the pretty girl with a sudden lighting of the sleepy eyes. He was thinking to himself what a marvellous difference her coming had made in the aspect of the dim, solemn room. All day long he had roamed about the house and grounds with the eerie feeling of being alone in an enchanted castle, where a spell of sleep was laid on the occupants. Wherever the eye lighted, some rare and costly treasure greeted the sight; the great rooms opened one into the other, while rare Venetian mirrors reduplicated the tapestries on the walls and seemed to open out fresh vistas before the eye. It was a palace among houses, a very storehouse of treasures, but the want of life chilled the blood in the young man's veins. Not a human soul to be seen but the silent-footed servant with his foreign tongue, and the crippled master, dead already to all that makes life worth living! All day long he had been alone, struggling with a depression which seemed to close more and more heavily around him; but here, at last, was a creature like himself, young, radiant, full of life, with the glow of health and happiness on her rosy cheek. His glance was so undisguisedly friendly that Nan responded to it with a smile, and seated herself forthwith on her accustomed chair. Shyness not being a complaint by which she was troubled, she saw no reason for refusing the stranger's invitation, or for disguising the keen interest which she took in his own individuality.

"Thank you; I'd like to stay," she said frankly. "I am so pleased to meet you, for I know all about you. 'Gervase Farrington Vanburgh',"—she checked off each word on uplifted fingers, and nodded her head with an air of triumph at the completeness of her information.

"'The Boundaries, Lipton, Devonshire.' I have posted ever so many notes to you, and once I addressed an envelope. Perhaps you remember my scrawly writing, with long tails to the letters? We were dreadfully disappointed that Mr Vanburgh had no daughters, for we have not many friends of our own age, but he tried to console us by saying that you were coming to pay him a visit. I asked him especially to arrange it for June, for we shall have our brother home then, and several things going on which will make it livelier than usual. We have made all sorts of plans for your amusement!"

"That is kind; I appreciate it very much. I have heard of you too, and of the pleasure which your acquaintance has given my uncle. He was giving me an account of you all last night, from which I have no difficulty in recognising you from your sisters. You are Miss Lilias!"

"Lilias!—I! Good gracious! Whatever made you think that?" gasped Nan, staring at him with eyes so clear and honest, that, though an adept in the gentle art of flattery, Gervase Vanburgh found himself incapable of explaining the reason of his mistake. He could not tell Nan Rendell that, after hearing Lilias described as the beauty of the family, he had at once identified her with the charming figure whose presence had brought sunshine into the gloomy house. He murmured some vague excuse, while Nan proceeded to expatiate on the difference between herself and her sister. "Lilias is fair, and I am dark; she has golden hair, and is quite grown up and staid and proper. I am supposed to be grown up too, in the afternoons and in the evenings, but the mornings are my own, and then I am disgracefully young, and behave as badly as if I were a child again. I wish I were! I shall never be so happy again as I was in the dear old school-days." Nan's eyes roamed wistfully across the road to the porch room, where Elsie's sleek head could be seen bent over her work, with Agatha and Christabel vaguely outlined at the table; then suddenly her face lit up with mischievous smiles. "If they could only see me!" she told herself ecstatically. "If the girls could see me sitting here talking to this strange young man! They'd have a fit! They'd go crazy with excitement! I must, I must lure him to the window, and let them see us together! They will never believe me unless I do." She looked up, to meet Gervase's eyes fixed upon her, and found inspiration in his first remark.

"You are looking at your own house, are you not? It is exactly opposite this, I think. My uncle pointed it out to me last night."

"Yes, just opposite. It stands on the road, as this one does, but we have a lovely garden behind. You can see a little bit of it from here!" and wily Nan led the way to the window, secure of bringing Gervase in her train, and keeping him in evidence until it pleased her to finish her explanations. The appearance of her own light dress was sufficient to attract Elsie's attention; but what of the agitation of the three at sight of her companion? Elsie fled into the background—"The better to see you, my dear,"—and Nan's keen eyes could discern the three patches of white made by the gaping faces, the while she smiled and posed, far more for their benefit than that of her companion. Presently Elsie disappeared, and Nan knew as well as if she had heard the words spoken, that the object of her flight had been to bring the opera-glasses from the drawing-room, when the three would take turns to stare at the stranger, and speculate as to his identity. In the first mischievous enjoyment of the moment she found it impossible to face her companion, but when at last she did venture to meet his glance she was vastly impressed by his appearance. A superfine specimen indeed, this Gervase Vanburgh, with his frock-coat, well-creased trousers, and immaculate linen. Even Nan, the unnoticing, noted the faultlessness of detail which characterised his attire, and had an instant perception that Ned Talbot would look rough and countrified by his side, and even Jim himself suffer from the contrast. Evidently this was a dandy of the first water; yet, despite his languid bearing, his face was full of intelligence, and decision of character was proclaimed in the large nose and square, clean-cut chin.

"What a mercy I tidied my hair!" sighed Nan to herself; and at that moment the door opened, and in came the Italian servant, pushing his master before him in the wheeled chair in which he was moved from one room to another. The invalid was looking more death-like than ever, but his face lighted with pleasure at the sight of Nan, while she ran to the sofa and arranged his cushions with loving solicitude. When he was settled she knelt beside him to exchange greetings, putting her hand on his with a caressing gesture, and he held it firmly while he replied, as if gaining strength from the contact. Gervase Vanburgh thought he had never seen so typical a picture of youth and age as that made by his uncle and the bright-faced girl, and mentally contrasted this welcome with the one given to himself the day before. His uncle had never shown such pleasure on his arrival; but he felt no jealousy of the girl who was so evidently preferred before himself; for, whatever his faults might be, he was free at least from any tinge of self-seeking. The lazy smile lingered on his face as he listened to the exchange of question and answer.

"This is a pleasant surprise, little woman! When did you come across? I did not hear of your arrival."

"Bounced in ten minutes ago, and had such a fright to find a stranger here instead of you. Why didn't you send at once to tell me that you were worse?"

"Because I could not have seen you if you had come. On my bad days I am best alone; but I am pulling round again, and am glad to have Gervase's company. You have made each other's acquaintance, I see! I suppose neither had much difficulty in guessing the identity of the other."

"He thought I was Lilias!" said Nan, glancing at Gervase with laughing eyes. "Think of that! He will be surprised when he sees her, won't he? But I knew who he was in a moment. Now, tell me honestly, would you rather I went away? I came meaning to stay to tea, but if you don't feel able to talk to two people at once I'll come again when you are alone. I won't be a scrap offended!"

Mr Vanburgh smiled.

"I am sure you would not, but I should like you to stay, please. We want you to pour out tea for us; and I won't attempt to talk, but just lie still and amuse myself listening to you."

"But I never can be amusing when I try,—can you?" said Nan, appealing to Gervase with a friendly smile. "The girls at home think I am amusing, because I generally say the wrong thing at the wrong moment, which may be entertaining to them, but is very poor fun for me. Maud says I speak first and think afterwards; but what can I do? I once made a vow to cure myself of being impetuous by counting twenty slowly before I began to speak, and I kept it religiously two whole days. They seemed like a month; and if I had persevered I should have become dumb, for by the time I had counted twenty the conversation had hopped on to another subject, and any remark was hopelessly out of date! So now I have gone back to my old ways, and say my say, and take the consequences."

"You don't look to me as if you were given to making painful remarks," Gervase remarked in a conciliatory tone, and Nan straightened her back in defence of her own behaviour.

"Wouldn't hurt a fly! That's the worst part of it. For I am so soft-hearted over other people's woes, that I shed tears regularly every time I meet a tramp, and he tells me that he is a discharged seaman who has lost his certificate, and only needs four and sixpence to take him to a port where he is certain to find fresh work. They always have lost their certificates and want a railway fare, but I can't help relieving them and handing-over last Saturday's money. But a tender heart is not much use if you make awkward remarks and quote people's own doings to their faces, as capital jokes against somebody else! I got into terrible trouble in that way with a caller only the other day, and if I had had any sense I should have stopped in time, for I had plenty of warning. Her face grew all stiff and rigid, and I wondered what in the world had given Elsie such a cough all of a sudden. Is there any cure, do you think, for a habit like this—anything I could do to make myself careful?"

There was a pause while the two men looked at the eager face, smiled, and grew sober, as the question awoke memories from their own past.

"A practical kindness of heart, Nan, which is not satisfied with facile tears and offerings, but takes continual thought of the feelings of others!"

"Or a severe lesson!" added the younger man thoughtfully. "If you wounded some one very near and dear, and saw them suffer through your thoughtlessness, you could never forget it. I learnt that for myself long ago, when—"

But Nan heard no more of what he said, for, with a flash, her eager mind had leapt to the solution of the mystery. More love! That was what was needed. Love, the cure for every human fault. She applied the test to her own experience, and found it abundantly proven. Had any word or deed of hers hurt Maud through the period of ultra-sensitiveness through which that dear sister had passed? Ten thousand times, no! On the contrary, she had been quick to ward off blows, to turn dangerous conversations into new channels, to stand between the sufferer and the world. Where she loved it was obvious that she could show both care and tact; it was want of love which lay at the root of her thoughtless acts and speeches. Gervase looked up at the conclusion of his story, to find the girl staring blankly across the room, with a glimmer of tears in the brown eyes, and was at a loss to guess the meaning.

"I'll begin this instant, and love every one in this world!" Nan was saying to herself determinedly. "It will be fatiguing, but so good for my character. I'll think of what they will like, and what I can do for them, and spend my time in good works. What can I do now for these two men? It's no credit pouring out tea, for I want some myself; but I might do something for that poor Gervase to-night, when Mr Vanburgh goes to bed, and he is left alone. He looked dolefully dull when I came in, and I believe he would enjoy coming across and seeing us all, as he has heard so much about us. I'll ask him anyway, and see what he says."

The idea was so pleasant that the dimples came back to greet it; she looked across at Gervase with a brilliant smile, and struck amazement to his heart by inquiring blandly—

"Would you like to come to dinner with us tonight?"

Gervase Vanburgh stared, as well he might, at so informal an invitation. His uncle also struggled with a smile, and Nan, tardily conscious of her lack of formality, plunged headlong into explanations—

"I meant to say that it will be lonely for you after Mr Vanburgh goes to bed, and I am sure mother would be delighted to see you. We have Ned Talbot, a friend of Lil—of my brother Jim staying with us, so that there would be two other men to keep you company. When father and Jim are away, we never ask gentlemen to the house, for mother says seven women at one time are too great a tax on any man's nervous system; but you wouldn't be afraid of us when there were two other men, would you? The schoolroom girls don't come down until after dinner, so we are really only three."

Gervase Vanburgh laughed aloud, and Nan looked up with a quick flash of approval, for a laugh has a tell-tale sound, and this one rang unmistakably honest and true.

"I am not in the least afraid," he cried boldly. "I'd like to see you all, school-girls included. It is most kind of you to think of it, and if Mrs Rendell will really allow me, I shall be delighted to accept your invitation."

So Nan ran across the street, and entered the house with the great news that Gervase Vanburgh had arrived, and—given a formal invitation—was coming that very evening to make the acquaintance of the family.

Chapter Twenty
Among the Roses

By no one was the news of Gervase Vanburgh's advent greeted with more enthusiasm than by Lilias herself, for, truth to tell, the day had seemed interminably long in the company of a depressed and anxious lover. The points of view from which Ned and herself regarded his position seemed to grow more hopelessly far apart the more it was discussed, and the consciousness that he was disappointed by her lack of sympathy did not tend to raise Lilias's spirits. If the question at stake had not touched the all-important subject of future comfort, she would have been willing to sacrifice her own wishes in order to preserve Ned's approval, but in this crisis of their fate she would allow no such weakness. If her own parents seemed to place Ned's scruples before her interests, if Ned himself were so ignorant of what was due to his *fiancée* as to talk calmly of accepting the position of a clerk on a few hundreds a year, it behoved her to be firm, and make Ned understand that she would never be his wife until he could provide something more than the bare necessaries of life. Nevertheless, the task of opposition was far from pleasant, and the grave wonder of his glance cut like a knife into her vain little heart.

It was a relief to know that the presence of a stranger would prevent further reference to the subject for this evening at least, while the Vanburgh nephew and heir was in himself a sufficiently interesting person. Lilias put on her prettiest dress, and sat trifling with a book until the company had assembled in the drawing-room, and the time was ripe for an effective entrance, when she glided into the room, and smiled sweetly at the stranger, while Nan watched his face with mischievous enjoyment. He was surprised—there was no mistake about that! When Lilias raised her face to his, he gave a distinct little start of surprise, and the sleepy eyes looked for once quite wide-awake and animated.

"And the stupid fellow actually mistook me for her!" chuckled Nan to herself, with that pride in her sister's beauty which the Rendell girls shared so loyally, looking upon it as a family possession which reflected credit on one and all. "That's one mistake he will never make again, however much confused he may get among six sisters!"

Conversation at the dinner table was of a general character; but every now and then Nan found an opportunity of exchanging a few quiet remarks with Gervase Vanburgh, who sat next herself, the result of which was to assure her that she had found a character as diametrically different from her own as it was possible to imagine. She was full of energy, he was languid to the verge of apathy; she had hard and fast opinions to offer on every topic, known or unknown, while his "Don't know!" and "Couldn't say!" repeated themselves with wearisome echo. She was afire with ardour, with enthusiasm, with the burning desire to right all wrongs, redress all evils, bring peace on earth, and start the millennium without a moment's delay; judging from appearances, he seemed incapable of any sort of emotion, and possessed with the conviction that nothing was really worth taking any trouble about.

Nan grew irritated beyond measure, wriggled about on her seat, shrugged her shoulders, and crumbled her bread, unconscious alike of her father's smiles and her mother's frowns, and, when actions failed to relieve her feelings, was forced into emphatic speech.

"Nothing interests you, nothing gives you pleasure! You care for nothing, you hope for nothing! I wouldn't be like you for the whole wide world!" she declared; and Gervase Vanburgh fixed his melancholy eyes upon her, and said tragically—

"And I would give the whole wide world if I could once more care and hope like you!"

This was disconcerting. Nan had not expected so speedy a concession, and she followed her mother from the room oppressed by the remembrance of that melancholy look, and consumed with curiosity as to its cause. Money anxiety it could not be, seeing that Mr Vanburgh's heir need never fear want; but a broken home, disappointed love, and faithless friendship held out wide avenues for speculation. Nan sat and pondered, listening meekly to her mother's reproofs, while inside the dining-room Mr Rendell could not resist putting a home question to his visitor.

"You were amused by my little girl's enthusiasm! I saw her growing hot and eager, and had a strong suspicion that you were leading her on! She is a most fervent young person, and cannot understand being less than in deadly earnest over any question."

"She is er—refreshingly young!" replied Gervase in his soft, drawling voice. He took no notice of the charge made against himself, but went on peeling his fruit with an air of pensive exhaustion, at which the two elder men exchanged glances of amusement. He looked at once so young, so healthy, and so prosperous, that this affectation of depression had somewhat of a ludicrous air to men who knew the world and had acquaintance with real and pressing anxieties. Ned Talbot looked across the table at the handsome youngster, and heaved a sigh to the memory of the good old days when he also was happy enough to invent troubles, and philosophise darkly concerning unknown woes. He had come south with a heart heavy with care, yet with an expectation of comfort which had taken away half the sting, but that hope had been doomed to disappointment, and on the morrow he must return to his work with an added fear in his heart. Could it be that he had been mistaken in Lilias? As a man eating a soft bloomy peach jars his teeth suddenly against its stone, so had Ned found himself confronted with a hardness in his *fiancée's* nature which had brought with it a shock of disillusionment. Surely, surely, if a girl were ever to be sweet and sympathetic to the man whom she had promised to marry, it was when he was threatened by misfortune; but Lilias evidently refused to believe in his version of affairs, and cherished a grudging conviction that he was sacrificing her to romantic scruples. He had talked, and pleaded, and reasoned—it was like hitting one's self against a wall. She never swerved from her position, her voice never lost its tone of studied toleration; and now he sat, the poor fellow! listening dreamily to the conversation between the other two men, too weary and depressed to take any active share in it himself.

When a movement was made towards the drawing-room half an hour later, however, Lilias was discovered leaning against the lintel of the window, looking so young, so sweet and fragile, that every chivalrous instinct rose up in her defence. Such a girl was not made to endure hardships, Ned reflected tenderly. The man who was lucky enough to own her should be prepared to carry all burdens on his own shoulders. He was ready! Oh yes; if Lilias would but love him faithfully, he would work for her with the strength of twenty men. He was eager to tell her so, to apologise for his harshness of the afternoon; and, stepping past into the garden, he caught her hand in his, and tried to draw her away.

"Come, dear, come! Let us walk round the garden. I want to speak to you alone."

Lilias laughed, gave a caressing little squeeze to his hand, but stood firmly in her position. Gervase Vanburgh and her father were approaching, and a general conversation seemed at the moment more interesting than a *tête-à-tête* with her lover. So far she had had little opportunity of speaking to the stranger, and his appearance both interested and perplexed her. The air of languid elegance which provoked Nan, filled her sister with admiration, yet there was something baffling in the expression of the sleepy eyes. Lilias had an uncomfortable impression that those eyes might be very keen on occasions, and would have suspected a quizzical expression at the present moment, had the idea not been so palpably absurd. Why should Gervase find anything amusing in her attitude? It was surely a most natural thing that she, as the eldest daughter at home, should wait for the gentlemen, while her sisters went out into the garden, and, that being so, where should she stand, if not by the window? Nevertheless, the slow, quiet smile which followed his glance around, sent the blood into her cheeks, and seemed to intimate that he was as well aware as herself of the appropriateness of the background, and the care which had devised that seemingly careless pose! So disconcerted was she that she would have been inclined to retire in Ned's company had he pressed his request a second time, but he was silenced by the first refusal, and the little group stood together exchanging commonplaces, until a white dress appeared among the rose-bushes, and Nan's voice called out an unabashed summons—

"I thought you were never coming! Why don't you come out? It's perfectly lovely here. The roses smell so delicious in the dusk; and oh, father, there are two whole flowers on the little pink-belled saxifrage you brought home from Norway!"

"No!" cried Mr Rendell in tones of incredulous ecstasy, which stamped him on the spot as one of the noble army of gardeners. He hurried forward to inspect the new treasures, while Nan went down on her knees to hold up their tiny heads and expatiate on their fragile beauty. When she arose five minutes later, she found two surprises awaiting her, the first being the presence of Mr Vanburgh by her side, and the second, alas! two large green stains on her white skirt, in the middle of the front seam, where she had knelt on the dewy grass. Her face of dismay as she pointed downwards evoked a laugh from the two men, but Mr Rendell checked himself, glanced over his shoulder towards where his wife paced to and fro, and said quickly—

"Better run upstairs, dear, and change it. No need to be distressed; you have plenty more, I suppose, and it will wash."

Nan groaned in a sepulchral fashion, and shook her head.

"You don't understand! It's an evening skirt with trimmings, not an ordinary piqué. My very best too! I put it on because Mr Vanburgh was coming, and now it's spoilt!"

"Oh, surely not! Don't say that; it makes me feel so horribly guilty. Let me try if I can rub it off," cried the visitor eagerly; and, before Nan could protest, out came a superfine hemstitched handkerchief, and Gervase began rubbing the damaged skirt with such vigour, that the stains grew larger and larger, and increased their borders so rapidly that they met and blended in one great whole. His face lengthened with horror as he withdrew his handkerchief, and gazed upon the results of his labour; and Nan said dismally—

"Thank you so much! It's much worse now! Wish I were old enough to wear black always, and not be bothered. My life's a burden to me because of my clothes!"

"For the mother's pride the child must suffer pain!" cried Mr Rendell, laughing. "That is what Kitty said, isn't it, when her mother insisted on pinning down the end of her collar? Better confess at once, Mops, and get it over! Tell your mother she can send it to the cleaner's, and I'll stand the racket."

"Come and tell her yourself. D–oo, ducky darling! Sweetest father in all the world, come and plead for me!" coaxed Nan, hanging on to his arm, and rubbing his face with her soft cool cheek, while he affected to push her away, and in reality allowed himself to be led where she would take him.

Mr Vanburgh followed, stroking his moustache to conceal his smile, and Mrs Rendell's quick eyes saw their approach, and fixed themselves sternly upon Nan's ruined skirt.

"Another accident, Edith, worse luck! The grass would get damp, and Mops and I were so interested in looking at our plant that we forgot everything else, and—"

"So I observe! It is a pity, but I am not surprised. What can one expect from Nan, but destruction!" Mrs Rendell spoke with melancholy resignation, while the assembled sisters looked on with solemn eyes. Dainty Lilias, pensive Elsie, kindly Agatha, Christabel the immaculate, they stood gazing in a solid phalanx of disapproval, while Nan the culprit hung her head and flushed with embarrassment. A moment later Mrs Rendell had turned the conversation into another channel, unwilling to prolong the present discussion in the presence of a stranger, and Nan seized the opportunity to escape to the far end of the garden. Gervase Vanburgh stood in her path, and spied the glimmer of tears on the dark eyelashes as she passed by. Then she disappeared, and Elsie's chin dropped with amazement as she saw the elegant stranger deliberately mark a stone on the path, and kick it savagely with the toe of his patent leather shoe.

"Bland of exterior, but concealing beneath the surface secret and violent impulses!" Such was the character given to Gervase Vanburgh in Miss Elsie Rendell's diary that evening; and perhaps for once the youthful author was not far wrong in her conclusions!

Chapter Twenty One
A Vow of Friendship

The next morning at ten o'clock the Italian servant was entrusted with a message from his master which created a wild excitement in the Rendell family. Mr Vanburgh was restored to his usual health, and wished to celebrate that fact, and provide at the same time a little entertainment for his nephew, by giving an *alfresco* luncheon in the garden, to which he invited his friends at Thurston House. The meal would be served under the beech-tree on the lawn, and Mr Vanburgh hoped to welcome his guests at one o'clock precisely.

"But not all of us! There are six of us—six women—not to mention Mr Talbot. Mr Vanburgh cannot mean to include the school-room party! The elder ones will be delighted to accept, but—"

"*Mother!*" gasped Christabel. Agatha laid hold of the back of a couch, and prepared to faint on the spot, and the Italian looked from one to the other, a gleam of amusement showing in the dusky eyes.

"My master would be much disappointed, madam. He wishes especially the young signorinas. I am to bear an invitation also to Mrs Maitland and to Miss Kitty."

That settled the matter! If Kitty were going, it would be nothing short of cruelty to keep her companions at home, so Mrs Rendell sent a general acceptance to the invitation, and shrugged her shoulders resignedly as each of the five girls hugged her in turns, and deafened her with questions.

"Mother, what shall I wear?"

"Mother, my piqué skirts have not come home from the wash! I wish you would leave that horrid laundry. It's the third time—"

"Mother, will my pink blouse do? It's the nicest I have, and it's only a little bit soiled on the sleeves, and if I wore clean cuffs—"

"Mother, need I change? Can't I go as I am, and be happy? I might want to climb over a fence, and it's such spiky work."

"Mother, I think we should all go dressed alike in white dresses and blue ties, and march across the road in a crocodile. Do let's! It would be such fun!"

Mrs Rendell pressed her hands to her head in distracted fashion.

"If every single one of you is not out of this room in two minutes from now, I'll retract, and send a refusal instead! Get away to your work! I'll see you separately later on, if you want instructions, but surely girls of your age ought to be able to dress without my assistance! The only thing I bargain for is that you are *not* alike, for that would only accentuate your number, and as it is I feel ashamed to appear with such a battalion."

"Lilias, need we go?" Ned Talbot slid his hand through his *fiancée's* arm, and drew her into the garden. "If the party is too large, why should we not reduce it by two, and have a quiet little lunch by ourselves? I must leave before four o'clock, and if we go to the Grange it will mean that we have no more time together, for we cannot run away immediately after lunch. Mr Vanburgh would understand our position if we sent an excuse."

"Oh, Ned!" cried Lilias, and the tone of reproach was so eloquent that there could be no mistaking her wishes on the subject. "Oh, Ned, the first time we have been asked! Our first invitation! You couldn't really wish me to refuse it. I should be so dreadfully disappointed. You don't know how much we have longed to be asked, or what castles in the air we have built about this day!"

"Very well, dear; don't trouble yourself. We will do just as you please," said Ned wearily. He tried to convince himself of the reasonableness of Lilias's position, and to show no sign of resentment; but the jar was there all the same, and seemed to set up a barrier between them in all they did and said. If any one had foretold that he should feel time drag heavily in Lilias's company, and cast about in his mind for subjects on which to talk, how he would have derided the idea! yet, alas, it had come true, for he felt a distinct sense of gratitude towards Nan when she thrust her head out of a bedroom window and summoned Lilias to her assistance. When there is no sympathy in the great principles of life, small talks become increasingly difficult, as this poor fellow was discovering to his cost.

Punctually at one o'clock the door of Thurston House was thrown open, and Mrs Rendell was discovered standing upon the threshold, issuing final directions to her flock.

"Stop talking! My dear, good girls, if you insist upon speaking all together, how am I to make myself heard? Pray calm yourselves, and behave like reasonable beings. Don't let me have the humiliation of taking about a crowd of excited children who might never before have been outside their own gate!" Then she marched majestically ahead, with the demure Elsie as her companion, while the engaged couple followed, and each of the three remaining girls fell back in turns to cast a critical glance at her companions. Half-way across the road Nan's belt was discovered to have parted company with the skirt, and the most strategic measures were necessary in order to secure it before her mother reached the door of the Grange.

"And remember, all of you, not to put your arms round her waist! The pin will stick out, whatever I do with it," said Christabel darkly; then the door was thrown open, and the butler led the way across the hall towards the entrance to the garden. Each member of the visiting party was consumed with curiosity to examine the beautiful objects on either side, but had too much ado to keep her footing on the slippery oak floor to have any attention to spare. Lilias clung to Ned's arm, Mrs Rendell and Elsie minced along with tiny footsteps, and Nan waited until no one was looking, and then gave giant strides from one mat to another, or clung to a friendly rail to help her round slippery corners. Then at last the garden was reached, and there, beneath the trees, stood an enchanted table, laden with everything that was beautiful in the way of glass and china, and banked up with a wealth of pink roses.

Mr Vanburgh's couch was drawn up at its head, and Kitty Maitland sat at his side, bearing herself with that preternatural solemnity of manner which she invariably adopted along with her best dress and hat. A moment later Mrs Maitland and Gervase appeared from behind a tree, and the elders shook hands and murmured the meaningless speeches common to such occasions, while Kitty took an early opportunity of stepping to Chrissie's side, and calling her attention to the splendours on the table in a series of awed and breathless whispers.

"Gold spoons! Venetian glass! It breaks if you look at it! I daren't drink a drop out of those tumblers, and I'm so thirsty! Such cream! Such strawberries!—big as peaches, my love, and such lots of them. I feel like the Queen of Sheba. There's no spirit left in me, it's all so grand and gorgeous."

"I like it. It suits me! I was born to splendour!" said Chrissie, with an air. "I call it awfully sweet of him to do the thing so well. But what a dreadful number of knives and forks! I shall never know which to use. I wish I had asked mother about it before we came, for I do so detest making mistakes. Before a butler, too—so humiliating! And yet I don't want to refuse anything I can help!"

"Don't refuse! Take all that comes, and crumble bread until you see how other people eat it. That's my dodge when I go out to lunch with mother. I say, how do you like the nephew? Doesn't he look ex-actly like the tailor's advertisement that you see in the shop windows? I have never seen any man look like that before, and want to pinch him, to see if he is real. Do you suppose it's possible to be so handsome, and yet as nice as if he were ugly, like Jim?"

"Jim! Jim ugly!" gasped Jim's outraged sister furiously. "Gwendoline Maitland, you are raving! Jim is the best-looking man I know, and I'll tell him the moment that he comes home that you said—"

"Jim won't mind. I told him so myself last year. He asked how I liked his moustache, and I said it was 'stubbly,' and he said moral worth was better than brilliantine. There's none of your nasty pride about Jim."

Chrissie glared, but Kitty refused to be annihilated, and crinkled her nose in sauciest defiance, whereupon her companion stared into space with an expression of disdain. An onlooker would have concluded that a serious quarrel had taken place; but such small interludes were of common occurrence in the friendship of these two young women, and five minutes later they were pinching each other in the most amicable manner, and whispering, "Sit by me! Sit by me!" as if true happiness could not be enjoyed apart.

During the meal which followed there was ample opportunity of "crumbling bread," for the Vanburgh cook had received instructions to eclipse himself for the young ladies' benefit, and the succession of curious unknown dishes which he sent to table would have puzzled more experienced "diners out" than the members of the present party. A prettier scene could hardly be imagined than the table under the trees, with the green lawn sweeping away on either side, the foreign servants flitting to and fro, and the six girlish faces of the guests beaming with delighted approval. Elsie's eyes grew large and dreamy, as she mentally rehearsed the most appropriate language in which to chronicle the event in her diary. Such expressions as "Arabian Nights entertainment," "Green sward," and "Princely Splendour," figured largely in the description, which ran to an inordinate length, and still seemed to have left half the wonders untold.

Nan spoke little during the meal, but, like the proverbial parrot, noticed much. She noticed that, though the utmost courtesy was maintained between uncle and nephew, the elder man was evidently annoyed by the persistent nonchalance of the younger; and she had a shrewd suspicion that Gervase knew as much, yet did not trouble himself to rectify it. She noticed that, while Ned was depressed, Lilias's mood was of the gayest and sweetest; and she noticed that Gervase noticed as much, and studied the lovers narrowly from his point of vantage across the table. She heard dear old Agatha discussing politics with her host, and quoting her father wholesale in her gallant attempt to be grown up and important; and she chuckled audibly over the two schoolgirls' enjoyment of the fare. Then at last the meal was over, and she heaved a sigh of relief that all had passed off without catastrophe and with credit to the family. No one had broken the fragile glass, no one had betrayed a plebeian ignorance of the *convenances*, nor showed ill-bred surprise. They had examined the *menu* with an understanding air, as though every other name was not as Greek to their ears, and had refrained from any signs of approval more noticeable than pressures of feet under the table, and occasional sly joltings of elbows.

'I NEVER TOLD YOU,' CRIED NAN IN AMAZE.

The two ladies stayed beside Mr Vanburgh, while the younger members of the party strolled about the grounds, Gervase Vanburgh first walking with Lilias, and then making an excuse to cross to Nan's side. He smiled as he came, and his first words showed that he had grasped the situation without any need for words.

"I shall get myself disliked if I stay there any longer! Mr Talbot leaves in another hour, I think, so it is hardly fair to him to engross your sister."

"But how do you know anything about Mr Talbot? I never told you," cried Nan in amaze; and Gervase smiled in his aggravating, lazy fashion as he replied—

"Oh no, you simply said that 'a friend of Lil—a friend of my brother Jim' was staying with you at present. That was all, I think. You gave me no information."

"Which means that I did, of course, and blurted out everything in my stupid, headlong fashion," sighed Nan dolefully. "It doesn't matter much in this case, for a good many people know; but mother wishes it kept as quiet as possible, because—"

"Just so. But I assure you that even without your hint I should have discovered for myself that they were at present engaged; so there is no necessity to blame yourself."

Nan wheeled round upon him with flashing eyes.

"Why do you say 'at present'?" she demanded; and Gervase smiled in impenetrable fashion.

"Did I say so? Foolish slip! They are engaged, of course. I wish Miss Lilias every happiness, and congratulate Mr Talbot on his good taste. She is certainly a lovely girl."

"Oh, isn't she?" cried Lilias's sister gladly. "I knew you would say so. You see now how absurd it was to mistake me for her, and what a difference there is between us! I knew quite well you would be surprised."

Gervase Vanburgh put back his head, and stared at her with a scrutiny which was not without a touch of cynicism; but the eager face he met was at once so frank and so honest, that the sneer faded from his lips and gave place to a smile.

"Yes," he said slowly, "there is a great difference. I cannot imagine two people more unlike. You are complete contrasts in every respect."

"She is so fair, and I am dark," sighed Nan, a trifle abashed by so vehement an assent, but striving loyally to conceal her discomfiture. "Lilias is our beauty, and we are all very proud of her; but you cannot really know the family until you have met Maud. Maud is the eldest sister, and the best and sweetest of them all. She isn't pretty, but she is such a dear that every one loves her. 'Maud of all work' Jim calls her, because she is always helping other people and forgetting herself."

"Most exemplary, I'm sure. Excellent example!" drawled Gervase with a yawn, at the sound of which the last trace of Nan's patience gave way. She stood still in the path and fixed him with a glittering eye; but the speech which swelled in her throat was slow in coming, choked back by very excess of emotion. Gervase, in some alarm, demanded the cause of her agitation, and received a straighter answer than he expected.

"I don't care to speak about Maud to a person who only sneers at her goodness. If you don't mind, I'd rather talk about the weather, and the garden, and things that don't matter; and then I can keep as indifferent as you are yourself, and we sha'n't quarrel."

"I sneer! I beg a hundred pardons, Miss Nan, if I have appeared to sneer at anything you say; but I assure you that I have never yet voluntarily sneered at goodness; so that in this instance at least you are doing me an injustice. You must believe me, please, for I am thoroughly in earnest."

"Yes, I see you are. I'm sorry that I misjudged you."

"And I am sorry too. You are sorry, I am sorry, we are both sorry, so now suppose we drop this subject and start afresh. I'd like to be friends with you if you will; for I expect we shall see a good deal of each other in future, and it would distress my uncle if we disagreed. Do you think you could sign a treaty of friendship with me?"

"Well," said Nan slowly—and then paused, too honest to pledge her word without counting the cost—"I could, but I'm not sure that it would last. We are so different. Would you mind answering one personal question?"

"I'll answer fifty with pleasure if it's in my power."

"Then have you known some awful trouble? Has something dreadful, heart-breaking, happened to you, which you are trying to cover up and hide from the world?"

Gervase stared at her in amazement, which ended in a laugh.

"Certainly not! I have had an absolutely smooth life—too smooth, I am afraid, for the growth of character. Now I wonder what made you take such an idea into your head!"

"I thought perhaps your heart was broken, and that was why you took no interest in anything that was going on."

"Do I take no interest? I was under the impression that I took a great deal—sometimes; but I have learned to conceal my feelings. You may not perhaps be aware that English boys are educated in this fashion, nowadays.

At a public school it is considered 'bad form' to be enthusiastic on any subject. 'Not bad' or 'pretty decent' are the superlatives of praise, and anything more emphatic is sure to be snubbed. Perhaps I have been too apt a disciple in that school."

"I call it a hateful school! and if I had a hundred sons I would not let one of them be trained under such an influence. If a boy is not to be enthusiastic when he is young, when will he be, pray? Youth is the time for noble dreams, for enthusiasm which carries all before it. It is the enthusiasm of youth which keeps the world moving. None of your languid half-measures for me!" declaimed Nan dramatically, backing into a flower-bed in her earnestness, and trampling half a dozen begonias beneath her heels. "Life is real—life is earnest!"

"It is indeed," cried Gervase, laughing; "and so, if you will permit me to say so, is my uncle's gardener, when he is roused! Begonias, I fancy, are his special passion. Miss Nan, you will have to be friends with me whether you will or not, for our natures are so different that we could be of infinite service to each other. You could inspire me with your own enthusiasm, and I, in my turn, could curb and restrain you."

"But, dear me," cried Nan, "I don't want to be curbed!" Then she looked at the begonias, and her face fell. "But I suppose, like all disagreeable things, it would be good for me; so I'll be friends, if you like, Mr Vanburgh, and take my share of the discipline."

"I feel much honoured. It shall be my endeavour to be as little disagreeable as I can," said Gervase Vanburgh, with his courtly bow; and thus were the deeds signed in a friendship destined to have far-reaching consequences.

Chapter Twenty Two
Lilias Interferes

Nan's compact of friendship with Gervase Vanburgh was announced to the family, and received with acclamation by the younger sisters, and with shocked disapproval by grown-up Lilias.

"Most improper!" she pronounced it. "You ought to remember, Nan, that you are no longer a child in the schoolroom, and that such an intimacy with a man of Mr Vanburgh's age is simply another word for flirtation. It is all very well to call it friendship, but everybody knows perfectly well what it means!"

She stopped short with an expressive wave of the hands, and Nan glared at her with flashing eyes.

"If there is one thing more than another that I loathe—and detest—and scorn—and despise," she replied, dropping out each word with vindictive emphasis, "it is looking upon every man one meets in the light of a possible husband, and taking for granted that you can't be civil to him without making a fool of yourself! I don't know quite what you mean by 'flirting,' unless it is giggling and making eyes, as some idiotic girls do; and I am quite sure that I am in no danger of following their example!"

"You know perfectly well, Nan, that it means much more than that; and Mr Vanburgh is a man of the world, and understands exactly to what you are lending yourself. Judging by his manner, I should call him an accomplished flirt!"

"Very well, then, I will ask him about it on the first opportunity. I will tell him what you say, and find out what his ideas are, before things have gone any further."

A gasp of dismay sounded round the schoolroom, for the listeners knew that Nan was perfectly capable of putting her threat into words, and, moreover, that in her present state of indignation it was certain that she intended to do so. Lilias broke into angry protests, but Nan's icy, "Don't be alarmed! I shall not mention your name," showed that the true reason of her discomfiture had been gauged, and she could only hope that no opportunity would occur for the putting of such a question before Gervase left the Grange. In this hope, however, she was doomed to be disappointed; for Mr Vanburgh invited Nan to tea on the following day, and she departed, primed with determination. It seemed at first that she would have no opportunity of broaching the all-important subject; but when tea was over, Gervase proposed a walk round the grounds, and Nan was no sooner clear of the house than she gave a preliminary little cough, and said, in sententious accents—

"Mr Vanburgh, we have agreed to be friends, but I should like to hear, as a preliminary measure, exactly your definition of the term. What is a friend?"

Gervase's eyes twinkled and his lips twitched beneath his moustache, but he made a gallant attempt at seriousness, and replied—

"A friend is a comrade who is faithful not only in words, but in deeds. My friend is one who will make personal sacrifices to ensure my welfare; who will not hear me maligned behind my back, but will reprove me to my face when I have done wrong. My friend is one who cares for me for myself, apart from my circumstances, and will be most loyal and loving in the time of trouble!"

"Bravo! Bravo!" cried Nan enthusiastically. "That's good! I like that! Those are exactly my own sentiments, only I could not have put them into words. I had no idea you were so eloquent. Now, another definition, please. What is a flirt?"

"A flirt!" An expression of the most complete amazement passed over Gervase Vanburgh's face as he echoed the word, for this was, indeed, the last question which he had expected to hear from Nan Rendell's lips.

"You want me to define a flirt? That is a little more difficult, but I will try what I can do. 'One who practises the art of flirting,' the dictionary would tell us, with its usual admirable candour, but that doesn't seem to give much enlightenment. A flirt, I should say, is the antithesis of a friend, for he affects more than he feels; he flatters and makes pretty speeches, while in effect he may be critical and disparaging. He thinks of himself and his own amusement, and is so much concerned for the gratification of his own vanity that he often inflicts serious wounds on the hearts of others."

"So bad as that? Horrid things, how I despise them! I can't imagine how people can make themselves so contemptible. Well, whatever may be my faults, I can honestly say I am not a flirt; but some people are so suspicious that they are always imagining mischief. Some one said to me—I mean, I've heard it said—that when a man and a girl like you and me agree to be friends, it is just another way of beginning a flirtation. It made me very angry when I heard that; but now that I have asked you, I am quite satisfied, for it seems impossible to mix the two things together. You can't flatter a person when you have agreed to tell him his faults; you can't feign a sentiment which is real. I knew I was right, though I could not argue it out; but for the future I sha'n't mind a bit when you say nasty things to me, for I shall feel they are a proof of friendship; and I shall find fault with you on every possible occasion, just to show that I am not flirting, and have only your own good at heart."

Nan stopped short, quite out of breath with eagerness, and Gervase looked at her with a scrutinising smile.

"So!" he was saying to himself, "Somebody said, did she? I wish Somebody would mind her own business, and not put foolish ideas into your innocent little head. Somebody has her own hands pretty full, I imagine, and might be better employed looking after her own affairs;" but aloud he said simply—

"We will make a compact that we will never flirt with each other, but be the truest and most candid of friends; and, to begin as we mean to go on, lay your instructions upon me now for my conduct during my absence. You know my life—an idle one, unfortunately—living in my own place, among my own tenants, in a sleepy little corner of the earth, which affords no opportunity for adventure. I fear I shall come back with no heroic deeds to recount!"

> "'Do the work that's nearest,
> Though it's dull at whiles,
> Helping, when you meet them,
> Lame dogs o'er the stiles!'"

quoted Nan impressively. "That's one of my pet verses, which I quote to comfort myself when I am burning to do great deeds, and have to hem dusters instead. Be thankful you are a man, and have not to hem dusters; and try to take an interest in your tenants, and help them over their stiles. I'm sure many of them are lame, and longing for you to come to their aid; and really and truly it would do you all the good in the world to think of something beside yourself!"

"I have never yet found any one who interested me so much; but I will make the effort. And for yourself—look where you are going, think what you are doing, be a trifle more circumspect in coming downstairs and bicycling round corners, and I will hope to meet you again in health and strength and with as few broken limbs as may be at the end of another month. Goodbye, little friend! All good be with you!"

He held out his hand, and smiled upon her in the slow, kindly fashion which already seemed familiar in her eyes, and Nan felt a sudden warmth at her heart, as at the realisation of a new joy in life.

"Good-bye," she cried heartily; "and I'm glad I promised. I'm glad we are going to be friends."

Chapter Twenty Three
Jim Returns

"In work, in work, in work alway, let my young days be passed, that I may fade away and die, as I am doing f–ast!" sighed Kitty Maitland one afternoon a month later, as she sat in the porch-room, surrounded with a mountain of needlework, on which she was laboriously stitching labels, while the elder girls consulted together as to prices, and Elsie plied an iron at a side-table, smoothing away disfiguring creases and crumples. It was amazing to see the quantity of work which had been gathered together, and nobody was more surprised at the amount than the workers themselves. When the contents of drawers, ottomans, and cupboards had been gathered together and laid on the table, the girls had gasped with amazement. Who could have believed that their little efforts could have achieved such a whole? Who could have credited that friends would have come forward with such generous and ready help? During the last few days parcels had arrived by every post, and from the most unexpected sources; while good, kind Maud had come home from Paris with a box full of spoils from the Louvre and Bon Marché. Lilias declared that her heart leapt within her when she reflected that she had originated the beneficent scheme; but Nan vowed that it made her tired even to look at the things, and reflect how hard-worked she must have been; and Kitty, as has been seen, went in absolute fear of her life!

"I never want to see another pin-cushion so long as I live!" she announced tragically, as she tacked the label on the last of these useful articles, and tossed it impatiently to her companions. "If you charge more than one and six for that beauty, it's a cheat, for it's a regular museum of odds and ends. Heigho! this grows monotonous. Let me go out into the garden and begin preparations there. My master mind is wasted sitting here sewing on labels. I want scope—variety!"

"You can't get it then, until you have finished the work on hand. It ought not to matter to you what you do, so long as you are helping forward," said Lilias severely. "To-morrow morning will be plenty of time to arrange the tables."

"If it is fine! I am sorry to discourage you, but it is raining already. I see five drops on the window-pane," announced Elsie in a tone of satisfaction, born of the remembrance that she had "told them so!" months ago, and that they had refused to believe her; but her triumph was short-lived, for the girls only laughed at her five drops, called her their "faithful croaker," and altogether played such havoc with her dignity that she retired within her shell in displeasure. Had the occasion been less important, she would have flown to her room to pour out her woes to the ever-sympathetic diary; but no personal slight could be allowed to interfere with work to-day, for at four o'clock Jim would arrive, and never should it be said that the Rendell girls were engaged on their own devices when the one and only brother returned to his home! The first few hours after Jim's arrival could be spent in no other way than gazing upon him, in drinking in his words, and hanging around him in adoring admiration.

By four o'clock the porch-room was abandoned, and each sister, attired in her best blouse and freshest skirt, was craning her head out of the dining-room window, while Kitty Maitland hovered in the background, scarcely less excited than themselves. He came. He stepped out of the fly, paid the cabman, and lounged up the path, lifting his head to nod in patronising fashion to his adorers. He was no Apollo of beauty, no Samson of strength, but just an ordinary-looking young man in an ordinary grey suit, with ordinary irregular features redeemed from plainness by an expression of quizzical good humour; yet each of the eight beholders gave a gasp of adoration as she beheld him. His mother's eyes swam with tears as she embraced her boy; Maud felt a ray of pure, unselfish happiness; even Lilias overlooked the fact that his collar was of an unfashionable shape in the delight of meeting. As for the younger girls, they fell upon him, and hugged and kissed, and kissed and hugged again, until he was obliged to beat them off with his long grey arms.

"Now, then! Now, then! Leave a fellow alone! I won't stand being mauled to death!" cried the ungrateful male, scrubbing his cheek with his handkerchief, as if contaminated by the touch of so many feminine lips. "Take it easy, and I'll speak to each in turn, but I can't tackle the bundle together. Where's Maud? Where's my Maud? Come over here, Maud, and don't let these youngsters keep you in the background! Holloa, Nan, what's the matter with your back hair? Done it up, eh? Doesn't look half so well, you know, but I suppose you take it out in honour and glory. Best respects, Lilias; how's the young man? You kiddies are getting too tall—that's what's the matter with you. I shall feel quite an old man at this rate. Do you mean to say that is 'Cath-er-ine Maitland' I see before me? Kitty, my own! How *large* you have grown!"

"Jim, you rude man! Behave, if you can!" retorted Kitty with admirable promptitude. It was an old habit of these two to converse in couplets, though Kitty lived in chronic dread of an hour when she should fail to invent an appropriate reply. Her present success filled her with satisfaction, and evoked a burst of laughter from her companions; and though Jim rolled his eyes at her in threatening manner as he entered the drawing-room, he refrained from a further effort, and devoted his attention to the admirable tea provided for his benefit. His sisters waited upon him obsequiously, while his mother sat with folded hands gloating over the sight of the tall, masculine figure seated in state on the centre of the sofa. What joy to behold him again—her only son, her pride, her darling! How she glorified him, and exulted in him, and rejoiced in every evidence of his beautiful manhood! The sight of the thick-soled boots gave her a positive thrill of joy; she looked unmoved at the mud on the carpet, and did not even wince when he crumpled her best silk cushion behind his back.

Jim looked across, caught her glance, and flashed back an answering message which made her heart swell with joy. Her boy loved her, and had no fear to meet his mother's eye! That was all she wanted to know, and she knew it without further questioning. Jim was not given to words; and even if he wished to speak, how could the poor boy *get* a chance, with seven excited girls all talking to him at the same moment?

Jim listened blankly for some moments before he could understand the drift of the remarks, but gradually the words "Sale" and "Bazaar" disentangled themselves from the clamour and awoke a dim remembrance.

"Oh, the sale for the Mission! You did tell me something about it! Coming off to-morrow, is it? That's a bore! Why didn't you get it over before I came?"

The girls shrieked aloud in dismay, and, under cover of their protests, Maud whispered an eager—

"Take an interest in it, do! They have worked so hard, poor dears, and they want you to help!"—which had the effect of rousing him to the importance of the position.

"All right, girls, I'll see you through!" he announced, with the self-confidence which a man assumes as if by instinct in discussions with his womenkind. He had the vaguest ideas of what was expected, no knowledge at all of the difficulties of the position; but it never occurred to him to doubt his own ability to overcome these difficulties, and put the final triumphant touch on the girls' labours.

"I'll see you through!" he repeated; and his sisters chorused their thanks and murmured grateful acknowledgments, while Kitty Maitland kept silent and eyed him askance through her spectacles, registering a vow to speak faithfully on the subject of masculine vanity on the first convenient opportunity.

The next morning each of the six Rendell girls awoke with a start and a shiver of dismay. What had happened? For a moment they could not tell, yet a cloud of depression was there; and then, alas! in each case a glance at the window answered the question. Down fell the rain, splashing the panes, soaking the trees, turning the paths into pools of water, weighing down the heads of flowers, and scattering blossoms over the grass. Alas and alas! it was almost too dreadful to be believed, that after weeks of fine weather such a downpour should time itself to arrive on the very day of the long-expected sale.

"If Elsie says, 'I told you so!' I shall do her an injury. I shall—I know I shall! I sha'n't be able to help it!" protested Nan; but Elsie made no such statement. To do her justice, she deeply regretted her prophecy, and felt as much distressed as if she were to blame for its fulfilment, while her morbid mind had much ado to countenance such unreasonable behaviour on the part of Providence.

"I don't understand why it is allowed to rain when so much depended on good weather! The work won't look half so well cramped up in the house, and we can make no money on the river, and the people who live at a distance will think it too wet to turn out, and it will all be a dead, dismal failure. It seems to me very strange that we should try to do a good deed only to be frustrated by something over which we have no control," she lamented; and though the other girls snubbed her promptly, it was difficult to banish the same thought from their minds. If only, only it had kept fine, how different it would have been, and with what glee and zest they would have set about their preparations! As it was, they were all more or less depressed, and had it not been for Jim's presence they would have been a sorry company; but Jim rose to the occasion with such a succession of quips and jests, such schoolboy tricks and merry whistlings, as could not fail to be infectious. He was not much use, so far as arranging the work was concerned; but, as he himself expressed it, he played the part of beast of burden, dragging tables into the library, fitting them together to take the place of stalls, and undertaking a dozen onerous duties. With the best will in the world, however, it was impossible to make the room larger than it was, or to prevent an amount of crowding which left many precious treasures hidden from sight, instead of being displayed in the sunshine of the garden. The girls sighed, and resolutely turned their eyes from the window; and thus it happened that certain things took place which they were far from suspecting. Whether the rain had spent its strength, or was put to shame by the sight of the mischief it had already wrought, it would be difficult to say; but certain it was that the downpour changed gradually to a drizzle, the drizzle grew lighter and lighter until it ceased altogether, the clouds rolled away to the east, and through the grey of the sky there broke a feeble, struggling light. Brighter and brighter it grew, stronger and stronger, until of a sudden a ray of sunshine danced across the floor of the room, and electrified its occupants in the midst of their work.

"What's that? What's that? The sun! The sun!" cried every one in chorus, and a stampede was made to the door to see if the good omen could possibly be true. The ground was soaking with moisture, but oh, the freshness, the sweetness, the delightful earthiness of the scent which greeted their nostrils!

"Mff!" cried Nan, opening her mouth wide to draw in deep breaths.

"Ouf!" gasped Agatha rapturously.

"Do my eyes deceive me? Has it actually stopped raining?" cried Christabel elegantly; and Jim executed a jig of triumph on the doorstep.

"It has stopped indeed! The clouds have rolled away, the sun is coming out; in another hour it will be beaming, and you will have such a day as you have not had for weeks past. I told you so! If you had only listened to me, you would have been spared all your misery. I told you so—"

"Excuse me! You did nothing of the kind. You remarked to me on my arrival that it looked 'Jolly bad, and that it was going to be a brute of a day,'" interrupted Kitty severely; but Jim affected a convenient deafness.

"Now then," he cried, "all hands to the pumps! I'll set James to work to mow the lawn, and by the time it is cut and swept and the sun has shone on it for a couple of hours it will be as dry as tinder. We'll have the paths swept too, and put a few planks across where the water has settled, and all will be as right as a trivet. Put on thick boots, and set to work to undo all you have done this morning. There is no time to lose!"

There was not, indeed; but willing hands made light work, and a more cheery band of workers it would have been difficult to find. To see Nan rushing in and out of the house, clad in a short bicycling skirt, with snow-shoes covering her slippers, and Jim's cap stuck on the back of her head, was a sight funny enough to have cheered the most melancholy of patients; but when she executed a dance of triumph before her completed stall, her sisters held their hands to their sides in convulsions of laughter. A deeper laugh joined in with theirs, a lazy musical laugh, which could only have come from one person; and Nan, hearing it, wheeled round fully prepared to see

Gervase Vanburgh standing before her. Not one whit disconcerted did she appear at the sight; but, holding out her skirt on either side, so as to display the huge cloth boots to the fullest advantage, she dropped him a curtsey and cried, "Pleased to see you, sir! I hope you admire me!"

"I do!" said Gervase in his soft drawl; and there was an accent of sincerity in his voice which brought Jim's eyes upon him in curious scrutiny. A word from Lilias had introduced him to this heir of the Mr Vanburgh of whom he had heard so much, and now he eyed him narrowly, forming his own swift conclusion.

"Dandified! Affected! Fine face, though; good expression! Decent fellow, I should say, if the nonsense were knocked out of him. Uncommonly pleased to see Nan, too. This must be looked into!" Then he was obliged to laugh again at the downright fashion in which his sister demanded the reason of the stranger's sudden appearance.

"What have I come for?" Gervase raised his hand deprecatingly. "To see if I could be of any use, of course. My uncle was anxious to know if he could lend anything in the way of tents or bunting, or if you would like one of his gardeners to come across and help your man. A hamper of strawberries is to be sent over presently, with the palms and plants, and the cook is concocting something very special in the shape of ices, but you are to ask for anything and everything you want. He is most anxious to help."

"Bless him!" cried Nan devoutly. "Give him my love, and say that I shall thank him on my bended knees the moment the rush is over. The gardener would be most useful, for James has more than he can do, and we are all taken up with our own special departments."

"And for myself? Can I do nothing to help you? I came last night on purpose for this sale, so I hope you will make me of use." He looked at Nan as he spoke, but it was Lilias who replied, taking him at his word, with an assurance which virtually monopolised him for the entire afternoon.

"Oh, thank you so much; then will you please help me in the punt? I am going to take out small parties at sixpence a head, and intended to ask Jim to help me; but as he knows the people, it would be better if he were free to walk about, and make himself agreeable. Will you walk down to the river with me now, and have a little practice? Jim will send across for the gardener, and we ought to try how we get on together, oughtn't we?"

"Certainly we ought. It is most necessary," replied Gervase, and his face was absolutely devoid of expression. Whether he was disappointed or pleased, annoyed or elated, it was impossible to guess, but he turned aside without another word and followed Lilias down the path which led riverwards.

By three o'clock preparations were completed, and everything done that could be thought of to exhibit house and garden in their most favourable light. In the drawing-room the best cushions and table-covers were displayed in all their glory; in the dining-room the table was set out with the precious china tea-service, which saw the light only on festive occasions, while every silver article was polished up to reflecting point. Seven girls robed in robes of spotless white flitted to and fro in the garden, while Japanese umbrellas made picturesque splashes of colour amongst the green. The visitors were polite enough to declare that it was well worth paying the admission fee to see so pretty a scene, and were altogether in such an affable frame of mind that they were the easiest of preys. Nan's objects of "bigotry and virtue" were speedily purchased, while Kitty and Christabel did a roaring trade in toffee and confectionery. Agatha looked wistfully at their empty stalls while she displayed pinafores and petticoats to the county visitors, heard them murmur "Very useful!" and rustle on without dropping a solitary sixpence into her box; but she consoled herself by the reflection that her turn would come later, when the villagers arrived to make their purchases, and meantime frequent doses of strawberries and fruit salad helped to sustain drooping spirits.

Elsie smiled pensively across a mountain of fancy articles, Maud helped her mother to receive the newcomers, Jim flirted violently with all the prettiest girls, and Lilias was a vision of loveliness as she punted admiring crews up and down the stream.

Gervase Vanburgh had attired himself for his work in the most immaculate of flannels, and as he stood behind his companion plying his long pole, it is safe to say that every feminine beholder remarked to her own heart that the young people were made for each other, and that it would be a sin to divide such a beautiful couple! It was true that there was some talk of an engagement to an old family friend, but as it was not officially announced it could not be binding, and dear Lilias would do well to reconsider her position, now that this charming stranger had appeared upon the scene!

Dear Lilias smiled back with sweet unconsciousness as she met her friends' glances, but she was at no difficulty to read their meaning, and heaved a sigh for the contrariety of fate. If only, only, it had been Gervase instead of Ned—or rather, if the positions of the two men could be reversed! It would be delightful to float along the stream of life as they were even now floating down this sheltered river, a charming companion by her side, the eyes of friends turned admiringly upon her. How different from the life before her in the bleak North-country town, with poverty and anxiety for daily guests, and Ned's worn face looking sadly at her from across the table!

Lilias shivered for all the blazing sunshine, and her heart swelled with anger. It was not fair, it was not right that her future should be blighted in this fashion. Ned should realise that she was not bound by a promise given in completely different circumstances! It was some days since she had heard from him, for his letters had been less frequent of late; and though at the bottom of her heart she knew that her own chilly replies were to blame for this diminution of her lover's ardour, she chose to count his silence as still another offence. He was neglecting her, and she would not stand it. Like a flash of inspiration it darted into her head that she would free herself from this entanglement while there was still time. It would seem unwomanly to desert a man in the hour of misfortune, but she would act at once, and not wait until the worst happened. She would tell her mother that she was not happy; and though Mrs Rendell might disapprove her past promise, she would never persuade her to keep it in the circumstances. Yes, yes! she would be free, she must be free, and then—who could say what would happen then? The long summer lay before her, with its intimate friendship with one of the richest and most charming of his sex. Lilias raised her head with a gesture of determination, and met Gervase Vanburgh's eyes fixed steadily upon her. His glance did not waver as it met hers, and she blushed beneath it with a new and strange feeling of discomfiture. It was as though that steady gaze had pierced beneath the surface, and read her poor, unworthy thoughts.

Chapter Twenty Four
The Garden Sale

"Forty-three pounds seven and twopence, nearly fifty pounds, my darlings, in solid coin of the realm, and all of our amassing!" cried Nan three hours later, as the last visitor drove away from the door of Thurston House, and the contents of the cash-boxes were counted over by half a dozen eager workers. "Here's a triumph for us, for our hopes never soared above a modest twenty pounds, and where it has all come from, I don't know! A great deal of work is left, so that, I fear me, our friends must have wasted their substance on eating and drinking and riotous living, as exemplified by sails in the punt. I could have sold my carvings three times over, and the compliments which were showered upon me I would blush to repeat! My cheeks ache with smiling polite acknowledgments, and indeed I'm nothing but a mass of aches from head to foot. How on earth do poor girls manage to stand behind a counter all day, and not snap off the customers' heads? My poor feet are in a lamentable condition!"

"I'm sorry to hear it; but they look, if you will allow me to say so, considerably better than they did a few hours ago," said Gervase, glancing at the white shoes with an approving smile. "Why don't you sit down, if you are so tired? There is a delightful seat waiting under that tree, and no more work to do, so that I should say the sooner you take possession of it the better!"

"Oh yes, yes. Let's all go!" gushed Agatha, leading the way onward, unconscious of Gervase's look of dismay. "Let's go and rest, and talk it all over! The best part of an entertainment is when the people go, and you can quiz them, and make remarks, and—"

"Eat up the scraps!" concluded Kitty aptly, seizing a plate of cakes from a table as she passed, and illustrating her words with the aid of the daintiest morsel she could select. Christabel ejaculated "Kittay!" in a tone of dignified remonstrance; but the protest was for form's sake merely, for hers were the next pair of hands to rob the dish, and it was neither *one* macaroon, nor two, which satisfied her appetite.

"I really think it has been a great success," she said, munching away, and using an even greater amount of emphasis than usual in her elation of spirits. "The people behaved splendidly! Miss Shorter's behaviour I consider simply *noble*! Do you know what she did? Refused to buy anything at all, my deahs, until every one else had chosen, and then went about buying up all the old rubbish which no one would have. It would have made you *weep* to see her collection of atrocities, and the old dear beamed away as if she were quite delighted. I call it Christian to buy straw spill-boxes and cork frames for the good of your fellow-creatures!"

"But think of the ni-ice little fire they will make when the weather turns chilly!" said Jim wickedly, as he jolted Chrissie's elbow, jerked the plate out of Kitty's hand, and made a snap at Agatha's cake, held temptingly before him. He could never by any chance sit near the girls without teasing them in some such schoolboy fashion; and though they made a great show of indignation, they would in reality have been much disappointed if he had taken them at their word. In the present instance all three girls fell upon him at once, and, having reduced him to a state of submission, continued their song of jubilation.

"We took five pounds at the refreshment stall alone. It would make a scandal in the parish if I divulged how many plates of strawberries the vicar ate. Mrs Bolter bought up all the macaroons. 'Home-made, my dear? X-ellent! I must really beg the recipe.' Mrs Booth asked the price of everything, and sniffed, and walked away. What a woman! Mrs Raleigh seemed quite indignant because I had no eggs. 'Dear me! I quite *counted* on getting fresh eggs!' Mr Vanburgh had only one cup of tea. I don't call that helping the cause of charity!"

"I was busy in another direction, and if I neglected the tea, I did my duty nobly by the lemonade. I am afraid we did not make very much money, but, considering the low rates, it came to more than I expected. How much did we take altogether, Miss Lilias?"

"Two pounds, one and sixpence; and all pure profit, remember! We had no outlay to deduct," replied Lilias, with the shrewd little air of business which contrasted so strangely with her child-like looks. "Looking at it in that light, I think ours was the most profitable of all the departments."

"And I made nothing! I feel quite guilty among you all, for I took not a single coin the whole afternoon," said Maud the modest; but Jim would not allow his favourite sister to decry herself in his presence, and was up in arms in a moment in her defence.

"And why not, pray? Because you were doing the thankless work, as you always are, and fielding for every one else. That was my task, too; and let me tell these young people that they have to thank us for their success. You tackled the dowagers, and put them into a good temper by asking after their ailments, and I managed the girls. Bless their pretty hearts, they would do anything for me! You should have heard me complimenting 'em, and quoting poetry by the yard, and all the while luring 'em on towards the fancy stall. Then I'd nothing to do but remark, 'See that cosy? I drew the design.' 'Observe that cushion? that's my favourite colour,' and they fairly jostled each other in their eagerness to buy it. It was our gentle influence behind the scene which helped you on, young women; and don't you forget it."

Maud smiled; but the smile flickered out all too quickly, as her smiles had a habit of doing nowadays, and her brother glanced at her sharply. Maud was not herself, and he feared that he knew too well the reason of the change. The news of Ned Talbot's engagement to Lilias had smitten him dumb with surprise; but as none of the home letters breathed a hint of a like feeling, he had tried to persuade himself that he had been mistaken in his earlier surmises. This had been easy to do, for Master Jim was not given to distressing himself unnecessarily; but since his return home his fears had sprung into life again in unwelcome fashion. When Maud returned to the house he rose as if to follow, but, changing his mind, turned back and took possession of Kitty Maitland instead.

"What is the matter with my Maud?" he asked her the moment they had turned a corner and were safely out of hearing. "She hasn't half the life and go in her that she had last time I was home. What have you been doing to her, I should like to know?"

Kitty elevated her eyebrows until they were almost lost to sight beneath her curling hair.

"Personally," she said, "personally I have treated her with every consideration. Maud is Maud, and no one in this neighbourhood would dare to treat her otherwise. Of course if other people—from a distance—choose to make lunatics of themselves, and—and—"

'WELL, AND HOW HAVE YOU BEEN?' SAID GERVASE.

"All right—you need say no more! I thought as much; and as you and I had discussed the situation together last year, I wanted to see if your ideas agreed with mine. I could have sworn we were right, and can't imagine how this muddle has come about. It's a big mistake anyhow, and some one will find it out before long, or my name's not James Rendell. It's not my business, I suppose, but I—I should uncommonly like to kick somebody, just as a small relief to my feelings!"

"Oh, so should I—badly; but I'm afraid I couldn't kick hard enough," said Kitty humbly. "The worst of it is you have to be civil, because to show your suspicions would be the most unkind thing you could do. I know Nan agrees with us, and I think Elsie too, but the others seem quite pleased and satisfied."

"Well, let it be a lesson to you, never to allow yourself to be influenced by looks. 'Appearance is deceitful, and beauty vain,'" quoted Jim sententiously.

"That Vanburgh fellow, for instance, is, I suppose, better-looking to the casual glance than I am myself, but I don't need to point out to you the infinite superiority of my character. Whenever, my estimable Katherine, you meet with a man who is popularly styled handsome, take my word for it, he is a wolf in sheep's clothing, and ought to be avoided. People like you and me, with noble hearts and ugly faces,"—but at this point even Kitty's forbearance came to an end, and she stalked off to the house in a fume of indignation. Feminine fourteen does not find the consolation it should in nobility of character at the cost of plainness of feature!

Gervase and Nan, left alone on the garden seat, had meantime turned towards each other with inquiring smiles. It was the first time they had found themselves alone, and each was anxious to question the other concerning the time of absence.

"Well," quoth he, "and how have you been, and what have you been about all this long month?"

"Quite well, thank you; and I'm proud to say, slaving like a nigger for the good of my fellow-creatures. An ignorant man can hardly realise the amount of work it takes to get up a sale like this, but I shall bear the marks to my grave. Look at that!" and she held out towards him a pair of sunburned hands, shapely enough, but disfigured with sundry scars and bruises inflicted by hammer and chisel. Her look of pride in her wounds was comically in contrast to her companion's distress, as his glance wandered from the little hard-worked fingers to his own white hands,— almond-nailed, soft-palmed, taper-fingered, the hands of a man who has lived an idle life, and known little or nothing of the reality of work. Nan's eyes followed his, and she laughed in amused fashion. "Mine look like the man's, and yours like the woman's! The contrast makes mine browner than ever. How do you manage to keep them so white?"

"Don't!" said Gervase shortly. "I am not at all proud of them, Miss Nan. They have been useless enough hitherto, and if they find any work now, it is more your doing than their own. I have tried to turn over a new leaf since I saw you last, and to remember your axiom—"

"And did you find them? Did you help them over? Were many lame, and not able to walk?"

"Crowds! Dozens! Scores! The whole parish seems hobbling; and I foresee that that stile will keep me busy, now that I have begun. It was astonishing how many cripples seemed waiting for my advent, and what a lot of 'helping over' they required. When they had recovered from the shock of discovering that I was showing some interest in their affairs, they were not at all bashful about stating their desires. One man wanted a new roof to his cottage—his wife was rheumatic, and objected to the rain coming through on her bed. I had previously refused the request through my agent, but when I went to inspect the place, I could not deny that repairs were needed. The woman showed me her fingers, too—most unpleasant! I would rebuild the whole cottage rather than look at them again!"

He shrugged his shoulders, with a relapse into his old affectation of manner, which brought Nan's eyes upon him with a flash of indignation; but she refrained from remonstrance, as, after all, he had granted her request; and he continued his story uninterrupted.

"Another man begged for an extra strip of land where an invalid daughter might keep chickens, and so contribute towards the family-purse. Three widows had sons to place, and seemed to think that a word from me would be sufficient to secure positions with handsome salaries; half a dozen women demanded letters to hospitals. The school marm wanted an additional window in her cottage, which is about as gloomy a little hole as I have had the pleasure of entering; and the vicar, hearing reports of my new-found generosity, requested a donation towards a new organ, felt he would be the better for a second curate, and remarked *en passant* that he had had a lifelong desire to visit the Holy Land. I promised to pay the last hundred pounds for the organ when he had made up the rest of the sum, said that the parish was too small to allow two whole curates and myself to live together in peace and harmony; and congratulated him on his good fortune in not having visited Palestine. I have, and ever since my return have been strenuously striving to forget, and work back to my old dreams. He went away saddened and surprised; but as he is neither poor nor hard-worked, I did not consider that he came within my category. I was beginning to feel a trifle overworked, and was quite relieved to get away for a rest!"

"I think you have done splendidly, and am sure you have enjoyed it, in spite of all you may say. It gives one such a lovely, warm, glowey feeling to help other people! On the rare occasions when I have succeeded in doing it, I have just longed to be a philanthropist, for I felt so deliriously happy and pleased with myself. You can't look me in the face and deny that you have been far happier this last month, and far less bored and cynical?"

Gervase laughed, and shrugged his shoulders.

"Have it your own way! I deny nothing. I am considerably the loser both in time and money by the new arrangement, but perhaps that is wholesome discipline. I don't know that I have experienced much of the 'glow' as yet; which is, I suppose, because I have not your affection for my fellow-creatures; but I hope it is yet to come, for it sounds an attractive sensation."

"Don't laugh at me," said Nan severely. "I said glowey, and I mean glowey! No other word expresses the sensation. You'll understand some day when you have it yourself, and be sorry that you made fun of me. As for liking your people, the more you help them, the more interested you will feel, until in the end you will positively love them as if they were your own relatives."

Gervase looked dubious.

"If only they would refrain from exhibiting their deformities! I do so strongly object to looking at disagreeable objects," he sighed plaintively; then suddenly his face grew grave, and he added in a different voice, "It will be a long time, I fear, before I can reach your standard of loving help. So far it is a duty only, and a distasteful one in to the bargain; but I will persevere, in hope of better things. There is one person in the parish who has been set in the right way through your instrumentality. If the other efforts have failed, this, at least, has been a success, and it was time that some one took him in hand. An idle, loafing rascal who thought of nothing but his own comfort, and was the biggest waster in the village. He has set to work now, and he shall stick to it, or I'll know the reason why! I'll keep a stern hand on him, Nan, for your sake; for it was you, not I, who set this ball a-rolling, and I am only the executor of your orders. It is you who have played the good angel in his life, and he shall have no chance of slipping back."

"But you mustn't be too stern with the poor young man. You must make allowances, and be patient and forbearing. I shall be so interested to know how he goes on. It is nice to have a *protegé*, and feel that one has had some part in his reformation. Tell me his name, so that I may know what to call him."

Gervase looked at her curiously. The eager face was without a suspicion of embarrassment, but it coloured over with a quick flush of surprise as she listened to his reply.

"His name," Gervase said slowly, "you have heard before. His name is Vanburgh!"

Chapter Twenty Five
The Blow Falls

Two days later, Maud was sitting reading in the drawing-room, when the door opened, the servant pronounced a name which thrilled her with surprise, and, looking up, she beheld Ned Talbot standing before her,— Ned Talbot, or the wraith of Ned, for so pale did he appear, so worn and haggard, that it needed no words to tell the nature of his visit.

Maud had heard about the anxieties of the last few months, and had grieved for Ned in her tender heart, feeling an added bitterness in the lot which forbade her the privilege of comforting him; but now it would appear that Fate had led them to each other, and even her modesty could not mistake the relief in voice and manner as his eyes rested upon her.

"Maud," he cried,—"Maud, it is you! Oh, this is good, this is better than I hoped for, to find you here, and alone! I was longing for your help; but you are so much away nowadays that I seldom see you. Well, Maud, it has come—the end has come! I have thrown up my post, and have to face the world again, and the whole weary fight from the beginning. All these years have been wasted; the time has gone, and the money, and the strength, and here I am at the end, stranded and beaten! You may wonder how I have the audacity to show myself among you. If I had any pride left, I should have stayed away—"

He broke off with a hard, unnatural laugh, and Maud laid her hand on his arm with a soothing gesture, her own trouble forgotten in the necessity of soothing his.

"Come and sit down," she said gently. "Sit down, and tell me all about it. We are not fair-weather friends, Ned, and will only care for you the more because you need help. If you have lost this post, I am sure it is from no fault of your own, so you must not be cast down. Tell me about it—Or stay! Shall I call Lilias? She is at the Grange, but I could send for her at once."

She paused, looking inquiringly into Ned's face, and he hesitated painfully, the colour flushing in his thin cheeks, his eyebrows twitching nervously.

"I think—not!" he said slowly at last. "She will hear soon enough, and she is so young and inexperienced that she cannot understand. Let me first talk it over with you, Maud, and then—No! It was no fault of mine, though in the last instance it was I who gave in my resignation. I could not stay on longer, and keep my self-respect. Positions were forced upon me impossible to any man of honour. My post was deliberately made untenable, and to stay on would have been the act of a coward and a scoundrel. They had got what they wanted out of me, and I was of no further use. It only remained to get rid of me as quickly as possible,—and, mark you, by my own doing in the last instance, so that they might preserve some appearance of honour before their neighbours!"

"But can such things be?" Maud wondered incredulously. "Is it really possible that men, calling themselves gentlemen and, I suppose, Christians, can be so absorbed in the idea of growing rich that they can be so low, so base? To go to a young fellow who is fighting against hard odds, to propose a scheme which looks fair and smooth, to suck his brains and steal his business from him, and then—then—to treat him as you say, and send him out on the world alone! Oh, Ned, is it possible? One can hardly believe in such wickedness. Are there many such people in your business world?"

"Not many, thank God! but there are a few who are notorious for absorbing small firms, and treating their owners as I have been treated. They build up huge fortunes, and we are ruined; they succeed, and we fail, and the world goes on as usual, and no one sees any difference, or takes any thought of the poor fellows who have gone to the wall."

"God does!" said Maud softly. "God doesn't think they have failed! In His eyes they have succeeded, and are rich, while the others are ruined and outcast. Don't be cast down, Ned—don't lose hope! God is on your side, and has some good purpose behind this trouble. The clouds are dark to-day, and you cannot see it, but in years to come it will be plain. Keep a brave heart, and don't grieve too much over what is past. You have the future before you, and you are young and strong. You would not allow any one else but yourself to call you beaten, and I will not hear it from your lips."

"Oh, Maud!" cried Ned brokenly, "you always know what to say, you always say the right thing! How can I thank you? If girls only understood what angels they might be to men,—if they would remind us oftener that this world is not all,—what a help it would be! We are out on the battlefield, and it is difficult to remember these things, especially when we are so hard pressed that our thoughts are engrossed with the struggle. I felt hard and bitter when I came into this room, for it's a terrible thing to face ruin,—a girl cannot imagine how terrible, for she is shielded from such trouble,—but you have put fresh life into me by your sweet words."

Maud smiled faintly, her brows drawn together in painful fashion. She was saying to herself that she knew well what it was to see life robbed of its dearest hope, and realising, as many a girl has done before her, that one of the sorest features of her trial was that she could neither ask nor receive sympathy from her friends. The reflection brought her thoughts back to Lilias, and she was once more about to suggest sending a message to the Grange, when the door burst open and Lilias herself danced into the room. What a contrast to the pale and depressed couple seated on the sofa! Just returned from a delightful visit to the Grange, love of admiration gratified by Mr Vanburgh's courtesy and Gervase's elaborate compliments, her hands full of trophies in the shape of flowers and fruit, she looked the impersonation of happiness and prosperity, and singularly out of sympathy with her companions. She was half-way across the room before she recognised Ned, and the sudden change which then passed over her face was far from flattering to his vanity.

"You!" she gasped, in bewilderment. "Is it you? When did you come? I—I never knew. You said nothing in your letter about coming."

"No; I wanted to tell you the news myself!" Ned rose and stood beside her, not attempting any lover-like greetings, but holding her hand tightly in his own. His face was pathetic in its wistfulness, and dread of the pain which he was about to inflict, but it was in the tone of a father speaking to a child that he said gently—

"I have bad news for you, Lilias—the news which I have been dreading. I have sent in my resignation to the heads of the firm, and have practically said 'Goodbye' to the Works. It is a bad business, and very hard on you; but, as Maud has been reminding me, I am young and strong, and we must not be cast down by a first failure. If you will have faith in me, and will wait a few years, all will come right yet."

He paused, and Lilias stared at him with incredulous eyes. Her glance wandered from him to Maud, from Maud around the pretty luxurious room, through the window to the garden beyond, and finally back to his face. Her lips moved, and the words came out in spasmodic snatches.

"You have resigned? You threw it up? You did it of your own accord, in spite of all I could say—of my wishes and entreaties? It is your own doing?"

Ned dropped the hand which he held in his, and straightened his shoulders with a gesture at once proud and determined. His voice took a sharper edge, and the gentleness died out of his face.

"Yes, it is my own doing, Lilias, in this last instance, but you know what has driven me to it. I have told you in what position I was placed. I could not stay on without sacrificing every sense of honour. Surely you can understand and sympathise with me in my misfortune?"

Lilias laughed, a high, hysterical laugh, and threw back her head with a defiant gesture.

"Oh, I understand—yes! I have understood all the time. Your ridiculous quixotic notions have ruined your life, and you don't care if they ruin mine also. You think of your own feelings, your own discomforts, but you never think of *me!* If you really loved me, you would bear a few discomforts for my sake; but no! it must all go, you must throw it all away. I begged, I implored, I did everything that was in my power to prevent it coming to this. You can't deny that I did?"

"No, Lilias, I cannot. I am bitterly grieved to remember that you have systematically urged me to act against my conscience." It was an unexpected answer, almost awful in its unflinching sternness, and Lilias greeted it by a burst of weeping.

"Oh yes, yes, blame me! blame me! It's not enough that you have brought this misery upon me, but now you must begin to abuse me to my face! It is cruel and cowardly to turn against me like this!"

"Hush, Lilias, oh, hush, hush!" Maud stood before her—Maud's fingers gripped her arm in remonstrance.

"Think what you are saying. You are surprised and shocked; but you must not, you shall not talk so wildly! Ned is in trouble, and it is your place to comfort him. He has done what is right, and it is harder for him than for you. He needs your help!" But Lilias only sobbed the louder, making no attempt to give the desired comfort, and Ned said sadly—

"I ask no more from you at present, Lilias, than a fair judgment. Maud has given me her sympathy and encouragement, but that seems too much to hope for from you. Try to believe, if possible, that I was not indifferent to your interests. Maud would not allow me to say I had failed because I must suffer temporarily for conscience' sake; she believes that the day will come when I shall be thankful for this change in my circumstances. Can't you bring yourself to feel the same; to look forward to a future when I may meet with success instead of reverse?"

"No, I can't; how can I? It is contrary to reason. You said yourself that you could never hope to be master again, and situations are so difficult to find. I've heard father talking, and I know. Sometimes men have to wait years and years before they find an opening, and then it's a wretched thing with a salary of two or three hundred a year. And you have less chance than many, because your own Works didn't pay, and you have left these people after such a short time. It will count against you. People will think it is your own fault."

"Lilias!" cried Maud again, and this time her voice trembled with anger, and her eyes sent out such a flash as her sister had never seen before, "how dare you! How dare you be so cruel! If it were true a hundred times over, how could you have the heart to say so to Ned in the midst of his trouble? For pity's sake, think what you are doing!"

"Don't distress your kind heart, Maud. It is better that I should know exactly what Lilias has in her mind. She is right in her surmises. The changes will tell against me in public opinion, and it is quite probable that I may suffer for them. I would not for one moment deny it, so you see there is no injustice in the accusation. You are right, Lilias! My chance of being a rich man is sensibly diminished by this last misfortune, and it may be years before I can earn even a bare competency. I have never deceived you about my position, and I shall not begin now. I knew that my news would be a blow to you, but I could not have believed that you would receive it as you have, without a word of kindness or sympathy. Apart from the question of love, I should have thought any woman would have taken pity on a man in the first sharpness of his misfortune, and have spared him her reproaches. Maud has been an angel of kindness, but you have had no thought of my sufferings."

Lilias gave a gasp of mingled anger and mortification. This was what she had feared, this was what she had determined to avoid; but once again Fate had been too strong for her, and had precipitated the calamity before she had had time to obtain her freedom. Now every one would call her heartless and unwomanly; her parents would look coldly upon her, she would be branded before the neighbourhood as a girl who had forsaken her love when he most needed her devotion. A great wave of anger swept over her, her heart thumped against her side, and her breath came fast. She hardly knew what she was saying, but the words rushed out in a breathless string—

"Oh yes, Maud—Maud! Always Maud! I'm sick of hearing Maud quoted, and held up as a pattern! Maud is always right, and I am wrong. Maud is an angel, and I am an unwomanly wretch! Why didn't you get engaged to Maud, when you liked her so much better than me? If I have made a mistake, so have you, and you have no right to reproach me. I'll go away and leave you, since I make you so unhappy, and you prefer Maud's company to mine."

She was out of the room even as the last word was uttered, and the two who were left stared at each other with horrified eyes. Maud's face was crimson, from the tip of her chin to the roots of her hair, but she was the first to speak and recover some semblance of composure.

"Oh, don't listen to her! Don't listen to her! She does not know what she is saying. She is excited, and has lost her self-control. In a few minutes she will be sorry. Oh yes, I know she will; she will be wretched, and come to beg you to forgive her. Wait, wait, and don't judge her hardly. She is so young, as you said, and she didn't know what she was saying. Try to forget it."

But Ned sank down in a chair and covered his face with his hands.

"But it is true!" he moaned. "It is true, and I can't deny it! Oh, how blind I have been—how blind and foolish! I have ruined my own life as well as hers."

Chapter Twenty Six
A Milestone

It was all over. Ned had gone away, and the diamond ring no longer shone on Lilias's left hand. In a storm of tears and sobs she had declared to her mother that she neither could nor would keep true to her engagement, and Ned had received the intelligence with grave composure.

"She made a mistake!" he said quietly. "We both made a mistake. I cannot blame her, for I was in fault myself. What we thought was love, was but the attraction of youth and good spirits, which could not stand the strain of adversity. Don't be hard on Lilias, Mrs Rendell. I should be sorry that she should suffer any more on my account. It has been a painful experience for her."

But Mrs Rendell closed her lips in a stern silence, and had no word of pity for her daughter. It shocked her proud heart that one of her girls should have behaved in a manner so unworthy the precept which she had endeavoured to teach, for she knew well that Lilias would have felt no qualms in preparing for her marriage, if Ned's story had been one of success instead of failure.

What Mrs Rendell thought she was accustomed to say, and Lilias came away from the important interview smarting with mortification and wounded vanity. She tried to think that the worst was over; but the bitterest moment was yet to come, when she met her father—the gentlest and most forbearing of men, who was so slow to blame that his children could count the reproofs of a lifetime on the fingers of one hand—and he looked at her with a strange, cold glance, in which was no trace of the old fond admiration.

"What's this I hear about you, Lilias?" he asked sternly. "I'm not proud of you, my dear, not proud at all! I did not think that a daughter of mine could have behaved in such an unwomanly manner. Your affection seems good only for fair weather. Talbot is well rid of such a wife!"

It was not much, and it was the only reference to the broken engagement which she ever heard from his lips, but it pierced the girl's heart as no other reproach could have done. The relationship between a father and a daughter is a very sacred and beautiful one, and the consciousness of his pride in her, his barely concealed satisfaction in the admiration she excited, had been one of her most cherished joys. The thought that her father was ashamed of her made Lilias wince with pain, nor did her sisters' reception of the news help to restore her composure.

Maud's principle in life was to say nothing, if it were impossible to say what was agreeable; but Nan made up for this silence by the candour of her denunciation. The two girls came face to face at the top of the stairs, an hour after the great news had circulated through the house, and mutually stopped to gaze in each other's face.

"W–ell?" queried Lilias timidly. "You've heard! Mother has told you. What do you—what do you think about it?"

Nan closed her eyes, and tilted her chin in the air.

"Sneak!" she said shortly; and the other started back in astonishment.

"Wh–what do you say?"

"Sneak! That's what I called you. It's a mean, sneakish thing to desert a man just when he is in trouble and needs all the help he can—"

"It wasn't just then. I had been thinking of it a long time. If he had stayed away a week longer, I would have spoken to mother all the same. I had made up my mind. You don't understand what you are talking about, and you have no right to call me names. It's vulgar and unladylike."

"I am thankful for that!" cried Nan piously. "If your behaviour is ladylike, I'll be as vulgar as I can. I'd rather not talk, if you please, until I have got over it a little. I'm afraid of what I may say."

She went stalking downstairs, and Lilias turned into the porch-room and sat herself down in despair. Elsie was seated at the table engaged in informing the diary of the latest family event, and she turned a look of such sympathetic sorrow upon the new-comer, that Lilias felt that here, at last, she had found a friend in need.

"My heart is broken, Elsie!" she sobbed tragically. "Every one has turned against me. Father—mother—Nan—they are all cruel to me. Their words cut into my heart! I can never forget them—never feel the same again."

Elsie drew a sigh so long and fluttering that it was almost worthy to be ranked as a groan.

"No—never, never! A blow like this, coming in early youth, will cloud and darken all your life. You can never be a girl again. The remembrance of all you have suffered, and of the life you have wrecked, will haunt your dreams, and make you old before your time. You feel it now, but you'll feel it more and more, like a leaden weight pressing upon you, crushing out all your joy..."

"Dear me, Elsie, how you talk! You might be a penny novel, to prose away like that. You are a fine Job's comforter for a poor girl to come to in her trouble! It's hard enough for me as it is, without trying to make it worse. I shall drown myself, if this sort of thing goes on. Maud sulking, Nan raving, you croaking! What a prospect! And I shall have to endure it all my life too, for I shall never marry—now."

"No," said Elsie judiciously, "I suppose not. Not for love, at least. Perhaps, by and by, after years and years, when you are middle-aged, you may make a marriage *de convenance*, to some old man who could give you a comfortable home. People often do that in books, I notice, when they have had an unfortunate affair in youth. And look at Mrs Bailey! Her lover was killed in the Crimea, and when she was fifty-two she married that nasty old man with the snuff on his beard, and—"

But the rest of the sentence was spoken to the air, for Lilias had fled. The prospect of the old man with snuff on his beard was too much for her composure, and she rushed into the garden, to see if there, at least, she might find the much-desired solitude.

No, not yet! for the summer-house towards which she sped had already been occupied by the three schoolgirls, and there they sat staring at her with big solemn eyes, as if, forsooth, a girl who had broken off her engagement was a new and extraordinary freak of humanity.

Good-natured Agatha made room for the new-comer by her side, and glanced sympathetically at the tear-stained face, but, as usual, her remarks were not the most tactful in the world.

"Was it really your doing, Lilias?" she inquired, "or was Ned tired of you too? Kitty says he was, and feels sure he will not mind much."

That opened Lilias's eyes with a flash of anger, but Kitty had the courage of her opinions, and said stolidly—

"I never considered from the beginning that he was really in love. I've seen lots of engaged people, and he wasn't a bit like them. He used to ask us to go about with you, and be quite disappointed if we wouldn't, and most couples like to be alone, and make faces at one another when they think you are not looking, to say they wish you would run away. I've had experience, for last summer we stayed two months in a hydropathic."

"Perhaps he really did care for you at first, but was disappointed when he got to know you better!" This from Christabel; while Agatha chimed in with an eager—

"But you are glad, dear, aren't you, to think he is not heart-broken? It makes it easier for you when he doesn't care!"

Plainly there was no comfort forthcoming for Miss Lilias from the members of her own family!

Meanwhile Jim was seeing his friend off at the railway station, and administering such sympathy as was deserved for Ned's business reverses, while eclipsing his sisters in candour on the subject of the broken engagement.

"If you would be a fool, you must be prepared to suffer for it. Never was more surprised in my life than to hear of it, when it first came off. Thought you had gone off your head. When I was at home with you last, there was no sign of such nonsense. Can't think what on earth possessed you!"

"She was so pretty and charming, and seemed so much interested in all I did! Vanity was at the bottom of it, I suppose. I was flattered and interested, just when I was down on my luck, and needed it most. I—I—I must make a clean breast of it, Jim, and tell you the truth! Of course, it was Maud I cared for first; I can see now that I have loved her all through, but she was so reserved with me, and kept me at such a distance, that I thought she wanted to show me that I had no chance. Then Lilias came home, and I was captivated by her lovely face and pretty ways. She seemed to turn to me for advice and sympathy, to be so pleased to see me, so sorry when I left, that—that—ah, well, you know the rest! I was a fool, as I daresay many a man has been before me; and though I was miserable enough, I never discovered why, until Lilias herself pointed it out. She accused me of caring for Maud more than for her—in Maud's presence, too—when we three were alone together!"

Jim's lips met in a significant whistle.

"The little wretch! She ought to be shaken! My poor old Maud, that was rough on her. What did she do or say?"

"Begged me to take no notice, and pleaded for Lilias, like the angel she is. But I was knocked completely over, didn't know what I was doing, and told her straight out that it was true. Perhaps I should not have done it, but I could not help myself, and she gave me one look, just one! Oh, Jim, old man, if this crash has shown me the awful mistake I was making, it will be indeed a blessing in disguise. I will work like ten men, I will laugh at difficulties, I will do anything and everything, if only, only I can win Maud in the end. You will be my friend, won't you? You will help me, and tell her what I hope?"

"Not if I know it!" returned Jim, with masculine candour. "You have done quite enough mischief for the time, old chap, and had better lie low until things have blown over. I've a great deal too much respect for Maud, to suggest that she should adopt you as her lover the moment you are dropped by Lilias. Wait a year or two until you have made your position, and then come down and ask her yourself—"

"A year or two! And meantime she might think I had changed again, and had forgotten all about her—That's too much to expect! I don't ask you to say anything just yet, but in time to come you might drop a hint, or let her see one of my letters, show her in any indirect way you like that I know my own mind at last, and am working towards an end. It isn't much to ask from an old chum—I'd do as much for you if I were in your place."

"Humph!" quoth Jim concisely; but his grey eyes sent out a kindly gleam, and Ned Talbot went away comforted by the knowledge that his friend would be kinder in deed than in word, and that his message would not fail to be delivered.

He had another friend at court to whom he gave less thought, but whose loyalty was at least as strong as that of her brother. Nan had her own dreams of the future, of which she breathed no word to a living soul, but she set herself to work to clear away such difficulties as lay in Ned's path, with her accustomed energy and daring.

"If I were a nice old gentleman with heaps of money and nothing to do, I would give a good situation to a young fellow who was miserable and ill-treated!" she announced to Mr Vanburgh, at the conclusion of the story of the broken engagement; and that gentleman chuckled with enjoyment as he listened.

"Would you, indeed? And in what capacity? I don't quite see what situations I have to offer which would meet Mr Talbot's requirements. There is a good deal of machinery of one sort and another involved in the work of a house like this, but I fear it is hardly the kind which he is accustomed to superintend."

"Don't snub me, please. I'm too reduced. I don't mean in this house, but somewhere else where there are Works like his own. If you would just write to the people and say how clever he is, and what a good manager, and that you are sure they would like him!"

"But how can I be sure? I know nothing about Mr Talbot's business capacities, and should hardly recognise him if I met him in the street!"

"But I tell you! You can trust my word; and every one likes Ned, for he is so good and noble. He didn't want to go into the Works at all, for he is one of those quiet, studenty sort of men, who are never so happy as when they are in the country, alone with their books and their thoughts. He wanted to be a literary man, but his brother died, and there was no one else to help his father, so he gave up his own plans for the sake of the family. That seems to me very hard—to be unselfish and take up uncongenial work, and then to meet with nothing but failure and disappointment! I should expect to be rewarded by making piles of money, but poor old Ned has lost almost all he has. Dear, sweet, kind Mr Vanburgh, find him another opening—do!"

The old man smiled, and laid his worn fingers caressingly over the girl's hand.

"I would do a great deal to please you, Nan, if I could find the way, but my word is not so powerful as you imagine. I am afraid the managers of the great factories would pay very little attention to my recommendation; but if Mr Talbot is not set on continuing a business life, it is possible that something else might be found. I have a good deal of land which will come to Gervase in his turn, and meantime, as he engages my stewards for me and takes in hand most of the arrangements, you had better speak to him on the subject."

"Oh-oh!" cried Nan, and turned towards the young man with hands clasped together in supplication. "Oh! do you—do you? Then one of them is a bad steward, isn't he? I am sure he is! You want a new one; I am sure you do! Ned would make a beauty, for he loves nothing so much as a country life. He is a splendid shot. Jim saw him knock over twelve rocketers running, last time they were out together, and he goes in for all kinds of sport. His father had a beautiful country place when they were rich, and he is always talking of what he used to do. He looks so sweet in gaiters, too! He would make a lovely steward!"

Both men shook with laughter, but Nan's earnestness could not be shaken. She was pleading for Maud's future, for Maud's happiness, and neither ignorance nor bashfulness had power to check her. She insisted on the wickedness of the present steward with such determination, that Gervase was forced to come to his defence.

"Indeed, Nan, he is a most capable and clever fellow. I've not a word to say against him, except that perhaps he is too clever to stay with us much longer. Lord Edgeworth has been advertising for a steward, and I think it more than likely that he will get the post. If he should—"

"He will! He will!" cried Nan excitedly. "I feel a conviction. He will get it, and you will offer Ned his place. It would be defying Providence to do anything else. Oh, how happy I am—how pleased he will be! And is it a pretty house in a garden, big enough for us all to go down and stay with him? How soon will it be settled, so that I can tell them at home?"

So determinedly confident did she appear as to the success of her scheme, that it seemed an ungenerous act to pour cold water on such generous enthusiasm, and each man registered a mental vow to satisfy her, if it were within the bounds of possibility.

As his custom was, Gervase escorted the visitor on a tour of inspection round the garden before she took her departure, and took advantage of the *tête-à-tête* to express a more ardent sympathy with the home trouble than he had cared to show in his uncle's presence. The broken engagement had been no surprise to him, for he had summed up the character of Miss Lilias too accurately to have any trust in her stability; but it had evidently come as a shock to Nan's unsuspecting mind.

"She says now that she has been thinking of it for some time, and he says he was dissatisfied; yet neither of them spoke a word, but went drifting on and on, waiting upon chance. I suppose they would have married each other if this crash had not come, and regretted it for the rest of their lives. I can't understand such behaviour. If I feel a thing, I can't bottle it up, I simply cannot; out it must come, whatever is the consequence. And when it comes to pretending to love a person when you don't, and to be happy when you are not, that is worse than anything else. It's positively wicked!"

"I agree with you. I have always maintained that absolute honesty should be practised in these affairs between a man and a woman, and that far less trouble would arise if each side spoke out plainly as to what was in their hearts. I go perhaps a little further in my views than most people, but long ago I made myself a promise that when my own hour came I would act up to my convictions, and I am not going to draw back now. Months ago, Nan, you walked into my uncle's room to meet me, and I knew—I think I knew almost as soon as I met your eyes—that here was a new specimen of her kind, a woman who would play a great part in my life. I had never known that feeling before, but it has grown in strength ever since that day, until now it is difficult to imagine my life without it. You have engrossed all my thoughts—all my hopes—"

Nan stood still and stared at him. The colour had left her cheeks, and her eyes were wide and startled. She laid her hand on her throat and gave a little choking gasp.

"Do you mean that you—that you are—in love—with *me*?"

The amazement in her tone, the incredulity of that "me" was touching in its humility, and Gervase's smile was very tender as he replied—

"I think I am. I am, at least, travelling very fast in that direction. Does that alarm you so very much? Does it distress you? Have you no feeling of friendship to offer me in return?"

"Friendship! Oh yes, but not,"—Nan gulped over the word in wild embarrassment—"the other thing! It's too soon. I have just left the schoolroom—I have just put up my hair. I couldn't think of such a thing for years and years, until I am old, and have got some sense!"

Gervase laughed softly.

"You have more sense now than any girl I know; but don't be frightened, dear, I am not asking for my answer yet. You must have time, but I wanted you to know from the beginning what my feelings were. As you grow older and go into society, and meet other men, I want you to remember that there is one man who has already given his heart to your keeping, and is waiting in the hope that yours may be given to him in return. You are not bound-to me in any way. If you meet some one whom you can care for more than for me, I will wish you God-speed; but until that day comes I will wait in hope. I will not trouble you by referring to the subject again at present; for a year to come I will promise not to allude to it, but by that time you will be twenty, and will have had twelve whole months to think me over. You will not forbid me to speak to you again next July, Nan?"

"N–no!" sighed Nan dubiously, "I suppose not. You are very kind, but I am—frightened. Suppose I said 'Yes,' and then changed my mind like Lilias! That would be dreadful, yet how can one be sure? I like you very much, better than any other man, but still—"

"You must never say 'Yes' unless you have no doubt in your heart. No amount of liking will do. If the day ever comes when you feel that your whole heart goes out to me, as mine does to you, when you would choose poverty with me rather than riches with another man, then come to me, darling, but never till then. You and I are not the sort to be satisfied with a half-and-half happiness, and we will not risk failure. I want to make your life beautiful, not to wreck it!"

The tears rose slowly in Nan's eyes, and her lips trembled.

"You are very good to me; but I feel as if I must be a hypocrite to have deceived you so. I'm not worth it. I'm not, indeed. If you only knew what a wretch I am, you couldn't think of me any more. There are such lots of nice girls. If you would only choose somebody proper and sensible and accomplished and clever—"

"Oh, Nan, I don't want her. Don't force her on me, please. I've met her such scores and scores of times, and she bored me so unutterably. I want just you, and no one else; but don't trouble your head about me for another year. Live your own bright life. I would not for the world shorten your girlhood or make you old before your time. It won't be a very depressing thought, dear, will it, that somewhere a hundred miles away a man is loving you, and trying to live a better life because of his love?"

Nan could not answer, could only shake her head in a mute dissent. No; it was far from depressing—it was beautiful, inspiring—but, oh, what a responsibility! Gervase might say that he would not willingly shorten her girlhood, but, alas! had he not already done so? To feel that another heart leant on her own, another life depended on her for happiness—was this not a reflection to sober the most careless and most light-hearted of natures? Nan knew full well that this short interview was as a milestone in her life, and that at one step she had left behind the careless days of youth.

Chapter Twenty Seven
After Two Years

Nearly two years had passed by since Lilias had broken off her engagement with Ned Talbot, and Gervase Vanburgh had told Nan of his love, and a stranger passing along the village highroad one bright May day might have discerned an air of unusual excitement and bustle in Thurston House. The housemaids were hanging clean curtains in every window from attic to cellar; the gardener was bedding out plants; message boys besieged the house with trays of provisions, and the Parcel Delivery van seemed to empty its entire contents at the door. Nor did the bustle grow less as one entered the house, for the hall was banked up with plants, and seven girls enveloped in aprons seemed to be chasing one another up and down stairs, so rapid and unceasing were their movements. There would have been no difficulty in recognising our old friends, though the years had not passed without bringing changes in their wake. Maud's sweet face had lost its look of sadness, and blossomed into fresh youth; Lilias was still the professional beauty, whose very apron was donned with an air to effect; while, wonder of wonders! Nan had grown tidy, possessing hair as daintily coiled and hands as carefully kept as Lilias's own. In the old days it had been hazarded as an occasional conjecture that Nan was pretty; but there could be no doubt on that question now, for the plump face had moulded into shape, the complexion toned down to a soft pink and white, and the dark eyes shone with happiness. Happiness, indeed, seemed to radiate from Nan to-day, as she raced up and down the house, as hard-worked as any of her sisters, yet in some indefinable way distinguished from the rest, for she was given the precedence in all that went on, while every time that she and her mother came together, they embraced with fresh unction. For the rest, Elsie had reached her ambition, and the age when she might dress her hair as she chose, and by means of parting it in the middle and plastering it over her ears had given herself an appropriately funereal aspect. Even Agatha boasted a coil at the back of her head, while Christabel and Kitty wore skirts which reached to their ankles.

Advancing years had, however, by no means diminished the girls' powers of conversation; and as they banked up plants in corners of the staircase, and rearranged furniture in the sitting-rooms, the babel of voices was as deafening, and seemingly as inexhaustible, as of yore.

"Children, children, be quiet! Stop talking, for mercy's sake!" pleaded Mrs Rendell piteously. "I try to ask a question, and cannot make myself heard. You will make Nan's head ache if you go on like this. Go up to your room to write your letters, Nan dear. Don't attempt to do it here, but take the chance of half an hour's quiet when you can get it."

Nan rose obediently, and carried her writing materials upstairs; but it was some time before she sat down at her desk, for the dressing-room door stood open, and therein lay something which exercised an irresistible attraction, something which lay stretched on a sofa, swathed in careful wrappings.

Nan drew back the sheet with reverent fingers, and there it lay in all its beauty—a gleaming satin dress, the train folded skilfully in and out, bunches of orange-blossom catching up the lace, which was festooned with as much lavishness as if it had been modest Nottingham, instead of precious Brussels, of that rich mellow tint which comes from age alone. A bride's dress, and a bride's dress fit for a princess, and in the box beside it a veil of the same old lace, and in the safe in the corner a diamond necklace and stars which represented a fortune in themselves!

Could it be, could it really be that all this splendour was for her? And oh! lucky girl, that she was so happy in love given and received, that they counted as nothing, and less than nothing, in her rejoicings! Could it be that to-morrow morning—in twenty-four hours from now—in less than twenty-four hours, she would be transformed from Nan Rendell of the coat and skirt—Nan, the third daughter in a large family, in constant straits for money and anticipation of her dress allowance—into Nan Vanburgh in satin and diamonds, Mrs Gervase Vanburgh, with her country seat, her diamonds, her carriages, her expectations of even greater wealth to come! Oh, wonder of wonders! Oh, fairy tale in real life! Oh, dear and beautiful prince, to work such marvels in a poor girl's life! Nan bent down lower and lower until her lips touched the gleaming folds and her cheek rested lovingly against them, then she drew the sheet forward once more, and went back to her seat. To think, not to write, however—to think over the two years that had just passed, and all the events which they had brought. Had she really loved Gervase from the beginning, even as he had loved her? It seemed as if she had, for after that memorable interview in the garden she had known no doubt nor hesitation. It was right to wait and let time prove the stability of her feelings, but at the bottom of her heart she had felt no uncertainty as to her final answer; and oh, how long had seemed the last three months of the year, with what joy she had hailed July—what a happy; happy time it had been for all concerned! Mrs Rendell and Maud had been the only members of the family who had known of the intention which lay behind Gervase's frequent visits; and if the surprise with which the engagement was greeted was mingled with some envy and disappointment from one of the five sisters, the others more than made up for it by their unaffected delight.

Gervase had long received the sanction of approval; and once assured of Nan's happiness, it was impossible for the most unworldly of relatives to restrain a thrill of satisfaction in the grandeur of the alliance. The schoolroom party was inflated with pride at the thought of "My sister Mrs Vanburgh," and even Maud tilted her head and smiled with a complacent air when congratulated on the engagement. As for the parents, they were naturally delighted at the prospect of so prosperous a marriage for their dear girl, while old Mr Vanburgh shed tears of happiness over the fulfilment of a cherished dream.

"She will be the making of the boy!" he declared. "He has always been a good fellow, but too indifferent and lazy to make the most of his abilities. Nan's energy, Nan's enthusiasm will be his salvation! This is the best news I have heard for many a long, long year. It puts fresh life into me in my old age."

Everybody seemed pleased and approving; and not the least welcome among the many letters of congratulation was one from Ned Talbot, now some months settled as steward of the Vanburgh property, and his earnest, outspoken appreciation of his new employer.

When the subject of the marriage itself was broached, however, Mr Rendell obstinately refused to hear of any date within a year.

"When she is twenty-one—not a moment before," he said firmly. "I have a parent's right to my Mops until she is of age, and not one day of the time will I give up for you or any man living."

"And I've a husband's right to her after that, and not one day longer will I wait, so we'll fix on her birthday, the twentieth of May!" said Gervase, equally obstinate; and so it was settled. And the months had seemed as weeks, so rapidly had they flown past, until here was the day before the wedding, with Nan's new boxes standing in the corner ready packed for that wonderful journey to foreign lands of which she had dreamed all her life long.

When the gong sounded, Nan looked guiltily at the blank sheet of paper; but it was too late to begin letters now—she must go downstairs, and trust to good fortune that the girls would not discover how she had wasted the time! Lunch was a scramble meal to-day, served in the morning-room on three different tables, and in the midst of a medley of boxes and parcels; but that was part of the fun of the occasion, and added to the general hilarity. A formal meal in the dining-room could be had any day, but it needed a convulsion of Nature to induce Mrs Rendell to hold her plate in her lap, and actually—oh, horrors! to help herself to butter with her own individual knife! The girls chuckled with delight at the spectacle, and then turned to greet Nan on her reappearance.

"Well, 'Bride,' finished your notes? Hope you have been a good little honest girl, and said what was true. 'Dear Mrs Webb,—Thank you so much for the dear little pepperettes. It is so kind of you to think of me, and as I have already had seven pairs sent, I feel no anxiety whatever concerning my future happiness.' 'Dear Mr Cross,—Thank you so much for the vases which you have so kindly sent me. They are quite unique, I am sure, as I have never before seen anything like them. I shall put them in my drawing-room whenever I know you are coming, and keep them carefully in a cupboard when you are away.' 'Dear Mrs de Bels,—How kind of you to send me such a sweet little egg-boiler! We never use such a thing, but it will do charmingly to give away to some one else, and—'"

"It's to be hoped no one will send you wedding presents, Kitty, if that's the way you are going to receive them!" said Nan severely; but her reproof was received with bursts of derisive laughter.

"Ho! ho! ho! How innocent we are! how proper all of a sudden! Can you look us in the face and say you have not said as nearly that as you dared— that you have not deliberately disguised your true sentiments?"

"I can! I do! I have not written a single word this morning with which you could find fault!" cried Nan, with a boldness which betrayed her to her sharp-witted adversaries, for the cry was immediately raised—

"She hasn't written at all! She has been sitting dreaming about *him* instead."

"I think of thee by morn, my love!" chanted Kitty, rolling her eyes to the ceiling with a ridiculous affectation of sentiment; while Agatha and Christabel went through a pantomime of rapturous greeting, at which Nan laughed in unperturbed enjoyment. She had served a long apprenticeship to her sisters' teasing ways, and was too happy in her engagement to keep up any pretence of indifference. Nan, indeed, won universal admiration in the character of an engaged girl, for there was something inexpressibly winsome in her transparent enjoyment of her own happiness. She loved her future husband with all her heart, and saw no reason why she should feign an indifference which she was so far from feeling.

When Gervase arrived in person shortly after lunch, she went flying to meet him, and came back hanging on his arm, her face sparkling with happiness and contentment.

"He has come! He has come! Here he is!" she cried, in tones of triumph; and Gervase was promptly surrounded by his sisters-in-law-to-be, and escorted round the house to see the preparations for to-morrow's ceremony.

He said little, for the solemnity of the occasion had already laid its sobering touch upon him, but his eyes glowed, and every time he looked at Nan there came an expression into his face so sweet, so true, so tender, that Maud could not see it and keep back the tears. She was in a supersensitive mood this afternoon, for not only did the parting with her beloved sister lie ahead, but also a meeting of even more importance. Ned Talbot was to be Gervase's best man, and was even now at the Grange, waiting only to greet his host, before coming to pay his first visit for nearly two years. The winter before he had received an invitation to Thurston House, but it had been refused; and even after that formal intimation that the way was open, he had delayed his coming, modesty and self-distrust alike combining to make him dread that final putting to the test which should "win or lose it all." How much Miss Nan had to do with the choosing of the "best man" is one of those secrets which are best left alone. But presently there he came, walking across the lawn towards the spot where the tea-table was laid, just as he had done on another afternoon years ago; and there sat Maud, once more busying herself with the tea-cups to hide her confusion, though of a different and far happier description.

Not in vain had Jim dropped his words of reminder; not for naught had he handed over letters received from his old friend for his sister's perusal! Maud knew, and had known for many a long day, to whom Ned's heart was given; and Ned knew that she knew, and gathered fresh hope from her sweet, shy smile. For himself, he was looking a new man, and Lilias felt a stab of pain as she looked at him and met his calm, scrutinising glance. She had loved him once, or had come as near loving him as it was in her nature to do, and she was surprised to find how much it hurt to realise his disenchantment. She was as pretty as ever, — prettier, so her mirror told her, — but though admiration was hers in plenty, no one seemed to love her, or to turn to her for sympathy and counsel. Nan, her younger sister, was about to be spirited away to a life of luxury and affluence; Maud would certainly follow suit before long; and she would be left at home with the younger girls, regarded by them as a tiresome elderly person, who refused to move on and make room for her juniors. A pleasant prospect, indeed! yet she could not complain, for if there was little sympathy between her sisters and herself, the fault was her own, and in her heart she confessed that it was so. It is impossible to live a selfish, self-engrossed life without suffering for it in hours of loneliness, and Lilias was beginning to learn this lesson to her cost.

When tea was over, Gervase went back to the Grange to sit with his uncle, while Nan adjourned upstairs to superintend that last trying-on of bridesmaids' dresses which the younger girls declared to be imperative.

"My dear, you don't know what may be wrong! I slipped on my bodice last night, and it was two inches too tight. That doesn't matter—I'll have a slim figure for your wedding, if I die for it; but consider—just consider—how fe-arful it would have been if it had been too loose!" cried Agatha tragically; and after that there was plainly no refusal possible.

Mrs Rendell wished to interview the cook, Jim had a letter to write—every one, it appeared, had some important and pressing matter demanding attention, save only Maud and Ned, who were left to their own devices, and presently wandered off towards that portion of the garden most sheltered from observation. Both knew what was coming, and both were trembling with hardly suppressed agitation; then presently their eyes met, Ned held out his hand, and Maud's went out to meet it without a moment's hesitation.

"Do you forgive me, Maud? Can you believe in me again? Can you give yourself to a man who loves you with all his heart, and can never do enough to show his remorse for his own miserable mistake? I did you a cruel wrong, but I have suffered for it all these years... Could you find enough charity in your heart to forgive me, and give me another chance?"

"I have nothing to forgive!" said Maud simply. Dear thing! and she meant it too; for when she loved, she found it impossible to blame, and Ned had been her hero for so many a long year. "It was quite natural that you should be fascinated by Lilias, for she is so beautiful and charming. I did not blame you, even at the time; but oh, Ned, I was very miserable! I loved you so dearly, I longed so much to help you! There is nothing in the world which could make me so happy as to be your wife!"

Ned's words of love, of gratitude, of almost tearful remorse, are too sacred to be repeated. He had reached his goal at last, and, looking back upon the past, felt that all the troubles which had lain in his path were but a light price to have paid for the treasure he had won!

Upstairs at the window of the girls' bedroom Kitty Maitland peered through her spectacles at the flutter of Maud's dress behind the bushes in the garden, and knitted her brows, in her anxiety to account for the presence of a dark stain around the waist! Presently the bushes parted company for a few yards, and the stain was discovered to be neither more nor less than a coat sleeve belonging to Mr Ned Talbot! Kitty cleared her throat, and chanted in a high, clear tone—

"A marriage has been arranged, and will shortly take place, between Mr Edward Mortimer Talbot and Maud, eldest daughter of—"

A stampede towards the window interrupted the conclusion of the sentence, and the sisters stared at the unconscious couple with eager scrutiny. They peered to right and left, craned their necks to one side and then the other, rushed to a second window to obtain a better view, and finally turned back and faced each other with expressions of awed conviction.

"It is—for a ducat! Oh dear, what a nuisance!" cried Agatha pitifully. "What shall we do without our Maud? First Nan, and then Maud—the house will be lost without them!"

"Our loss is their gain. We must be resigned. It is what we must expect. One bird after another will fly away, and leave the old nest bare. It is the order of Nature," sighed Elsie sadly.

"Another wedding! Another bridesmaid's dress. How s–implay lovelay!" cried Christabel rapturously; but Nan stood apart with clasped hands, and dark eyes full of tears.

"The only thing," she sighed to herself—"the only thing I had left to wish for. Oh, how thankful I am! What a dear world it is! How good God is to us all!"